The First Meeting

As he bent his head to speak to her grandmother, Pippa saw a finely etched profile. As they came nearer, he turned his head to look at her. She caught her breath. His face was incredibly handsome, or so she thought. His hair was shining and dark brown, his skin was clear, his cheekbones sculptural, and his mouth beautifully shaped. His eyes were thickly lashed and intensely brown, and in them she swore she saw a sudden spark of such rich, deep intelligence and interest in her that it took her breath away. She felt her heart flutter, and yet she'd always believed that only happened to ingénues in novels.

Romances by **Edith Layton**

To Love a Wicked Lord
A Bride for His Convenience
His Dark and Dangerous Ways
Bride Enchanted
For the Love of a Pirate
How to Seduce a Bride
Gypsy Lover
Alas, My Love
The Return of the Earl
To Tempt a Bride
To Wed a Stranger
The Devil's Bargain
The Conquest
The Chance
The Challenge
The Choice
The Cad

To Love A Wicked Lord

EDITH LAYTON

AVON
An Imprint of HarperCollins*Publishers*

This is a work of fiction. Names, characters, places, and incidents are products of the author's imagination or are used fictitiously and are not to be construed as real. Any resemblance to actual events, locales, organizations, or persons, living or dead, is entirely coincidental.

AVON BOOKS
An Imprint of HarperCollins*Publishers*
10 East 53rd Street
New York, New York 10022-5299

ISBN 978-0-06-175770-9
www.avonromance.com

First Avon Books paperback printing: November 2009

Printed in the U.S.A.

10 9 8 7 6 5 4 3 2 1

To Martee Hensley, M.D., and Paula, and all the other good, patient, and kind souls at Sloan Kettering Hospital in New York City

Acknowledgments

To all my kind and gentle readers, thank you.

To Love a Wicked Lord

Prologue

England, 1783

The duke glittered. Sunlight streaming in the windows of his front salon made his diamond stickpin sparkle enough to hurt the eyes and set the gold buttons on his waistcoat afire. The silver buckles on his shoes flashed every time he crossed his long legs. The sun lit his ice blue eyes until they looked blind and only capable of radiating light. That wasn't why the boy didn't meet his eye, or why he looked down at his own shoes. The dazzle didn't bother him. He didn't stare because he was very careful around his father.

"Well, there he is," the duke said in a careless drawl as he waved a languid hand flashing with jeweled rings at the boy. "My first born. You wanted to see him. Not much to look at. He has seven years to his name. Surprised everyone by attaining his great age. Sickliest infant the world had ever seen. Nonetheless, she doted on him."

The boy looked up at his father's guest. The man was older than his father. He was mild-looking, soberly dressed, with an old-fashioned gray wig and not his own unpowdered hair pulled back in a queue the way his father wore it. But then his father was always in fashion, or so everyone said. Today he wore shining silk hose and gray breeches—and—but his son dared look no higher.

"Good afternoon, Lord Montrose," the older gentleman said to the boy in a kindly voice.

The boy didn't know the man's title, and so didn't know whether to bow or only nod his head. But since his father hadn't bothered to introduce him, he reasoned that the old gentleman was lower in rank than he was. So he sketched a short bow and then stood still again.

His father picked up a goblet of amber liquid. "Kind of you to call after all these years, Vicar. Kind of you to ask after my lads too. This one don't say much. To tell the truth, he don't do much either. Somber little fellow, always looking grieved. Always was little too. M'lady, m' late duchess, doted on him. She was a fragile creature too. Made me promise not to send him off to school until he was ten. Ten! A new boy at ten? He'd be easy pickings for the older, stronger boys. But she was dying, so I promised. She quite ruined him, if there was anything to ruin," he added as he drained the goblet again.

The other man gave him a sharp look. Of course all adults spoke freely in front of children. But this was the lad's own father. And his grace was getting thoroughly soused.

"I knew your lady well," the old gentleman said. "She was a fine woman, God rest her soul."

The duke waved his hand again. "Aye. Pretty as she could stare. A French doll. But she had no stamina. Died after birthing the boy."

The boy looked up again. He was a slight lad, with dark hair, finely etched features, and astonishing eyes for such a youth.

The vicar gasped. "But he has her eyes, your grace! The very mirror of them!"

"Aye," the duke said, signaling a footman to refill his glass. "Big, brown, and with his soul showing through. They looked better on a female," he muttered as he raised the refilled goblet to his lips. "This fellow has soul, all right, but no stamina. Still," the duke mused, "if this one succumbs to some infection as she did, or an act of fate, there's his brother. I'll send for him, you'll see what I mean. Two years younger than this lad and a yard stronger . . . I mean a foot taller. Solid as a rock. A different dam, but he's his mother's image too. She was a wild creature," he added with a half-smile. "Beautiful. Strong. She had health and courage but chose to ride a horse that didn't have any. Her son looks like her and has all the spirit this one lacks."

Nothing in the boy's expression showed he was listening. He wasn't heard and it seemed he could not be seen; at least, not by his father.

The older gentleman squirmed in his chair.

"Ah well, accidents can happen even to the strongest," the duke murmured into his glass. "Certainly they can happen easily enough to the weakest too. Or at least, so one hopes betimes."

"Your Grace!" The older gentleman cried, half rising, forgetting his host's higher station, and remembering his own offices. "The boy, your son, is still here!"

"Is he?" The duke waved his hand at the child. "Go away, Maxwell. Tell Nurse to bring your brother to me."

The boy ducked a bow, turned and walked stiffly from the room.

"Your Grace," the older man said sorrowfully, "surely it isn't meet that your son should hear you looking forward to some accident that might kill him."

The duke looked up blearily. "What? I? Never said such a thing. Dreamin', Vicar, that's what you are." He slumped back in his chair. "Ah, I've got the megrims. An' who'd blame me?" He ran a hand over his ice-colored eyes, covering them. "I've eight and twenty years and too much sorrow on my plate. Two wives within four years, both fine ladies, both dead," he murmured. "And now, this new one and I don't get on. I've no luck, Vicar. None at all."

After Maxwell Andre Sutton, Lord Montrose, told the butler to relay his father's message to Nurse, he left the manor house. He was free. Father was drunk, and Nurse would be busy, and his tutor was in the icehouse, tickling Dolly the undermaid. Maxwell made it his business to know such things. So he took the Whitt path, out of sight of the front salon, and paced down to the big square reflecting pool at the side of the house. He stared back at himself through the blur of golden fish that came swarming up to the surface to be fed.

His brother was not a foot taller than he was. Duncan was the same height, only sturdier; at least everyone said so. But he himself hadn't been sick since wintertime. His father's words stung. They weren't new. Nothing he'd heard was new. Except for the last thing his father had said. That didn't make him unhappy so much as it made him very frightened. He sat by the pool, deep in thought.

At last, he rose and walked toward the stables. The man he sought stood at the door to the barn, currying his father's favorite horse, a pale thoroughbred. The duke said he liked to ride him because then he was a pale rider upon a pale horse. Maxwell didn't understand this. It didn't matter. His father never looked for his reaction.

The man with his father's steed was a short fellow. Stolid and solid, the strongest man Maxwell had ever known. He was gruff, but kind and fair.

"Hello, Osgood," Maxwell said.

Osgood whipped off his cap and touched his forehead. Boy or not, this lad was the heir to the title. "My Lord?" he said.

"I need a favor. A great favor," Maxwell said. He raised his dark, serious eyes. "And it's to be a secret, between you and me."

Osgood's eyebrows went up. "Can't promise that until I hear the favor you'll be needing. Could be treason, y'know. Could be murder you're planning."

Maxwell giggled. It was a strange sound coming

from a boy who rarely smiled. It pleased Osgood.

"It's actually to prevent a murder," Maxwell said, suddenly serious.

"Whose?"

"Mine."

Osgood squatted down beside the boy. "I'll be your protector, if you want."

Maxwell shook his head. "A man has to be able to protect himself. You always say that. I'm being taught to fence and shoot like a gentleman. I want you to teach me more; all the other things you know. You always talk about how it was in the war against the Americans. I need to know how to hear people behind me who don't want to be heard. I want to learn what you did from the red Indians. I'm not weak. I was, I suppose, but I'm not anymore. I'm not big, but I can learn. Will you?"

Osgood nodded. He thought a moment. "You think someone wants you dead?"

Maxwell shook his head. "No. I know it," he said.

"Who?"

Maxwell remained silent, biting his lips. Then he blurted, "Can't say. But I know."

"You sure?"

Maxwell looked up at him. "Sure enough. And if I'm wrong, well, I'll be going to school when I'm ten years old. I'll need to know then, won't I?"

Osgood sat in thought. "It will be steady, hard work."

"I want nothing more," Maxwell said.

Osgood rose to his feet. "Tomorrow morning," he said. "Sunrise. Before your maths tutor arrives. Meet me here. Mind, I won't be easy on you."

Maxwell's face was illuminated. He smiled broadly, for the first time in a long while.

Chapter 1

Bath, 1803

"So he's gone? Just like that?" the thin young woman asked incredulously.

The young woman she was sitting with shrugged. "Like that," she said, snapping her fingers. "Or that," she added, opening her hands to show she had nothing in them. "He's gone. No one knows where."

"Impossible!"

"Quite possible. And true."

"Oh! Pippa, you poor thing," her friend said. "But don't grieve. He may return. It's not as if he ran away from you. That is to say, who would? Why, even here," she said, sweeping a hand to indicate the whole scene before them, "every male has eyes only for you."

Pippa looked around the room they were sitting in.

It was a vast public room with high ceilings, tall windows that let the sunshine stream in, and chairs, tables, and settees placed everywhere. Most of the people in the room, at least those not already in wheeled bath chairs, needed a place to sit. The Pump Room and the Assembly rooms—actually, the entire town of Bath, had once been the place to gamble and gambol, as one wit put it. That had been in the last century, and even centuries before that, when the Romans were said to have built shrines and holy wells here. But time had gone on, and Bath itself had not. Now invalids from all over Britain, not just from the aristocracy, came to take the waters, rather than to play and amuse themselves.

The hot, sulfurous-stinking waters at Bath were said to bring health. All that Pippa could see now was that they brought the ancient and the unwell looking for health. Her smile was sad. "Yes. Those males that can see; see me. Most can't see anything farther than their noses though. Or if they can, they're so old they can't do anything about it. And those gentlemen who are under the age of fifty have eyes only for each other, or their wealthy protectors."

Her friend hid a giggle under one gloved hand.

"It's all very well for you, Adele," Pippa said morosely. "You're married, and enceinte. But me?" She sighed. "Oh well, at least I'm out of the house at last."

"Shocking," Adele said, shaking her head. "That this could happen to you!"

Pippa didn't answer. To disagree would be foolish; to agree would be vain. She was neither. Phillipa Carstairs was absolutely lovely; so everyone had said since the hour she entered the world. She was now four and twenty, and even lovelier than ever, with silver-gold hair, tilted amber eyes, a small shapely nose, a mouth that was a jot too plump, and a slender figure that was astonishingly feminine. Any male that saw her saw that and often nothing more. She knew that, and regretted it. As for her own opinion of her looks: she felt it was silly to be proud of something she hadn't actually done, and equally silly to be unaware of it.

"It's been seven months?" her friend asked.

Phillipa nodded. "Going on eight."

"Well," Adele said, eyeing her friend's slender form, "at least no one can say you're in the dismals because he left you with bread in the oven!"

Pippa laughed as her friend blushed at her own outburst. "Not nearly. But he left me in a worse situation; I'm not a disgraced woman or yet really a jilted one. I'm nothing—just deserted almost at the altar. My case is an even a worse fate than being a widow. If he'd died and we'd already married, at least I'd be free in a year and pitied, instead of being wondered about and judged by everyone. I can't end the engagement yet. I don't know enough. I can't see other gentlemen without seeming to be heartless either. There hasn't been a word of him, or from him. Not a letter, not a message. He's simply vanished.

"The world's in turmoil," she went on, sighing. "In spite of this new peace pact with France, there are still spies and secret missions everywhere, or so Grandfather says." She looked at her friend with a hopeless expression. "It would be one thing if he'd simply jilted me, another if he was met by highwaymen and killed on his way to London to get things in order for our wedding, as he said he was going to do.

"But what if Noel is, or was, a patriot?" she asked. "I'd look fine, wouldn't I, trotting about, partying with new admirers while he molders away somewhere. He may be in prison on the Continent. He may be dead, for all we know. He may have wed someone else. Whatever he is, or was, I can't go on with my life until I know."

"You loved him so much?" Adele asked.

Pippa shook her head. "I thought so. Now, I don't know. To tell the truth I was dazzled by him, swept off my feet by his charm. He was nothing like the gentlemen I meet at home, and you know I never found anyone I wanted when I had my time in London. It had been years since London anyway," she added sadly. "My life was slow and pleasant. I didn't note the passage of time until Noel came to visit Grandfather; and when he did, he brought energy and excitement to my humdrum existence. In fact, I didn't even know it was humdrum until he arrived. Nor did I realize how many years had passed since I had come to live with Grandfather and Grandmamma.

"But you see, he'd been everywhere, and he seemed to know everything. He woke me to the world again. He made me laugh, and not only that, he made me remember I was a woman." She stopped and raised a warning forefinger. "But he never, ever trespassed or presumed. He was always a perfect gentleman. He was handsome, well groomed, and well educated. He made me feel as if he'd been waiting to meet me as long as I'd been waiting for him. Which was ridiculous, of course. But I was thrilled that he actually wanted me. I was eager to be married to him and be off to see his glittering world for myself."

She shrugged. "Grandfather approved. Noel's credentials were good, and though he was an orphan like me, he came from old stock. We put the notice in the papers, set the day, posted the banns. We had a great party to celebrate and invited everyone in the district and beyond. In fact, I invited you."

Adele blushed again. "I was newlywed, Pippa, and going on my wedding trip. The Lake District was lovely."

"I imagine," Pippa said. "But we had a fine party for our engagement. The last party I attended, actually. Because after it, Noel said he had some business to take care of before the wedding, and he rode off. He never came back. Too much time has passed with no word of him or from him."

Pippa's hands closed to small fists. "I can't even grieve for him. I don't know whether to hate him or weep for him. Did he desert me willingly? Or was he compelled? How shall I ever know? It's unbearable. Seven months, Adele! I've been living in waiting. I must move on. That's why we're here. Grandmamma said that the cream of Society comes here, and if anyone knows anything about his travels or his disappearance, this would be the place to find out about it."

"And have you discovered anything?" Adele asked.

"The cream," Pippa sighed, "has obviously curdled. We have one more gentleman to speak with, and then we'll move on. This fellow is said to know everyone and everything too or, at least, everything he wants to know. He does favors for his friends as well, Grandfather said. We'll see."

"Why don't you employ a Runner?"

"That way the whole world will know. This way, only the privileged few do."

"And if you find Noel is alive?" Adele asked.

"I'll kill him," Pippa said.

Her friend's eyes opened wide. "You're joking, of course."

Pippa only sighed again. She glanced around the room. Old women and old men, a few crushed relatives sitting with some of them, and a sprinkling of maiden daughters and sad-looking young men met her gaze. Then she sat up straight. "Oh!" she breathed. "Here comes Grandmamma."

Her statement didn't match the look on her face or the odd sound in her voice, so her friend looked to see what had so affected her.

Pippa's grandmother was short and shaped like a dumpling. The current style didn't suit her at all. Perhaps that was why she chose to have her short curling hair such a strange bright yellow color. This afternoon, Lady Carstairs was beaming and excited. That might have been because of the gentleman at her side. Pippa and her friend frankly stared. The man was slender, a bit above average height, dressed in the height of fashion. But they weren't looking only at his clothing.

As he bent his head to speak to her grandmother, Pippa saw a finely etched profile. As they came nearer, he turned his head to look at her. She caught her breath. His face was incredibly handsome, or so she thought. His hair was shining and dark brown, his skin was clear, his cheekbones sculptural, and his mouth beautifully shaped. His eyes were thickly lashed and intensely brown, and in them she swore she saw a sudden spark of such rich, deep intelligence and interest in her that it took her breath away. She felt her heart flutter, and yet she'd always believed that only happened to ingénues in novels.

"Pippa, my love," her grandmother trilled in an excited voice, "here is Maxwell, Lord Montrose. He's the gentleman your grandfather suggested we speak with. Isn't this a lucky happenchance? He says he'll be glad to help us in our search for poor Noel."

For the first time in a very long time, Pippa didn't know what to say. That was, not until Lord Montrose spoke.

"Utterly charmed," he drawled in a bored voice that belied what he said. He nodded in what might have been a bow. When he lifted his head, he took a golden eyeglass from his pocket and raised it to look at her. Pippa could no longer see anything but bright malicious amusement in his magnified eye as he examined her. "Delighted to be of service," he said in that same flat, insincere tone.

"Indeed," Pippa answered stiffly, ignoring him and turning to her grandmother. "He says he'll help us? But why ever should he?"

She'd been incredibly rude, reducing the nobleman to a servant or an object by talking about him in front of him, but he only smiled at her. Their gazes locked.

"For your grandfather's peace of mind, of course," he said, his voice again belying his words. "And for this delightful young lady," he added with a wry smile directed down at her grandmother, which made the lady titter.

No, Pippa thought, and her grandmother positively simpered. The fellow was an affected popinjay of the worst sort. What was her grandmother thinking, becoming involved with the likes of such a creature?

"Indeed?" Pippa said again, keeping her expression calm, and ignoring his gaze. "And here is my dear friend Mrs. Standish," she said, in as bored a tone as she could muster. This time, his lordship bowed his head.

"Mrs. Standish," he said.

Adele colored, and ducked her head.

But his lordship smiled at Pippa again. "Well met," he said, and lowered his eyeglass.

She pretended not to be aware of it. "And so," she asked her grandmother, "how do we start this quest? Have you told him our objective?"

"Of course," he said, not giving her grandmamma a chance to answer. But he glanced curiously at Adele.

"Yes," Pippa said, embarrassed, but her head still high. "Quite right. This is neither the time nor place. I'm so sorry to involve you in this Adele, and so near our teatime too." Now she gazed directly into Lord Montrose's eyes. "This is such a personal matter, my lord. Can we not perhaps meet somewhere more private to discuss it?"

"Certainly," he said. "At dinner? At your hotel, so as to avoid comment? Which would certainly happen if you came to my rooms."

"Excellent," Pippa's grandmother said.

"At eight then," he said, bowed, and left them.

They watched him walk away.

"Now, there's a fascinating fellow," Adele breathed.

"So charming," Pippa's grandmother sighed.

"He minces," Pippa said.

Pippa inspected herself in the glass. She wore a simple pale pink high-waisted gown flowing down from beneath her breasts to her slippered toes. A pink ribbon held up her flaxen hair, and a shell pink cameo rested on her snowy breast. She nodded. Shell pink and lily white, a perfect English lady. She turned and inspected her derrière in the glass. A perfect fit. She looked fashionable and self-assured, and yet appealing. The subtle flow of the gown flattered her high breasts and pert derrière without emphasizing them. Still, there were other frocks in her wardrobe that made her look even better. But this one was so simple there was no way to know she'd spent an hour trying on gowns to find one that made it look as though she had no intention of impressing anyone.

"Perfect," she told her maid.

Then she picked up her hem and made her way down the dim hallway of the inn to her grandmother's room. It was time to go to dinner, and since that would be the first time she'd been alone with that lady since they'd met Lord Montrose, it was past time to find out why she approved of him. Whatever he'd said, he wasn't the sort of gentleman her grandfather would have cared for. Of that, Pippa was certain.

Her grandfather had worked in politics and won himself a title for service to His Majesty long before he'd retired to the countryside. He didn't move in Society, but he had inherited a fine manor house, the Old Place, and more. They had enough funds to be welcome anywhere, if they ever went anywhere. He now devoted himself to the scholarly pursuits of research and writing and was much respected, not least of all by his wife and orphaned granddaughter.

He was quite old, but not infirm. Still, he seldom traveled farther than his front gate these days. But the world found a way to his front door. That was how Pippa had met Noel. He'd been making an inquiry about a fourteenth-century poet as a favor to his own grandfather. Peasants, poets, statesmen, and politics; her grandfather was known to know everything, and he gladly shared his knowledge with the world and his granddaughter. Pippa believed she had as good or better an education than any man, thanks to him.

Now she paused at her grandmother's door.

Lady Carstairs wasn't a flighty lady. Although not very interested in philosophy or politics, she was as clever and in her own way as wise as her husband. So her being enthralled with the arrogant nobleman they were about to have dinner with was surprising. Pippa thought it might be the effect of having left the remote countryside after so many years, and finding herself in the world of fashion again.

"You look charming!" her grandmother exclaimed when her maid opened the door.

Pippa wished she could say the same. Lady Carstairs wore a silver gown that Pippa had never seen before. It was, doubtless, because the gown had been last worn before she was born. It was too tightly laced, too overly adorned, and too silver. Low cut, it belled out at her corseted waist and was supported by many petticoats, as had been the fashion in past years. Lady Carstairs also wore an ornate necklace that would have been lovely had the diamonds not been of such an old and heavy cut. She had too much rouge on her round cheeks, and her hair had been combed monstrously high and contained sparkles. But she was smiling, and somehow, oddly, the ancient fashion suited her.

"My, my," Pippa said. "We're very formal tonight, aren't we?"

"Needn't take that tone with me, my girl," her grandmother said. "I know I'm dressed to the teeth. But such a gentleman! I want to make a good impression on him."

"Grandmamma," Pippa said. "Why make such an effort? I mean to say, he's not very cordial; in fact he seems amused by us. I don't think the queen herself could impress him. Why bother to try?"

"He's very *comme il fault*. And your grandfather recommended him."

"But why should a fine nobleman act like a Bow Street Runner?" Pippa's eyes grew wide. "Is grandfather paying him a fortune? I won't have that!"

"You will have what your grandfather says," Lady Carstairs said haughtily. "Anyway, Montrose doesn't charge a penny-piece. The man's rich as a heathen king. They say he wanted to fight on the battlefield, but can't because he's the heir. So he does what he can for his country where he can. As for his airs? That's how all fine noblemen behave."

"No, it's not," Pippa argued.

"Well, if not, then it's how they used to behave," her grandmother said, snatching her wrap from her maid's hands, and marching out the door. "All strut and pose and airs and graces."

"Grandfather? Never!" Pippa exclaimed, shocked.

"Well, not he, perhaps," Lady Carstairs admitted, taking her granddaughter's arm. "But all the rest, to be sure. They were forever drawling their words and posing like a pack of poets." She sighed. "Still, it suited their looks. They wore diamonds and pearls, brocades and silks, powder and paint, buckles and clocked hose, even high-heeled shoes, not the shockingly casual clothes gentlemen wear now. The French have a great deal to answer for. They discarded elegance when they started chopping off fashionable heads. I don't know why we let their Revolution shape our fashions," she complained.

"Anyhow, Pippa," she continued, "if you want to find Noel, Montrose is the only man left that we can appeal to if we hope to discover anything. Your grandfather vows he knows all and everyone. And," she added as they approached the stair, lowering her voice, "just be grateful he isn't like his father, the duke. Now, there's a cold fellow. Handsome as he could stare, and he wore wonderful clothes and jewels and wigs. He had airs, and yet no graces, at least not when I met him. Of course, the poor man had cause for his megrims. Lost two wives in a row, and wished he could lose the third one. At least his son is charming."

"To some," Pippa grumbled.

"Yes, he was sweet to me, wasn't he?" Lady Carstairs asked, visibly preening. "But he wasn't nasty to you, Pippa my dear, and I can't see why you've taken such an instant dislike to him?"

"He seems to be amused by me," Pippa said.

"Ah, that," her grandmamma said, relaxing. "He obviously mimics his father. That's only his way. You would have despised all the men of that time. I vow you'd have remained a spinster had you lived in my day. Oh," she said, stopping and looking suddenly stricken. "You realize I meant nothing by that. Of course, you aren't a spinster. You're spoken for. You are engaged, but in waiting."

Pippa laughed. "What a lovely way to put it! And true. That's why I'll endure your most affected lordship Montrose." Her expression became serious again. "He may drawl and pose and ogle the world through his eyeglass all he wants. He may think whatever he likes too. If he can find Noel, I vow I will love him."

"Oh my heavens, no!" her grandmamma exclaimed. "Even in my day, we were only allowed one husband apiece."

Which was why when the ladies entered the private dining room the Marquis Montrose had engaged, the two of them were laughing merrily.

The marquis rose, and bowed. He was, as before, impeccably dressed, but this time in formal evening clothes. The black-and-white attire suited his grave good looks. But he still surprised Pippa when he spoke, because his tone was as light and bored as ever.

"Good to see you in such high spirits, ladies," he said, bowing as he greeted them. "And in such high good looks as well. I am a lucky fellow. Will you be seated? I've ordered the most delectable meal for you."

He held a chair for Lady Carstairs as a footman did the same for Pippa. The footman, Pippa realized, wasn't from the inn, he was in house livery, evidently that of his master, Lord Montrose. The gentleman who, Pippa thought darkly as she sat, had taken it upon himself to order for her. Noel had always asked her what she wanted. But Noel was a true man of the world, and one of her generation. This fop was obviously a throwback to his father's era. She vowed to bite her tongue and be silent about it. If it took a fool to find Noel, so be it. She'd already trusted wise men to do the job and they'd all failed.

Pippa smiled at her host. "Thank you, my lord,"

she said sweetly. "We are so pleased you've taken our commission."

"Ah, but I have not yet committed myself, my dear young lady," he said. "I don't wish to appear rude, but neither do I want to give you false hopes. I must hear more."

Pippa nodded. "We're ready to tell you about my missing fiancé if you wish."

His looked at her as he sat down, his expression bland. "Of course I do. I must hear all. But I'd prefer we do that after we dine. Is that all right with you?"

He meant that they should discuss Noel out of the earshot of servants, Pippa thought. She was well bred enough to know that even if he implied she was committing some kind of social solecism, he was wrong. She had often heard grandfather and his friends, gentlemen of birth and title, discussing much more serious things over dinner. But she wasn't the marquis's friend, she reminded herself, and whatever his reason, important or whimsical, she had to placate him. He might be able to help her.

"Yes," she said, casting down her gaze, "of course."

"Good," he said. "Now, shall we dine? We can speak of lighter things, of course. Later, we can speak of graver matters. An excellent meal deserves our concentration, don't you agree?"

She didn't, but she nodded, forced another smile, and kept her mouth closed until she was served her soup. Then she opened her lips, but only to swallow the soup—and her temper.

Chapter 2

"Now," Lord Montrose said, when their table had been cleared of dishes and the private dining room of servants, "tell me how I may assist you ladies."

"I thought my grandfather had done that," Pippa said.

"So he did," her grandmother said, looking puzzled.

Lord Montrose smiled. "Indeed. You're right, my lady. But I need a bit more information. I only know that your granddaughter has misplaced her fiancé."

"He never said it quite that way," Pippa's grandmother protested, her objection laced with titters.

Pippa scowled. "I know he didn't, Grandmamma," she said and glared at the gentleman. "Not really, my lord, not quite. Rather it seems he's misplaced himself. He left our house almost seven months ago, just before our wedding was to be, and hasn't been seen or heard from since. Well, there was one letter from London, three weeks later, in which he said he regretted how long his business was taking him, and promising to be back soon. I've heard no more."

Before he could say anything, she raised a hand. "We've asked after him everywhere and heard nothing. He simply hasn't returned."

Seeing a slight quirk on his lips, she added defiantly, "He showed no inclination by word or deed of wanting to sever our engagement. If he'd wanted to be free, he'd only to ask me and he knew it. The months passed, and I—we—began to worry about his having met with mischief.

"We asked locally, and then decided to go further. Grandfather has many knowledgeable connections here and abroad, you know," she went on. "He tried to find out more, but couldn't. An inquiry was sent to justices of the peace along the route from here to London and there've been no unidentified men found injured or dead. Even his horse, his favorite, a highly trained roan named Trueheart, hasn't been spied—and he'd go nowhere without Noel's command. When the trail went dry, grandfather suggested we leave and make inquiries of our own. He gave us your name, among others, of course. And here we are."

"Indeed, so we are," Lord Montrose said thoughtfully. "So then, what can you tell me about him?" he asked Pippa. "I know little but his name: Noel Nicholson. What more can you tell me?"

Pippa sat up straighter. He wasn't mocking her now. It made answering him easier, and her attitude became less hostile.

"What would you like to know?" she asked.

"His appearance, for a start," he said. "Can you give me a mental image of how he looked when you last saw him? Better yet, have you a miniature of him? Many lovers give them as remembrances before they embark on long journeys."

"No," she said, shaking his head. "Because he wasn't going on a long journey. He said he just had some business to clear before our wedding." She closed her eyes, concentrating on an interior image. "He was—is, I mean—about your height, with black hair. His eyes were—are—brown, and his face is considered very handsome, with no scars or pitting."

"Lucky lad!" his lordship said merrily. "He must look exactly like me!"

She opened her eyes and stared at him dispassionately, although she wanted to jump up and stalk from the room. "Not a bit like you, my lord," she finally said through gritted teeth.

"Then," he asked simply, "where is the difference? I can't go about asking people if they've seen my twin, you know."

She glowered at him.

He waved a hand. "Never mind. A horse's colors can be changed, along with his name, no matter how obedient he is. A fellow can alter his appearance even more easily if he wishes. He can grow military whiskers if he has none, or a beard if he wants to look ancient. He can color his hair, wear different clothing, even shave his head. He can alter his height by the boots he wears and the way he walks in them. Average height and dark-haired, then. What of his family? Where are they situated?"

Pippa looked down at her hands. "He was an orphan, like me; brought up by his own grandmother, but she passed away years ago. He said he'd only a few cousins left and those, far-flung."

"I see. And where did all this tragedy occur?"

She looked at him blankly.

He sighed. "Where was he born? Where did he pass his childhood?"

"Oh!" she said, coloring slightly because she

hadn't understood him. Then she sat up straighter. "He was born in Maidstone. He was seven when his parents died in an accident. Then he went to West Houghton to live with his grandparents."

"West Houghton?" her interrogator mused. "That's between Folkestone and Dover. Both busy ports to and from France when we are not at war. And," he added with a slightly twisted smile, "perhaps even more so when we are."

"Are you implying that he was a spy, or a smuggler?" she asked incredulously.

He waved a languid hand. "Oh, everyone is said to be a spy or a smuggler these days."

"Even you?" she shot back.

He smiled. "Aye, even I."

"I can't believe that."

"Why not?" he asked with interest.

She bit her lips.

"Because I am personable?" he asked. "Or because, with more honesty, I am considered a fribble? You mustn't judge a book by its cover. Why, just look at your lost love, Noel . . . if you could, of course. He seemed forthright and true, didn't he?"

Pippa bridled, trying to think of something unspeakable to say, after she'd make it more speakable, of course.

Her grandmother interrupted excitedly, "But, my dear Pippa, his lordship could only be pretending to being a fribble, like that fellow in my youth, oh, what was his name?"

Pippa winced.

Her grandmother didn't notice, she was obviously thinking too hard. "You know, my dear, the nobleman who dressed in exquisite laces and satins and pretended he hated to get his toes wet, when all along while no one was watching he became France's greatest enemy because it was all a hum. It was a disguise. He was really a brave spy and brilliant at freeing trapped English persons from French prisons. He was a fine duelist and the blight of the French secret police. Oh, what was his name? Percival or Perry or some such."

"He was a legend, a rumor, a fantasy," Pippa said flatly, refusing to look to see how the fribble seated opposite them was taking this. She doubted he was insulted. Or if he were, that he would let anyone see it. She didn't know what got her angrier, his boredom or his interest. She thought his amusement was worst. "No one knows if he even existed, Grandmamma," she said gently. "But the nation needed such a legendary hero then, King Arthur or Robin Hood."

"Oh, but King Arthur was real," her grandmother protested. "There are so many books about him and shrines dedicated to him and his knights. And what of Merlin? You're not saying he didn't exist? I'm surprised at you, my love. Robin Hood was real too. Your grandfather wrote a famously brilliant discourse on him. It appeared in the *Gentleman's Magazine*."

"Indeed," Lord Montrose said. "I read it."

Pippa ignored him and smiled at her grandmother. "Whatever the case, I am positive our guest is not such."

"Your host," Lord Montrose put in, "I do not let the fairer sex pay for my dinners."

"Exactly what I expected your attitude toward our gender to be," Pippa said with satisfaction. "So be it. I excuse you of spy-Dom, my lord. In fact, I'd bet against it, and I'm very good at cards."

"To be sure, and to my regret," her grandmother said. "I owe her twenty pins at Snap, my lord, and twice as many for Patience."

"Impressive," Lord Montrose said, his eyelids seeming to grow heavy, shielding the boredom in his eyes.

"Don't worry, Grandmamma," Pippa said. "I don't mean to call in my debts yet." She turned to their guest, or host, or whatever he wished to be.

She didn't know why she wanted to disagree

with him so much this evening. But she longed to say something to wipe that supercilious smile from his lips or shake his composure. It was distracting that such a good-looking fellow could be so artificial and condescending. In spite of her contempt for him, she found him attractive. But he didn't seem to think the same of her. She found that demeaning. She was generally considered very attractive. His lordship didn't appear to notice. Perhaps he didn't care for females. Perhaps he was hiding it. They were speaking of real people, and she suddenly yearned to see the real man behind his affect, if there was one.

"So, my lord," she said, "to get back to what we were saying, you believe Napoleon is still a threat, even with the peace pact at Amiens signed and declared?"

"Especially with the peace declared," he said languidly.

"You don't believe it will last?" she asked with amazement.

"Of course not. Bonaparte has no use for peace. Peace won't help him rule the world."

Lady Carstairs watched their exchange with growing worry, her head turning to note each combatant in turn, as though she were watching houseguests playing badminton.

"Napoleon Bonaparte is a Republican," Pippa said coldly, reining in her emotions. "He wants to better his country, and perhaps, yes, the world, in time. He believes in equal rights for all citizens. That is revolutionary and was bought by war; it's true, in both America and France. But he didn't start either revolution and I can't see it being part of his plan. Have you read his doctrines?"

"Of course," his lordship said. "That does not mean I believe him. By the by, have you read his latest screeds?"

She shook her head.

"You ought," he said. "I believe you'd be surprised. And you will recall, he is no longer merely a general but has named himself 'First Consul.'"

"Better than King," Pippa retorted. "Although, of course, I mean no disrespect to our king."

"Of course," he said calmly. "But though I dote upon gossip, and politics is, after all, only elevated gossip, we are going far off topic. Noel is the fellow we're supposed to be discussing. Unless, of course, it is Napoleon you prefer? Then I suggest you abandon Noel as he did you, and travel to France to become a true follower of the man you admire most."

She glowered. "I am an Englishwoman. I have no wish to see our king deposed. We have no need of it. We wrested a Magna Carta from a king centuries ago. That allows us to rule our lives more than the French or the American colonists ever could. We have no need for revolution. And because of that, I'm allowed to have my own ideas. And I do."

"And did Noel agree with those ideas?" he asked with what seemed to be real interest, at last.

"We didn't discuss politics much," she said, looking away from him.

He sat back, seeming satisfied. "Ah, yes. *L'amour* in any language chases out reason, or so I hear."

Pippa swallowed her retort. She began to believe he was deliberately seeking her hostility. She wouldn't be baited. She refused to give Lord Montrose the pleasure of showing him how much he annoyed her.

"Well then, onward," he finally said.

She was pleased with herself because of the faint hint of disappointment she thought she heard in his voice because she didn't rise to his bait.

"What of Noel's education? What schools did he attend?" he asked her.

"He was schooled at home and then went to university. He attended Oxford," she said, her head high again. "We didn't discuss that either. We laughed, my lord, and we rejoiced in our commonality of spirit. And by the by," she added as coolly as possible to answer his inference about *L'amour*, "Noel was too much the gentleman to indulge in that with me before we were wed. He respected me."

"Of course, a true English gentleman," Lord Montrose said, obviously holding back a yawn. "And his friends?" he asked.

"I met some of them," Pippa said. "They came to stay with us for a day or two. Remember, Grandmamma? Mr. Arnold and that charming Martin fellow—Martin West! And he often spoke of his good friend, Charles August."

"They lived in London," Lord Montrose said flatly. "And you haven't seen or heard from them since."

"Why, yes," she said. "How did you know?"

"It follows," the gentleman said obliquely.

"Well then, did he have an occupation?"

"Of course not," Pippa said. "He inherited an adequate income from his late parents and grandparents."

"What of Noel's interests?" he asked. "Why did he seek out your grandfather?"

"He was doing research on the last century," Pippa said, "to try to find traces of his family."

"Did he?"

"No," she said. "At least, he hadn't yet."

There was a silence.

Pippa spoke up at once. "But he came to us recommended by Lord Bellamy, who thought highly of him."

"Bellamy," Lord Montrose mused. "And I suppose he's abroad now?"

"Why yes. Do you know him?" Pippa asked.

"Many do," Lord Montrose said, his expression becoming bored again. "So here we have your fiancé, Noel Nicholson, who comes from Maidstone and West Houghton, and went to Oxford and thence to London and then to your grandfather's house. How long did you know him before you became engaged?"

"Two months," she said. She raised her head and looked at him directly. "Two wonderful months. Noel was—is—kind and thoughtful, well bred and well educated. Best of all, his wit was so keen he made everyone merry, even grandfather, and he's not been very cheerful of late."

"He's been distracted, my dear," her grandmother put in. "He often says he has so much to do and when he considers his age, he realizes how little time he has to do it in. I can't nudge him out of his moods, but your Noel could."

"How old is Lord Carstairs now?" Lord Montrose asked.

"He has two and eighty years on his plate," Lady Carstairs said quietly.

"And doubtless many long years left to him," Lord Montrose said quickly.

She nodded her head in thanks.

"But with all his knowledge," the marquis asked, "after your own investigations failed, his advice to you was to send you two to search for yourselves and, thence, to me?"

Both women nodded.

He rose from the table. "As I feared. I'm sorry, my dear ladies, to disappoint you, and dislike making Lord Carstairs lose faith in me. But as there's nothing more for me to go on, there's nothing more I can discover for you. I can tell you that yours is a hopeless cause. This Noel Nicholson of yours leaves no trail. He's a true will-o'-the-wisp; a dashing gent who appears and disappears at his own pleasure. I only hope, for your sake, Miss Carstairs," he added with a look at Pippa, "that whatever you say, it was not entirely at his pleasure."

Pippa's face turned pink and her eyes flashed, but before she could say anything, he spoke to her grandmother.

"And I must say," he said, "that I'm surprised you and your husband let this affair go on, Lady Carstairs. Lord Carstairs may have been distracted, and you may have been amused, but the fellow really had nothing to recommend him and no more background than a shadow."

"He had my grandfather's recommendation," Pippa flared. "And that's good enough for me, and half the nation," she added wildly. "Grandfather's famous for his cleverness and intellect, and judgment, and access to information of all sorts. Politicians and authors and poets and . . . why, even the prime minister has visited with him for advice! Certainly, if Grandfather thought Noel was a fit companion for me, then he was!"

"Possibly," Lord Montrose said. "But now he's gone, and were I you, I'd be glad of it. Really, the whole affair has a bad odor. Let him go, my dear Miss Carstairs. Place an advertisement in the paper requesting information about him and when there's no honest reply, which there won't be, have your grandfather place a notice canceling your engagement. And then get on with your life and consider yourself lucky."

Pippa rose from the table, her flushed face showing her fury, as did her suddenly sparkling eyes, lit by tears of fury. "Very well, we'll find him without your help."

He was expressionless. "There's folly. But I hear that's also love. You love him so much then?"

"I no longer know," she said with honestly. "But I must know if he's in difficulty. I know he'd do the same for me."

"Would he?" his lordship murmured. "Forgive me. I hope he would. But two women, even protected by servants and stout footmen, off alone on a quest throughout England?" He shook his head. "It will not do, ladies. You're sure to be taken in by practiced sharpers, men with no conscience, who merely want money. Not only men, but women and children too. Two females alone, throwing gold around, trying to find out what happened to a missing man, will doubtless encounter many such vile opportunists. The consequences will raise your hopes and then dash them, and put you in danger as well. I hate to see such things befall you."

He bowed. Then he shook himself as though from a long nap. "There's no help for it. I'll have to help you, will I, nil I. Mind, I'll need any papers you've gotten from previous investigations. You must have sheaves of them. I need to see them, all of them, including the letter Noel sent to you. I can't proceed until I do."

"We have them with us," Pippa said.

"Wise," he said. "I expected no less of you."

She was inordinately pleased at this mild compliment. "I'll have them sent down to you directly," she said, her shoulders relaxing.

He bowed. "Very good, I'll wait, I'll read them this very night. I'm staying with a friend nearby and will see you in the morning, if you wish."

Pippa nodded. "We do."

"I only ask one thing of you two ladies," he added. "When and if I tell you there is no hope, you must believe me and not keep on your mission. I may find amusement in strange places, and I admit I poke fun at many things. But I never lie about such things as life and death."

Pippa opened her lips and then hesitated. He was, for the first time, deadly serious, his handsome face set as in stone.

"Continuing to follow a path that leads nowhere will be exhausting as well as perilous for you," he added, shooting a look to her grandmother. Then he gazed steadily at Pippa. "I am good at what I do, Miss Carstairs, whether you choose to believe it or not. Your grandfather does. What I find or don't find should be conclusive. I don't go on fools' errands, or do errands for fools. So. Do you accept this? And if so, may I have your word on it?"

Pippa's shoulders drooped farther, but not from relaxation. She took in a deep breath. "Agreed," she said. "You have my word."

"My lady?" he asked Lady Carstairs.

"Oh yes, of course," she said, standing and looking from him to Pippa. "A very good idea, to be sure."

His smile was faint. "Then I'll wait here for your documents. And tomorrow, if there's anything to do, we will begin to do it."

Chapter 3

The large swarthy gentleman sitting in a deep chair by his hearth looked up as Lord Montrose came into his salon. "You're back? So early? Sick?"

"To the death," Maxwell said as he unceremoniously plunked himself down in a chair opposite his host. He stretched out his legs and laid his head on the back of the chair. "Why does everyone think I can do anything?" he asked the ceiling.

"Because you'd be insulted if they didn't," his host commented. "Need a drink?" he asked, waving a goblet of liquor in his guest's direction.

"Yes. But I need a clear head in order to go through some papers first."

"You're taking on Carstairs's commission after all?" the swarthy gentleman asked. "Working to help a female whose fiancé flitted? You said you'd never touch it. Or is it that you want to touch her?"

"Couldn't even if I wanted to," his friend said glumly. "Carstairs's granddaughter. I'm not ready to be leg shackled yet."

"A beauty?"

"Better than that," Maxwell sighed, closing his eyes. "And with a mind like her grandfather's, a temper like a teakettle, and a tongue sharper than an asp's."

"Sounds just your cup of tea."

"Is she? Why then did her betrothed ride off like his coattails were on fire to avoid his wedding day? And why in any god's name would a respectable woman go haring off after him, no matter the time spent or money cost?"

"Maybe because he left her holding something, so to speak, and she wants to be sure it's legitimate."

"No," Maxwell said, waving his hand. "Too much time has passed and no evidence has shown. In fact, I heard the lady's figure has always been a thing of loveliness. She isn't an ingénue, but she's far from being considered the shelf. Not with that face and form. So I wonder why she's doing it. Vengeance? Love? Hurt pride? Or does he know something he shouldn't?"

"You see spies everywhere," his friend said. "But I suppose our leaders do too or else they wouldn't have sent you along on her wild goose—that is to say, wild fiancé—chase."

"Unlikely," Maxwell said. "It's a favor between gentlemen. Her grandfather is a sage of some repute."

"So then I don't see the danger for you. I thought she was looking for her fiancé, not just for anyone to be her fiancé."

"I am not anyone," Maxwell said. He opened his eyes again, looked at his host as though seeing him for the first time, and visibly recoiled. "Gads, Whit. What do you have on?"

The gentleman ran a hand over his wide chest, which was covered by a bright crimson robe. "A banyan," he said proudly. "A new one. Nice, eh?"

"For the circus. Crimson silk with embroidered leaves, and big enough to be a horse blanket."

"You don't like it?"

Maxwell shuddered. "It doesn't like you. A large man should wear quiet garb, Whitney. I thought I taught you that."

"You tried," the man he called Whitney said cheerfully.

"How can I play the fop if even my best friend ignores me? Prinny listens to Brummel, why can't you pretend to be awed by me?"

"Who else will see me in my robe?" his friend

protested. "No one that anyone will credit. The females I consort with in this style have no style. And I certainly don't share my house with anyone else but an old friend like you, Maxwell."

Maxwell, Lord Montrose, sighed. "You're right. My pose doesn't work in any of its aspects. It's an ancient gambit, trying to be the bored milksop while really being the interested spy, but they insist. What was good enough for that Percy fellow in the last generation seems fine to them. But it's stale to me."

"Too bad," his friend said unsympathetically. "But everyone suspects everyone these days, so it doesn't matter."

"I suppose you're right," Maxwell said.

"So," Whitney said, "let's have the truth. Are you doing Carstairs a favor or do you think the girl's fiancé might be involved with something else?"

"As you said, these days everyone's suspected of being involved with something else," Maxwell said. He sat forward, clasped his hands together, and looked at his host. "Damme, but I'm weary of gossip and tattle, Whit. I'd give anything to get out there with a saber and a musket and do some actual good. This travesty of a peace isn't going to last much longer. We'll be at war again soon. And here I am, supposedly sniffing for spies, but about to work for an acid wench who probably frightened away her fiancé. In Bath, of all places. I'm taking tea with grannies and amusing the gouty, rheumatic, and antique of the realm. For tuppence I'd run away to sea and make myself useful."

"No, you wouldn't," Whitney said. "You wouldn't live to. Your father would murder you first. You're a nobleman, Max. You have the inheritance and the head that will someday hold his title. You can't get it shot off. Let your brother Duncan play soldier. He loves it. How is he, by the by?"

"He flourishes," Maxwell said absently. "And I'm happy for him. Osgood tutored him too. He's a good lad and a well prepared one."

"And the fiend?"

Maxwell's smile became curled. "Both my siblings thrive. One's playing soldier, the other is too young to do anything except try to dismantle my father's estate brick by brick, and is damn near succeeding. I'd say my father deserves at least one child like that, but I don't actually dislike the man except for the fact that he holds me back. I don't like it, Whit. It begins to bore me."

"Too bad," his friend said. "Last I heard Lord Talwin and his superiors thought the world of the work you're doing. You know you've done well for us. Still, if you don't want to play with this particular beautiful, witty, and sharp-tongued young female, I'd be happy to help. I know old Carstairs too, y'know."

"That's the point," his friend said seriously. "Carstairs may be old, but from all I hear, he's not doddering. His wife, who accompanies his granddaughter, is perhaps a trifle addled. Maybe she was always giddy. I don't know, nor does it matter. Carstairs does. He knew everything at one time, and still knows everyone. He's wise, better yet, he's clever, and he keeps his ear to the ground even though he hardly stirs from his estate. The world beats a path to him. His granddaughter's fiancé did too. One Noel Nicholson. He appeared out of nowhere. He came, he socialized, he became engaged. Now he's vanished. It may mean nothing but the fact that he came to his senses and escaped the wench. It may mean more. I'm pledged to find out. But it won't be easy."

"Nothing worthwhile ever is," his friend said seriously.

Maxwell levered up from his chair and began to pace. He shot a look at his friend as he did. "Worthwhile? The world is about to catch fire and I'm sitting by the hearthside with sweet old ladies and spoiled spiteful young ones."

His friend watched him pace. "But, Max, who

else can do what you do?" he asked. "Look at me. What have they set me to do? Watch over you. While it's worthwhile, I can't say it's exciting. I can swing a saber and flourish a foil and shoot with the best of them. I can ride like a demon, I'm good with my fives, and can probably wrestle a dancing bear. But you can do that too, plus you can floor me with a blow and a twist of your shoulders, as you have done. And no one knows it until you choose to let it be known. There's your strength.

"Osgood taught you well," Whitney went on. "You're lethal."

"At the time I thought I had to be," Maxwell said. "I was a child and heard something said in a drunken rant that terrified me. By the time I'd learned it was only inebriation speaking and certainly no danger to me, it was too late. I'd asked Osgood for help, and he obliged. I enjoyed my tuition too much to stop. I also learned that the fellow who had frightened me, my father, by the by, would have gladly cut out his tongue for it when he sobered up. Instead, he asked my forgiveness and cultivated my trust. That began a true friendship in spite of all obstacles. So I didn't have to become lethal, as you put it. But I'm glad I did."

"So is your country," his friend said. "And best of all, you don't look as though you can do anything but gossip and tattle. So people confide in you. Look at me. Would anyone in their right mind confide in me?"

"I do," his friend said.

"Well, I mean besides old friends and seriously drunken ones," Whitney admitted. "Well-bred females make me nervous and they return the compliment. Old ladies may lean on my arm crossing the street, if I offer it. But otherwise I look too fierce to approach, much less confide secrets to."

Maxwell cocked his head to the side. His friend was huge: long-boned, with large features in a craggy face. "I don't know. You look trustworthy. Females like to lean on you."

"And I on them," his friend laughed. "But the well-bred ones? They might run to me in a panic, but they don't trust me otherwise."

"Odd. I don't find you fierce, nor does anyone who knows you above five minutes."

"At any rate," Whit went on, "I'm only here because you are. This house is an inherited one. True, I have to visit it from time to time to make sure it doesn't crumble to the ground. But I'd rather be otherwise occupied. Bath was once the place to be; now it's the place to be old. And all I can do here is keep an eye out for you."

Whitney shot his friend a bright look. "How do

you think I'd look perched on a little chair, taking tea in transparent cups and nibbling on wafers with the old darlings? Absurd, that's how. No, you're best for that. There are some who may think you're a spy playing at being a dandy, like that mythical Percy fellow a generation ago, but many more doubt you care about anything but the shine on your boots. Even Frenchmen find you shallow and foppish. You're invaluable just as you are."

"And if I'm tired of being that kind of invaluable?"

Whitney shrugged. "I don't think there's anything else you can do, old friend. You can quit the whole business, of course. But I don't think you'd care for that, would you?"

"No," Maxwell said, sinking to his chair again.

"Nor would I, which is why I don't, bored though I may be. So find the errant fiancé, send the girl home, and get you to London," Whitney said. "When you're there you can ask to do something else. Maybe this peace will last, and you won't have to do anything more."

"And maybe the newly self-proclaimed First Consul for Life Napoleon Bonaparte will retire and cede France to our king after kissing our beautiful prince on both cheeks and wishing him long life," Maxwell said, staring into the blazing hearth.

"Then we can build a bridge to Paris and live as one nation, happily ever after."

"Some people think that may be."

"Some people," Maxwell said, "think the moon is made of cheese. I'll have that brandy now, thank you. Then I'll scan these reports. You can go over them too and see if I've missed anything. I don't think our missing lover is a spy. Nor do I think he's anything but wise to be shut of this lady. But I promised to look, and I'm a man of my word. And who knows? He may be Bonaparte in disguise."

His friend rose and went to a sideboard to pour another goblet of golden liquor. "You think the peace is temporary?"

"I think it may be over by the time I finish reading these papers. I know Napoleon wants to rule the world, and I don't care to be under his thumb or his foot. Although, come to think on, I wouldn't have to be. Because one of the first things he'd do would be to detach my head and those of my family and friends, as the Revolution did for my mother's relatives. He has an aversion to the nobility, remember? I'd take tea with three thousand dizzy dowagers to prevent that."

Maxwell accepted a goblet of liquor from his friend and sighed. "Thank you. But whatever else I do, I must find out what Carstairs's granddaughter's suitor was doing, if only because I hate loose ends. And then even if I have to give up the case because there's no end to it, I'll go to London. You'll follow I suppose."

"I should be honored to," his friend said, sitting down again.

"As well you should be," Maxwell agreed, settling down to read his papers.

"That is quite the loveliest gown I've seen you wear in a long while," Lady Carstairs said, gazing at her granddaughter.

Pippa's gown was a long-sleeved column of saffron-colored silk, embellished with tiny gold rosettes. Yellow roses had been woven into her gilded hair, and a simple golden locket lay at her white throat.

"And yet all we're doing is meeting the marquis for dinner," her grandmother mused.

Pippa's fair skin showed pink at her momentary discomfort. Then she shrugged. "It's April, it may soon be too warm to wear it."

"There is that," her grandmother said cheerfully. "And certainly the marquis will find it beautiful. Then perhaps he won't be so snappish with you. Do you think he's come up with Noel's whereabouts?"

"I don't know, Grandmamma. It's been three days since we met with him. That's why we're going to dinner with him this evening."

"He might just want to see us again," Lady Carstairs said brightly. She gazed at her reflection in the looking glass, and preened. "He may seem cold to you but there's no question he likes me. I may have aged a bit but I still attract the gentlemen." She positioned her diamond necklace so that it lay perfectly on the very rounded breast of her blue gown and smiled. There was no self-mockery in her comment or her smile.

Pippa bit her lip. There was no question that her grandmother's conversation was growing strange. But then, she thought guiltily, it may have been so for months now. She hadn't noticed. First Noel had taken up all of her time, and then she'd been absorbed in the mystery of Noel's leaving. This was the first time she'd passed in the sole company of her grandmother in a very long while.

Perhaps that was the real reason why grandfather had insisted his wife accompany Pippa on her journey. Grandmother was suddenly happier than Pippa had ever seen her: giddy and vain, flirting with every attractive gentleman she met, regardless of age. Had she been like that at home lately? If so, it must have hurt grandfather to see the love of his life diminish, if she, indeed, was diminishing. Or maybe he only wanted Pippa's opinion on the matter. Grandfather moved in mysterious ways. She'd have to listen more closely to her grandmother to know how her mind was working now. But tonight she had to listen most closely to Lord Montrose.

It was true she'd got herself up like a lady on her way to a grand ball. She knew the gown flattered her to the point that even she caught her breath when she'd seen her reflection. It had been designed to show off her curves. But he didn't have to know that this was her newest and best gown. And in truth, where else could she wear it? She wasn't invited to dances and balls anymore. She was an engaged woman whose fiancé had disappeared. She didn't know if she was expected to mourn or to go into seclusion any more than her friends did. She wasn't available, and so she couldn't dance or flirt because then she'd seem to be fishing for unattached gentlemen. So she was left to herself except for the occasional invitation to tea.

And, she admitted, she wanted to see Montrose's reaction to her tonight. Surely, he couldn't remain unmoved. If he continued to be snide and sarcastic, she'd know that he simply didn't like females. If he made up to her, he'd be a cad. She froze as a new thought came to her. Maybe he was married! She felt weird relief, and vague disappointment.

But whether he was a woman hater, a cad, or a married man, she likely wouldn't see him again soon, and so she'd not experience that curious tug toward him coupled with the urge to flee from him. She didn't know if that pleased her or not.

"Come, Grandmamma," she said. "He'll be sure to say something unpleasant if we're late."

Her grandmother rose. "Not to me, my dear," she said.

Pippa took her arm and looked down at her. That was when she noticed that her grandmother had a dusting of rouge on her wrinkled cheeks, a smudge of blacking above both eyelids, and a glaze of color on her lips.

"Grandmother!" she said. "You're wearing paint!"

Her grandmother winked a sooty eyelid. "I'm not so old as to forget how to make up to my best advantage. It was all the rage in my youth. I gave it up because your grandfather never noticed after we were wed, so what was the point? You know, my love," she said, peering up at Pippa, "you could do with a pinch of color in your face too. Lord Montrose looks like a judge of female beauty. You do want him to notice, don't you? Why else would you have worn your grandest gown?"

Pippa swallowed her answer.

"There," her grandmother said. "Now you're nice and pink. Shall we go?"

They made their way down the stair to the downstairs dining room. The place smelled of antique wood, polish, woodsmoke from many hearths, and the lingering scents of dinners long past. It was oddly homey and comforting, but Pippa couldn't see the point to staying on here much longer. That meant she'd go home and remain in seclusion. It made her want to scream or saddle a horse and ride off into the night. She'd seldom felt so powerless.

Pippa steeled herself for the coming encounter. Maybe she'd discover it would all be over soon: Noel found, her future restored. She doubted it, though. She didn't want to creep home in defeat, whatever happened. She'd started on an adventure and was loath to end it however it was to end.

Whatever news the bored nobleman had to share and whichever attitude he chose to display while doing so, Pippa promised herself she'd deal with it. And yet when she and her grandmother entered the private dining room, Pippa was startled by the sight of Lord Montrose's unexpected, warm, welcoming, and glad smile.

Chapter 4

The flickering candles on the dining table's top, the glow of the wall sconces, and the gleaming light from the lamps made the private dining room at the inn look snug and inviting, as did Lord Montrose's welcoming smile. He was casually and yet very well dressed, in hues of gold and brown. The fashionably tightly fitted clothes showed he had a lean muscled frame as well as excellent taste in clothing. In all, Pippa thought darkly, tonight he looked almost unspeakably handsome, and she was sure he knew it. For once, she didn't know quite what to say. She ducked a bow and used the moment to try to interpret the sudden, unusual warmth she'd seen on his face when she'd appeared in the doorway.

"Good evening, ladies," he said, bowing to them in return. "Please have a seat. I've taken the liberty of ordering dinner. The desert is said to be delicious, but I've even tastier news for you."

Pippa straightened instantly. "You found him!" she cried.

"Not quite, not yet," he said as he pulled out a chair for her grandmother. "But soon. I'm on the trail."

"Tell us, please," Pippa said, taking her own seat and gazing up at him with delight.

He hesitated.

"Oh, please don't make us wait until after dinner," she pleaded. "I won't be able to eat a bite until I know."

"I didn't mean to make you giddy with my success," he said as he too sat. "Because it isn't quite that. But I've heard news of him and will follow that trail. In short," he went on before she could ask more, "I heard that a fellow resembling him was here, and left. I hear he's gone to Brighton. I don't know if that was your man, but there's no trace of him left here so that's where I'm bound next."

"Brighton?" Lady Carstairs asked eagerly. "You mean the old village of Brighthelmstone? Oh, but wonderful. That was what they used to call it. It was a charming fishing village. The waters there were said to be quite as good for you as they are here. The king used to go there for his health. And then, in eighty-seven, our prince finally transformed it with the completion of his monstrous erection."

Pippa stared.

Montrose pursed his lips.

Lady Carstairs giggled. "Well, that's what one observer wrote about his new Pavilion, and we were all so tickled, we couldn't stop quoting it. I'm sure the architect, Mr. Holland, wasn't so amused. But we were. Ah me. Those days seem so long ago. Just the place I'd wish to go now."

Pippa frowned. Her grandmother had never talked so warm before. Was it the freedom of travel that made her do it? Or was it something more sinister?

"This place is short of amusing company," her grandmother went on. "No wonder we can't find Mr. Nicholson here. I vow the gentlemen here make me feel young again! Not in the best way, but anyone compared to them would feel youthful. And won't you be pleased to leave here, Pippa? She hates Bath," she confided to their host. "No, child, you hide it well, but I know," she said, shaking a gnarled finger at her granddaughter.

Then she smiled. "Imagine, she complains that all the streets in Bath are uphill! She says it's actually changed the people who live here and that's why the sedan chair porters who carry the chair in back are shorter than the ones in front. Their legs have become shorter because of their jobs, she says. So it seems, though I can't believe it's true. And I won't even tell you the naughty things she says about the visitors here."

Lord Montrose's expression seemed caught between amusement and annoyance. Amusement won out. "All the streets uphill? It does seem that way. But I promise you that what goes up does come down, eventually. And the porters are usually the same size, limbs and all. It's an optical illusion. A porter who carries a sedan chair in the back and goes uphill has to crouch for leverage. That makes the fellow in front seem longer-legged. Still, if you watch them going downhill, you'll see they reverse positions . . ." He paused. "Or at least, I thought they did. You may be on to something there, Miss Carstairs."

He smiled at Pippa, and she couldn't help grinning back at him. The moment passed quickly.

"That said," he added more seriously, "the truth is that there's no need for you ladies to accompany me to Brighton."

"Of course there is!" Pippa snapped. "I'm the one who knows what Noel looks like, and if he's there I'm the one who needs to speak with him. Nothing's changed that."

"True," he agreed. "But it's a long journey. Surely you and your grandmother would be happier ensconced here. I'll return with news soon as I have some."

"Oh my, no," Pippa's grandmother commented merrily. "I long to see Brighton again, my lord. I'm sure many of my old friends are there. They're certainly not here. And to see our prince again! I hadn't hoped for such felicity. I knew him when he was young; such a handsome lad, hair of gold and the bluest eyes. We all called him Florizel—a prince from out of fairy tales, and so charming, always. I know age has changed him; it was doing so even then. I yearn to see him again. We must go with you."

Pippa hid a smirk. She knew Montrose would rather be accompanied by a troop of bagpipers. But she also knew he respected her grandfather, and so might allow them to go with him. Pippa prayed that would happen. She'd just stuck her toes out the door and discovered that she wanted to take longer steps. The world was fascinating.

"But it's a long journey," he protested. "A long way from here. Down into Sussex, and toward the sea."

"It always was," Lady Carstairs said blithely. "We never let a little road or two get in the way of our pleasures, not in my day. How else to see the world? I can sleep in the carriage if I get weary. My dear husband would be shocked if I let a mere matter of miles cancel a journey I wanted to take. Time enough to rest when I'm dead."

Lord Montrose looked hunted.

Pippa knew her grandmother could be immoveable on some issues. They were usually household matters. Now, after seeming content to stay in one place for decades, it appeared that she was feeling the same sense of newfound freedom her granddaughter was experiencing. The farther they went, the more moveable her grandmother wanted to be. Pippa hoped her grandmother was healthy enough and, prayed, was in her right mind, because she so wanted to leave this place and solve Noel's mysterious disappearance. But Pippa had little part in this decision. She sat back, waiting to hear what Montrose would say.

"But your age, dear lady," he began.

Pippa shook her head. He wasn't as clever as he appeared. He'd said the worst thing for his cause.

Her grandmother seized on it. "I am as old as I am, and not one day more. I do hope you don't find me ancient!" she added coyly.

He put a hand on his heart. "You know I don't. I only had a care for your well-being, and my own. Your husband would slay me if you returned to him in any way less vibrant and lovely as you were when you set out."

It did the trick. Lady Carstairs beamed at him. "No need to worry. My goodness! I'm not confined to my bed or my chair. I know my dear husband would approve. He sent me away and bade me return with an answer. How poor spirited I would be if I went home because I was afraid to go on. This is England, not some barbarian land. I will be quite safe. Safer to be sure, with you, dear sir," she said with a flirtatious smile that made Lord Montrose blink and her granddaughter worry.

"But if you don't care to accompany us, my lord," Lady Carstairs added with sudden dignity, "I'd appreciate it if you would recommend someone who would."

He sighed. He spread his hands out in front of him. "I'd never do that. I trust only myself with your care. Then so be it. We'll go on together, if you are certain."

"Certain?" Lady Carstairs asked in puzzlement. "I am always certain."

Montrose nodded. "As I see. Very well. Now, shall we dine?"

The dinner was delicious, but no one dining seemed to notice. Each was wrapped in a cocoon of silence, so thoughtful that they didn't notice that no one else was speaking. They ate absently. Every so often one of them opened their mouth to say something, and then closed it again over a bite of food. The waiter serving them cast a significant look at the serving wench, and they both shrugged. The quality was strange, that was something sure.

When all the dishes had been cleared and the servers gone, the company in the private dining room looked at each other again. Pippa's eyes widened. Her grandmother looked exhausted, gray and fatigued, as though she'd walked a mile not just consumed a meal.

Pippa leapt to her feet. "Grandmamma!" she cried. "Come, it's time for bed. You can lean on my arm."

Lord Montrose strode to the older lady's other side.

Her grandmother shook off Pippa's hand. "Nonsense," she said. "It's not yet midnight. I just need a bit of rest. That chair near the fireside looks comfortable," she said as she rose to her feet. She made it to the chair with Montrose's assistance. "Ah," she said, settling back into it. "Just what I need, a chance to rest my eyes. Go on talking, my dears. Make plans. I'll be ready to leave tomorrow at first light."

"After breakfast, surely," Montrose said.

"Very well, then," she agreed, and closed her eyes.

Both Pippa and Montrose stood, looking down at her.

"I am not deceased," Lady Carstairs said irritably, though she kept her eyes closed. "Go away. I'll be right as rain in a few minutes."

Pippa and the marquis took chairs nearby, sat, and stared at each other.

"Ill advised," Montrose said in a low voice.

Pippa nodded. "True. But it will be worse if we refuse her."

There were a few moments of silence broken only by Lady Carstairs's increasingly deep breathing, the pop and hiss of it, and of the firewood in the hearth.

"The truth is, and I'm not happy to be saying it," Montrose finally said, watching Pippa, "but I must. Although we go to Brighton, you must realize that your Noel may already be in an unmarked grave anywhere along the road anywhere in England."

Pippa swallowed hard and nodded. "I know,

but I don't think so. He's an experienced traveler. He's been to France, Italy, and so many other places abroad, he knows enough to travel inconspicuously."

Montrose's dark eyes glittered in the lamplight. "Indeed? Why so much travel, do you know?"

"Because he was a spy," Pippa said in annoyance. "No, of course not," she said as Montrose's eye's widened. "A jest. He wasn't, I'd vow it, and so would Grandfather. Noel was—is—just a man filled with curiosity. He even said that the only bad thing about marrying was that he'd have to stop traipsing round the planet. I said he wouldn't have to because I wanted to see the world too, and couldn't he please take me somewhere someday? He readily agreed. We laughed, and so that was that."

"Would your grandfather have known if he were a spy? He's been living in isolation for years."

"No, he hasn't," Pippa said wearily. "Everyone from cabinet ministers to royalty to local fishermen come to him for advice all the time. I daresay he knows more about everyone in England than anyone in England. In fact," she added pointedly, "I wouldn't have landed myself and my grandmother on you unless he had specifically asked me to. He said you'd find Noel or no one could.

That was high praise coming from Grandfather. Are you a spy?" she asked curiously.

"Absolutely," Montrose answered in bored tones.

"Well, it doesn't matter," Pippa said. "In fact, it might even help you find him. I must. It just makes no sense for Noel to have left me. I'm not saying that I'm so utterly desirable. I am saying that he has manners. I believe he's alive and something is preventing him from reaching me. Lord Montrose," she said suddenly, urgently, "I can't go on as I've done. I'm neither widow nor jilted fiancée. I'm no one, living nowhere. I can't socialize. If I did, I'd look cruel and uncaring, but I can't continue to live in an empty jar the way I do now."

"You want to marry," Montrose said flatly.

"I want to live a normal life," she retorted. "You may remain unattached and you do so. I can't. I love my grandparents and owe so much to them, but I can't live with them forever. I want a life of my own." She looked over to see if her raised voice had woken her grandmother. The lady slept on. Pippa sighed. "Do you think she can bear the journey?"

"I was going to ask you that," he said.

"She's sturdy, and determined. As for the rest? I'm not sure I know her anymore," Pippa admitted. "But then, I've been too involved with my own troubles lately to notice little things about her behavior as I do now. Still, if she wants to go, and I refused to go with her, there would be nothing I could do about it short of writing to Grandfather and asking him to stop her. I don't think he would. He made a decision. He expects it to be carried out."

Montrose sat back and stared at Pippa. "The saffron and rose colors of your gown suit your eyes and hair perfectly," he said. "You're fair as an elfin child, but very much a woman. Your figure is magnificent, not too voluptuous, but neither are you too fragile-looking. You are very lovely, you know."

She couldn't have been more surprised if the chair she sat in had suddenly started complimenting her. She'd noted his attractiveness from the moment she'd clapped eyes on him. But she'd thought he was far more interested in Fashion than any female.

"Of course, you must know," he went on in soft, musing tones. "Beautiful women always do. That presents a problem for me. You came down tonight and looked so alluring you staggered me, and knew it. Your cheeks are flushed now by my praise, and when you begin to take such deep angry breaths as you're doing, your breasts rise magnificently."

She was as flattered as confused, and sat listening to him, entranced.

"It makes me wonder," he went on. "Do you think your grandfather wants you to attach yourself to me if we discover that Noel met with bad fortune or cold feet?"

She blinked and then glared at him. "No!" she spat. "No and no! Grandfather is clear in all his dealings. There's no secret purpose on his part, or mine."

"You don't find me attractive?" he asked in piteous tones, as though she hadn't spoken.

She was momentarily silenced. He was jesting, and then she was certain he was not. She lifted her head. "You are, as you must know, my lord, a very attractive fellow. But I prefer gentlemen with a bit more *man* and a bit less *gentle* in their natures. In short," she said defiantly, "I don't know whether you're pretending to be a popinjay or really are one, but whichever you are, it matters little to me. I have no designs on you, my lord. Let it go at that. Or," she asked shrewdly, leaning forward, "are you trying to alienate me so that I leave in a huff and find someone else to take me to Noel?"

He smiled. "Oh do, please. I've never seen anyone leave in a huff, though I've heard about it. I've seen people leave in a rage, which moves so fast it's hard to describe. But if you've a huff standing by, I'd love to see it."

Her lips turned up in spite of herself.

"Of course," he added, "I find your grandmamma very desirable as well; it must run in the family."

Pippa shot a glance to her grandmother. The lady's eyes were still closed, her expression hadn't changed, but her breathing wasn't yet the full-throated snoring Pippa knew she eased into when she fell fast asleep.

"But I'd never risk your grandfather's anger," he went on. "And I'm sure he would never dangle her in front of me as a lure."

"Few men would do that to you where it concerns a female," she said angrily.

His shapely mouth grew a slow, curled, and very wicked grin. It changed the appearance of his face, making him look as eerily provocative as a depiction of the devil come to tempt mankind, and womankind.

"Are you sure of that?" he asked her. "Interesting. You find cleanliness and interest in fashion and a certain niceness in my speech as meaning I don't desire women? Are only bluff fellows in bad clothes your idea of virility? That will certainly make it easier to find your Noel. We can sniff him out. He must be a stranger to soap; I daresay even a bit heady? Did he clap you on the shoulder to congratulate you whenever you looked as lovely as you do tonight? Did he growl, 'Give us a kiss, lass,' and give you a hearty buss on the lips before clapping you on your shapely rump? That's the way of those hearty fellows."

He lowered his voice until she had to strain to hear him. "Or did your Noel spread his hands and run them slowly along the silkiness of your gown until he touched your silkier skin, murmuring his delight in the warmth and smoothness of you? And was his kiss only a slight suggestion of a touch upon your lips at first, and then, when you relaxed, was it a slower, sweeter delving into the increasing sweetness he doubtless found in your mouth?"

"Stop! You shouldn't say such things to me!" Pippa said, knowing her protest sounded girlish and insipid even as she breathed it. He'd only praised her with words, but they bordered on lovemaking. He might only be trying to refute the snub she'd made to his masculinity, but she was scandalized, and to her dismay, aroused. His voice beguiled her. His words stroked her, soothed her, tempted her. She didn't know whether to be flattered or outraged. "It's disturbing and makes me feel uncomfortable," she added, sounding prissy even to her own ears.

"Then I won't do it again," he said unapologetically.

"Why did you?" she persisted.

"To see how you'd react. Or maybe I meant it. But if you don't care for it, I won't continue. Some ladies consider such flattery enjoyable and expect it, like a game of cards after dinner. Some don't. But you believe I'm uninterested in females?" he asked more briskly. "Interesting. Would you care to wager on it?"

"No," she said in a shaken voice, because the mere thought of testing his masculinity was dismaying. And he knew it.

The only thing she might wager on was that he probably smelled even better than she did, and spent more on his wardrobe. The idea of actually kissing him made her anxious. Was he testing her, teasing her, or trying to frighten her back home?

No matter, she was only going in one direction—with him, until she found out what had happened to Noel. And so she said as she rose from her chair. "And all the provocative talking in the world isn't going to deter me," she added.

He shrugged. "I thought not. But are you sure that was why I said such things?"

"You certainly weren't going to propose marriage to me, and I can't do anything else with you," she said bluntly. "Of course you were trying to get me to go home."

"You don't think I find you desirable?"

"It wouldn't matter. You know the rules. That's not how you speak to a well-born unmarried lady."

He smiled. "Certainly not. You're right. I was trying to discourage you. You tell me that nothing will stop you?"

"Nothing," she said clearly, "will stop me."

"Then I apologize," he said seriously. "Sincerely. It was abominable of me. It won't happen again." His smile was crooked. "The least you could do would be to look disappointed."

She laughed because she was relieved. But she discovered herself disappointed too.

"Let's have peace," he said. "Forgive me even though my behavior was calculated to be unforgivable. Shall we stop fencing?"

"I'd like to," she said honestly.

"Done. Where are you going?" he asked as she stood.

"Upstairs, to bed," she said.

"Aren't you going to wait here by the fireside with me until your grandmother awakens?"

She dared not, in spite of his reassurances not to continue his seductive behavior. The night, the hour, their proximity was too much for her now. "My grandmother," she said with more certainty than she felt, "isn't sleeping. She said she was only resting her eyes, and so she is. It's time for us to go upstairs, Grandmamma," she added more loudly.

Her grandmother opened her eyes. She smiled. "Such a lovely little doze I had. Have I missed anything?"

Montrose rose and came to her side. He smiled down at her. "Not a thing, my dear lady, as you know. You're sly as a tabby, and just as tempting to pet. But your husband would have my hand off at the wrist if I tendered it to you for anything more than to help you to your rightful night's rest."

Lady Carstairs gave him her hand and began to rise. "Wicked fellow," she tittered.

He bowed. "I can but try, my dear lady."

Pippa scowled.

"Gentlemen used to speak as you do, when I was young," Lady Carstairs said as she leaned on Montrose's proffered arm. "All innuendo and suggestive. Damned shame they don't talk that way anymore. It kept a lady on her toes. Or her back," she added.

"Grandmother!" Pippa gasped.

"Such a bland generation we have bred," the lady told Montrose. "We had more fun then. A gentleman's attentions made a woman feel wanted even if she didn't care to indulge."

"I'll wager Grandfather didn't speak that way," Pippa said wrathfully.

Her grandmother shook a finger at her again. "Don't wager on what you don't know, missy," she said. "You weren't so anxious to take up a gamble with Montrose here a minute ago, were you? So don't start now."

Her grandmother and Lord Montrose shared a conspiratorial smile.

"You were not sleeping," Pippa said crossly as she trudged up the stair behind them.

"Don't wager on that either," her grandmother cackled.

It was time, Pippa thought as she followed them, to write a letter to her grandfather. The message would have to be deftly phrased and imply more than it said, but she felt her grandmother should have been outraged at how Lord Montrose talked to her, if she'd heard it. And Pippa was sure she had.

Pippa brooded. She was off on a hunt with her beloved grandmother, who was longing for a past generation, and who might be failing in her wits, accompanied by a treacherous gentleman who had too many wits and likely no morals.

But Pippa discovered that the thought didn't sink her, and certainly wouldn't stop her. In fact, she decided it was both too late in the night and too early in the day to compose such a letter. She could do it tomorrow night . . . or the next one.

Chapter 5

"I haven't offended anyone, have I?" Lady Carstairs asked.

The two gentlemen at the card table with her shook their heads in denial.

"As if you could," Maxwell said smoothly.

"I assure you, you have not," his friend Sir Whitney said.

Pippa stared down at the cards in her hand. She hadn't just been offended by her grandmother's offhand remark; she'd been shocked and embarrassed. The topics, words, and phrases coming from her grandmamma's mouth these days would have earned her a smack or a soapy mouth if she'd said them when she'd been a child, and lord knew her grandparents had been liberal to the point of spoiling her badly. Now Pippa's cheeks felt hot and her mouth was dry. Grandmother had just spoken of sexual matters as though she'd been born in a barnyard. The trouble was that she also spoke about bodily functions the same way these strange days.

But then, they'd all been drinking wine since dinner had ended. Maybe her grandmother was flown, drunk as an owl, soused and trying too hard to sit upright to mind her tongue.

No, Pippa admitted, Grandmamma seemed happier than usual, and that was usually the case these days. And she was coherent. Too coherent. Nor did she slur her words or list to one side. She was sober, and utterly abandoned.

"Good. Thank you, gentlemen," Lady Carstairs said happily. "There's not enough plain speaking these days. You two gents aren't poseurs or mealy-mouthed Puritans. Why, look. My granddaughter gets red as a rose whenever I utter a word these days. Mind, it's a charming effect, but she doesn't need beautification, does she?"

Both gentlemen agreed Pippa did not need any cosmetics. They did so without looking at her, paying attention to their cards instead. This didn't surprise Pippa. At dinner, they paid attention to their plates, and Grandmamma. After dinner, they'd blown a cloud together outside, put out their cigars, and then came in to play cards with Lady Carstairs. Though they played cards with her too, Pippa began to think she had somehow become invisible. Her grandmother was the only one that noticed her. At least, tonight she did.

She and her grandmother had traveled together for days now. There was no longer any conversation between them. Grandmother caught up on her sleep as they drove on. When she did speak to her granddaughter, Pippa was pleased that her conversations weren't lurid when they were alone together. She'd have been better pleased if they at least had been different. But the only things she heard were the same old stories and conjectures about her vanished fiancé. Still, they'd been locked up together in a swaying coach so long Pippa realized that she'd have been sick and tired of the angel Gabriel's company by now, had he been traveling with her.

She might even have welcomed some warm talk. But as though proving she wasn't growing addled, Lady Carstairs never said an embarrassing word—until she was with the gentlemen. And they never rode in the coach.

They rode on horses beside the coach and seemed to be having lively conversations. They chatted and laughed together as they rode down the long road to the sea, and Brighton. Whenever the coach stopped to change horses, the gentlemen were merry with each other as they hurriedly ate so they could get back outside again. Pippa resented their good humor, when she herself was bored all the day long.

Sir Whitney was a charming man. He had manners and presence, and never made an unseemly comment to her, although like his friend, he too flattered her grandmother to bits once he saw how starved she was for praise. Or, at least, Pippa thought that must be the reason the two men spent so much time with her.

For the first time in her life, Pippa began to worry about her appearance, or at least how she appeared to others. Noel had swept in like a clean cool wind and swept her up in his attentiveness and enthusiasm for her. Pippa now realized she must have been as starved for company and praise as her grandmother so obviously was. Noel had loved her looks and her wit, he'd said. She'd felt prettier and wittier when she was with him.

But perhaps she was boring to other men? Maybe her fair good looks were out of fashion? She'd heard that brunettes were all the rage in London. Or perhaps, all her years with her grandparents had changed her. She might seem dull-witted, provincial, and too blue-nosed for the company of any lively young gentleman. That might be the reason Noel sheared off so suddenly and never returned to her.

"Bad hand, eh?" her grandmother cackled. "Look at her face, my lords, and know why she never can beat me at cards."

"Maybe she's playing a deeper game," Montrose said. "She might have learned to keep her emotions from her opponents."

"Ha," Lady Carstairs said. "Not her. She's clear as glass to me. She owes me a thousand pins by now. I let her wager them because she ended up owing me so many pence she'd never have cleared up her debt."

"I never could pay my debt to you, Grand-mamma," Pippa said quietly.

"Ha," her grandmother said again. "As if you owed anything. Brightened our lives is what she did, gents, when she came to us. My husband lost his dear son in the same accident in which she lost her father and mother. But no one could have asked for a better legacy than the child they left to us. She was a charming surprise. She didn't cost much to keep. Ate like a bird, and sang like one too; a pretty pet for us to cosset in our old age."

Pippa felt her face growing hot again. She was far past the age of a pretty pet. Maybe that was the root of her problem. She'd been so spoiled she'd forgotten what grown-up men wanted in a woman.

"You're a lucky lady," Sir Whitney told her grandmother.

"But wouldn't her Noel have carried her off out from under your very noses?" Montrose asked.

"Not he," Lady Carstairs said contentedly. "He said that The Old Place suited him right down to the ground and that he would settle down there with our Phillipa so that we could have the halls ringing with children's laughter again."

"He did?" Pippa asked, sitting up straight.

"Of course," her grandmother said placidly. "Why else do you think we gave permission? He wasn't a rich gent, but a smart and good-hearted one. And we didn't want to lose our girl forever. At our age, *forever* is right around the corner."

"But he said we'd travel," Pippa protested. "And he spoke of a house by the river."

"Not to us, he didn't," Lady Carstairs said. She put down her cards and splayed them out. "Ha! Beat you again, my lords, and my little love. I haven't lost my touch. Want another game?"

"It's getting late," Pippa said, although she was wide-awake now. Why hadn't she known that Noel proposed living with her grandparents forever? Or had he? That was another question to include in her letter to her grandfather.

Lady Carstairs laughed. "Late? London is just getting the fun started at this hour, and from what I hear, Brighton is too. The balls and soirees, musicales and gambling all begin when the moon is high over the rooftops. You're too used to the Old Place, Pippa, my love, and you were too right about Bath. That was for invalids and old crones. Now we'll be living in a different world, like London itself in gaiety, and you may as well get used to it before you even think of going to London."

"Have you never been to London, Miss Phillipa?" Sir Whitney asked in surprise.

"Of course I have," Pippa said. "But only briefly. Grandmother had a heavy chest contagion the Season I was supposed to spend there, and the next year it was something else, and then I suppose," she said, her voice becoming lower, "it became foolish to think of myself wearing white gowns and playing a dewy young girl."

"Then your grandmother is right," he said. "Brighton's a good place to learn the evil ways of London, if on a smaller scale, should you ever want to go there again."

"Stop, Whit, you'll frighten her," Lord Montrose said. "And remember, she's only going in order to find her lost fiancé, not to learn to dance and drink and laugh the night away."

"But I am," Lady Carstairs protested. She was pink-faced from laughing. Pippa thought she looked years younger tonight in the ruddy glow of the firelight. The cheerful illumination erased lines from her face, smoothed out hollows and brightened her entire demeanor. She looked like a plump little robin.

"She can watch and learn," Lady Carstairs said. "As for me, I intend to make up for all the lost years. Not that I minded losing them, but I think I was gone from the gaiety of Society for so long I quite forgot it. You gentlemen bring it back to me. Not only the parties but also the people we knew, and the salons. My husband and I had quite a fashionable salon of our own in our day. Our parlor was stuffed with lords and ladies, and those females who wanted to be ladies," she added with a wink.

"We entertained politicians and artists," she went on, "as well as those in Society—the eccentrics and notorious as well as the famous. We even had visitors from the stage. Well-known ones, of course. We hosted royalty from every land, and diplomats, generals, and admirals, painters and even poets. Poets? Gads!" she went on, making a face, "I'm sorry I thought of them. I hear they're even more the vogue now, what with that lusty

Byron warming up all the ladies, he and all those other 'Romantic' layabouts."

Pippa smiled too. Times like these made her think that what was happening to her grandmother was only fond memory making her escape to a happier time.

"Take my advice," Lady Carstairs told the men, waving a ringed forefinger at them. "Never give houseroom to a poet. They languish and pose, trying to look sensitive and otherworldly. Most are handsome devils. But they're more lecherous than randy old men, and handier with females than sailors fresh from a two-year stint at sea. The housemaids' bottoms were black and blue, and not just because those poets' fingers were inky. They'll seduce anything that sits and listens to them long enough. We used to say you had to watch your lap dogs chastity when they were in your house. And mind, whether rich or poor, poets never put a pence in their host's pot, not the chamber pot nor cooking pot, and they eat like locusts too.

"But we'll avoid them in Brighton and have grand times with some real gentlemen. So learn to be like me," Lady Carstairs cautioned Pippa. "Sleep the day away so you can be bright and smart all night. We're looking for your Noel, remember, not a bloody poet."

Pippa blanched at the nasty word. The gentlemen didn't seem to notice. That was why, she thought with humiliation, they were gentlemen, after all.

Her grandmother went on, "We don't need the Old Place ringing with the noise of a rubbishy poet's brats, no matter how lusty the lad, do we, my love?"

Pippa cast down her gaze. She had to face it. She didn't know what was happening to her grandmother.

"But we ought to get some sleep now if we want to be at Brighton by tomorrow night," Montrose said. "Because we'll have to leave bright and smart early tomorrow morning."

"Ah well," Lady Carstairs said, reluctantly putting down her cards. "So be it."

For the first time since they'd met, Pippa really wanted to kiss Lord Montrose.

The wind held a hint of a tangy saline breeze from the sea. Pippa pulled her shawl more closely around her shoulders as she stood by the fence that enclosed the inn's kitchen garden. She looked out into the darkness. The world was quiet except for the trees sighing in the wind and soft insect sounds. She breathed deep and felt the cool touch of the wind calming her. Her bedchamber had been too hot, her grandmother had snored too loud, and her heart had been too heavy to get to sleep. She didn't know what lay ahead, and was no longer sure of what was behind her. She wished she could go home; and yet she never wanted to go back again.

There was only a thin spindle of a moon, and looking up, she felt as lost as a spinning star in the vast firmament above her.

"Sometimes," a velvety voice said from the shadows behind her, "on a journey, there comes a moment when longing for home conflicts with the desire to go on to a place where nothing is familiar."

She didn't have to turn around. Pippa knew that voice and the sweet smell of the cigarillo she now scented on the night air. "Is that how you feel?" she asked.

"No," Montrose said. He moved until he stood by her side. She saw the small red ember of his cigarillo in the utter darkness. It was a comforting glow in the deep night. "I always want to move on," he mused. "But I recall feeling that way when I was as young as you are."

"I'm no longer young," she said in a whisper.

"Oh no," he said low. There was laughter in his voice. "You are an old lady, to be sure."

She didn't answer him. It was wrong to stand in the dark alone except for a virile male. She was very aware of his masculinity even though he had never made an improper gesture toward her, and she doubted he ever would. Except, tonight, here in the darkness, she was no longer sure of that.

His voice came softer. "You've never seen her act this way before?"

She didn't pretend she didn't know what he was talking about. She shook her head, forgetting that he mightn't see it in the darkness.

But he did. "Have you written to your grandfather to tell him about it?"

She shook her head again, and shivering, tugged her shawl more closely around herself. "I don't want to turn back now," she said. "And if he thinks she's failing he may order us home. But I must find out what happened to Noel, and I know I won't be allowed to go on alone."

She spun to face him, her eyes wide and gleaming in the scant light of the ravaged moon. "Do you think she'll do herself some harm?" she asked. "When she's with you gentlemen she forgets herself, or remembers herself, I can't say which. It's only words, but what words! She was never vulgar before or ever said anything racy. She and my grandfather never uttered a word out of place to me or each other or the servants."

"She harms your sensibilities more than she does herself," he said. He cast down his cigarillo and ground it under his boot. "So what are you going to do?"

"If more than her speech changes I may have difficulty," she said. "But now? It doesn't matter what Society thinks of me. I'm not coming out on the Town. My grandfather's reputation matters, but he's secure in that whatever she says. So I'll go on until I know what happened to Noel."

"And then?"

She shrugged. "I don't know. If it turns out he wanted to be free of me, then he is. If it transpires that he wants to continue our engagement, I'm not sure I will unless there's good reason for his disappearance. And if he was harmed, or held captive, or is dead, I'll decide upon the circumstance."

"And so you're alone even if you do find him," he said.

She nodded, unable to speak against the huge lump she suddenly felt rising, clogging her throat.

He stepped near, and then nearer still. She turned and raised her head to try to see his expression. She scented wine and tobacco and leather, and unconsciously took a step closer to him because she was alone and he was the only real and whole and warm thing in the strangeness of this new and limitless night.

He lightly laced his hands behind her neck and bent to touch his forehead to hers. She was stunned into absolute passivity. He cupped his hands around her head, his two thumbs stroking her cheeks.

"Don't worry," he said as softly as the night around them.

She tried to think of what to say, but then felt his fingers playing with a small stray coil of hair at the side of her face and swallowed hard and closed her eyes, thinking of nothing but the sensation of it.

"Silk," he whispered, and on the dying sibilance of the word, brought his lips to hers.

She stayed still. His kiss was astonishing. It was comforting and startling, warm and sweet all at once. Unknowing, uncaring, she moved closer and opened her mouth against his. Their kiss deepened. Her breathing grew ragged even as her body reacted to the warm strength of the man.

It was too delicious. She needed more. That finally made her remember herself. She tried to pull away. But it was too late. His mouth was already gone from hers. His hand lingered a scant second longer and then left her.

"You shouldn't have done that," she breathed.

"No. Neither should you have. Don't worry. Not about me. Let me do that. I give you a good-night," he said and disappeared into the darkness again, leaving her feeling more starkly alone than she had before.

Chapter 6

"Shall I congratulate you, or saddle up your horse and help you ride off into the night?" a weary voice said from out of the darkness.

Montrose dropped the boots he'd just removed in the outer hall. He sank to a chair in the inn's bedchamber and stared into the darkness. "You're awake," he said.

"Of course. How could I sleep? You tiptoed out of here as quietly as a bull elephant. Not only was I awake," Whit said, rising to one elbow in the bed, "I was observant, out of curiosity and a care for your life. You will note, or would if I lit a lamp, that I am also dressed. There was scant moonlight but enough once your eyes get used to it. I saw you go out and watched you while you were outside. You weren't shot or kidnapped, so I didn't race to your rescue. But there was danger enough, I'd say.

You've been out playing with fire, old friend. Did you get burned?"

Montrose ran a hand over his eyes. "No," he said abruptly. "I should have insisted on a separate room."

"Much good it would have done. Then you would have slept in the loft in the barn with our valets," his friend said as he rose from the bed and began to remove his jacket. "There isn't another space to be found in this place. I looked. Lady Carstairs demanded her own room, and you were playing the Cavalier. You granted it to her. Miss Phillipa got her own room too. Other travelers hogged the rest. We are stuck with each other.

"You aren't the most charming bedmate I could have found," Whit went on, "but if I can bear it, so can you. In fact, this mattress tick is so overstuffed that if you get into bed, you'll discover it's difficult to get out of, much less roll about. So we won't disturb each other. Enough. Out with it. Are you compromised? Or did you compromise her?"

"It was too dark to see my hand in front of my face," Montrose complained. "How could you see her?"

"As easily as you did."

"I was whispering to her."

"Ah. She has ears on her lips. Talented lady."

Montrose rubbed the smile from his own lips, stripped off his neckcloth, and threw it to the side. "I suppose you wouldn't believe she had something in her eye?"

"Oh, that I do. It was you."

"She didn't cry foul," Montrose said, peeling off his jacket. "Neither do I. It was an impulse. A moment."

"Yours or hers?"

Montrose ignored him and pulled his shirt over his head.

"To frighten her away?" his friend asked as Montrose's head emerged again. "To chase her back home?"

"To comfort her. To comfort me. Who knows?" Montrose said, shrugging. "It was, as you so nicely noted, a huge mistake."

"Unpleasant, eh?" Whit said, removing the rest of his clothes except for his breeches.

"No, damn your so observant eyes, but it wasn't," Montrose said with a snarl. "Quite the opposite. Oh, well. I'll admit it. It was temptation and I succumbed, which surprised me as much as it does you."

"No surprise. I like her," his friend said, crawling into the huge bed.

"Then why aren't you courting her?"

"Because I noticed how you look at her," Whit said, "and the way you don't speak about her. Because she's a lady in distress, and that was always your weakness. Because she doesn't seem to have a protector or a real friend in the world, and she's intelligent, well spoken, and well bred. She's made for you."

There was no answer for a moment as Montrose stripped off his hose.

"Would you mind if I courted her?" his friend persisted. "I failed to mention that she is also rarely lovely. And though neither of us needs it, rarely wealthy too, I'd guess. Or will be. She's old Carstairs's only chick."

"She'll be wealthy if his slightly dotty wife doesn't up and marry one of the footmen if the old fellow passes first," Montrose commented sourly. "And yes, I'd mind. It would be interference. She wants to find her damned Noel."

"And so she kisses you?"

Montrose ignored that. His eyes having adjusted to the scant moonlight, he stalked over to the nightstand nearby.

"And if she doesn't find her Noel?" Whit persisted.

"She'll find another in time. She needs that time. As for me? She's charming and bright, and nevertheless I shouldn't have acted on impulse. I can't. I'm not ready to wed," Montrose said as he poured water from a pitcher on the nightstand into the basin there.

"And as for me?"

"You aren't serious."

"Neither are you."

Montrose cupped his hands and filled them with water, then splashed his face. "Brr. The least you could have done was to have the water reheated, Nanny," he complained.

He didn't say anything more until he'd scrubbed his face, bathed his bare chest, taken up a towel and was drying himself. "I said I'm *not ready* for marriage, not dead," he finally said.

Then, clad only in his breeches, he approached the huge bed. "I have nothing against marriage," he said. "And she is all you say. But I don't really know her and she doesn't really know me, and my job is to find her fiancé, not to be him. My only regret is that I may have ruined my masquerade. She may never think of me as a man milliner again. It was difficult even for me to pretend to be interested only in fashion at a moment like that."

"So it was a moment."

"Which is over now."

"You've nothing against marriage?" Whit asked.

"There's another surprise. I thought you were determined to remain a bachelor."

"Why?" Montrose asked, pausing at the other side of the bed, the outline of his slender figure tensed.

Now his friend foundered. "Well . . . because of your father, and his attitude toward you, and all that nonsense. I can't think you'd find the prospect pleasing. Don't forget, I've known you and your family for a long time."

"I can hardly forget that. Our Duncan thought you were another brother until he was out of short pants," Montrose said, relaxing. "But if my father was cruel it was only because he had no heart left to be kind. Was ever a fellow more unfortunate in his loves? My mother died before I could focus my eyes on her, and he couldn't forget her. I look like her, they say. Hence, it was a long time before he could bear the sight of me."

"You're very understanding," his friend murmured.

"Understanding someone is simple enough, there's no energy involved. Not all my affect of a fribble, a languishing lump of Fashion, is assumed, you know."

His friend's laughter was low and disbelieving.

"No, really, I'd like to be lazy and unconcerned, I

just can't help getting involved with life," Montrose complained. "But really, how can one not be sorry for my poor father? Anyway, he made it easier for me. He saw his attitude toward me for what it was, regretted it, and mended his ways. We're actually friends now. He tried even more; he sought to give me a mother and married again. He married Elspeth; she was a joy. He loved her as deeply as he had my own mother. She gave him Duncan and peace of mind, until she shattered him when she broke her neck trying to prove her horsemanship. And so then he married Celeste, whom he didn't love. Well, who would? A mistake. Better to have a heart broken than chipped away at. He's stuck with her and their Theo the Terror now, and he couldn't be unhappier."

His friend was silent as Montrose obviously thought of something and returned to his cast-off clothing. He bent down, searched in his discarded jacket pocket, and produced an object. It was a pistol. Osbourne saw it in silhouette, glinting in the sparse light as Montrose again approached the bed, and stiffened. He only breathed again when he saw his friend tuck the weapon under the pillow he would use.

"Insurance for the night," Montrose explained, as he got into the bed on the farthest side from his friend. "Never go to bed in a strange place without your breeches on, even if you've had them off for a sweet reason. And never sleep without cold steel of some sort under your head, so you don't get any in your brain. Gad. This mattress is so stuffed, I sink a foot."

"You'll be asleep in a tick," Osbourne murmured.

"Lovely pun," Montrose said, smiling.

"So then, if your heart is safe from being pierced, aren't you afraid of it being broken?"

"I am not my poor father, thank the deity. I've never had to worry about it. My heart remains seriously unscathed. I think because I think too much." He laughed. "My father is a more emotional fellow than I am, even if he never shows it. Don't fret, Whit. There's hope for me. If I feel desire I sate it. And if I have to do that with a different female than the one I really wanted, I can live with that if only because I don't fancy settling down yet. No matter how I feel, I'll be like a brother to the lady in the morning, and we'll be in Brighton by nightfall, so the danger of traveling through Britain with a winsome wench will be over, at least for me."

"If you find the elusive Noel? And what if he's dead? Won't you want to stay and comfort her?"

"I don't think he's dead," Montrose said as he settled himself. He crossed his arms on his chest and looked up at the ceiling. "More and more I become convinced he is not. He left too fast and for mysterious reasons. Mysterious equals suspicious. And he left hardly any trail behind him. Murder victims leave some sort of trail. He's vanished too completely. I begin to think that he's hiding and that there's more to this than I first thought.

"Old Carstairs was a force in the government in his youth," Montrose went on, thinking aloud. "He still is counsel to the royals, the thinkers, the planners and plotters, and more importantly, the politicians. He knows everything about the government; he's a fount of information. Consider the facts. We've been at war with France, king and consul, for almost half a century. Fifty years," he marveled. "Can you credit that?"

"Centuries before that too," his friend commented.

"Aye, but fifty years with little let-up? *Incroyable,* as they say. They've gone from king, to rabble, to opportunists, to the greatest one of them all: Napoleon, and from there to God knows where. They've been in turmoil for generations. My mother was born there. She was born to nobility and wealth and left in poverty. She escaped to come here and did with only her head on her shoulders, and lucky to have it."

Montrose paused, and his friend thought he'd fallen asleep, but then his voice came clear.

"We've been at peace with France for scant months," Montrose went on thoughtfully. "You know Bonaparte can't get what he wants if we remain so. But he needs information about us as much as he needs arms. He's a clever man. We may mock his size and his ambitions, but that's like whistling in the dark. He is *formidable*," he said, pronouncing the word with a French accent.

"He knows information is a weapon too. Our Noel may well have been sent to pick old Carstairs's brain. Becoming engaged to his granddaughter may have been the last lever he needed to win over Carstairs's last reservations. They talked. Perhaps the old man talked too much. Maybe he's as daft as his poor wife seems to be now. I hope not.

"The errant fiancé's trail seems to lead to Brighton. Why Brighton out of all England? Maybe because there are so many French émigrés there? They came in hordes during the Revolution as refugees; some stayed. But some came to England for other reasons. And some still do. Whatever it was that drew Noel Nicholson, if that's his real name, interests me as much as alarms me. He may have had a political contact there. For all we know he may be back in France by now, talking to our enemies, because don't doubt we still have them."

"You'd pursue him there?"

"To the ends of the earth," Montrose said on a huge yawn. "I gave my word. But not until tomorrow morning."

She thought she'd be up all night, tossing and turning, her lips still burning, but the moment Pippa put her head on her pillow she dropped off to the first sweet easy sleep she'd had in a long time. Lord Montrose's kiss had steadied her. Of course it had also aroused her. The fact of it, the nearness of his warm body, the taste and strength and scent of him had rocked her. But it had also comforted her. Not just because he'd found her desirable. She rejoiced, knowing that for a certainty now. That sort of electric kiss had to be real because it had shocked him as much as it had her.

But beyond that, there had been a connection made. An attraction acted upon in spite all effort to remain uninvolved. It had been there for him as well as for her. Of that, she was also certain.

His disregarding her as a woman had been a pose. His tenderness, the desire and yearning in his kiss had been real. That moment in the night had changed everything. She knew she wasn't alone anymore.

So she hummed as she bathed in the morning, and smiled as her maid helped her dress. She laughed aloud for no reason as her maid did her hair, and blamed it on a coil of hair tickling her neck. When she recalled the gentle hand that had caressed her neck, she shivered a little and smiled again.

She danced out of her room and went to collect her grandmother. Her grandmother was also blithe. But that meant nothing. She always was at this hour these days because it meant she might be joining the gentlemen again.

But they'd breakfasted earlier, the innkeeper said. They were already attending to their horses, their servants, and the coaches. Still, Pippa and her grandmother made a good breakfast and went outside into a rarely lovely spring day.

Pippa was glad she'd worn her yellow and green walking gown and had let her hair down, so it could reflect the sunlight. Her grandmother was pert and amusing. The gentlemen bowed and exchanged easy morning greetings with them.

Pippa dared a glance at Sir Whitney when they did. Her heart slowed to its usual pace. Nothing in his expression or calm gray eyes showed he suspected anything of Lord Montrose, or her. Montrose had been a gentleman. He'd told no one. But when she finally gathered the courage to look fully at him, neither did anything in his calm demeanor suggest that he remembered anything of last night. She knew he couldn't have forgotten.

She couldn't, but she too kept any trace of her feelings to herself. She'd relive that delicious moment, gloat over it, study it, and think about all the possibilities only when she was alone again. Pippa's heart was high as she stepped into the carriage. Brighton by evening! She'd certainly speak to him at dinner.

She settled herself in the coach and frowned. What was she doing? She wasn't thinking about Noel. Not at all, and hadn't since Montrose kissed her. No, she thought honestly, not since he'd come near her in the night. She was thoughtful but not gloating as the coach pulled off onto the main road again.

Her grandmother fell asleep almost immediately, so Pippa had time enough and to spare to do all the thinking that she hadn't last night. Noel had never kissed her like that. Well, she supposed he had, but it hadn't felt like that. Still, what folly for her to form a new tendre now, and especially for a man of so many affects and poses, secrets and moods! And yet, what difference did it make? It was a moment now forever gone. She knew she meant nothing to Montrose. Or did she? Pippa was lost in thought as the carriage rattled on toward Brighton, which might be the end of her search and, she realized, of her ambitions . . . that was, when she understood exactly what those ambitions now were.

Chapter 7

Pippa went to bed in the dark and awoke at dawn. She stretched herself, remembered where she was, and leaped up. She ran to the window and pulled back a curtain. Brighton! She was in a fine hotel in the center of town. Last night she'd noted that the hotel itself was clean, well furnished, and in good repair, but the darkness had obscured any real look at its surroundings. Nothing prepared her for the view out her high window.

A beautiful scene was before her. A long, oval, well-tended green swath lay in the center of the town, with lovely homes, inns, hotels, and shops on all sides of it. When she looked up she saw the glittering sea in the distance. When she looked into the middle distance, she saw the newly risen sun glinting off huge golden domes and minarets. Surely that was some ancient church, built by a foreign order. But then she remembered she'd heard that the prince was building a luxurious pavilion here. Could he have created it?

Buildings of many styles bordered the long swath of grass in the center of the city. Staid old homes sat snug, near the road. Older buildings tilting with age stood shoulder to shoulder with new gray and white town houses. It all fit, somehow, and gave the view an aura of charm.

When Pippa looked directly down, she saw that with the rising sun came fashionable equestrians, cantering out for their morning's ride, as they'd done in London that time she'd visited there. She stayed by the window, watching the well-bred, handsome horses and their equally well-bred and handsomely dressed riders.

Pippa put her elbows on the sill, and breathed deep. She scented the sea and the rare, fair spring morning. This was a far better place to be than Bath. The people she saw were young and able, or if not precisely young, then at least agile. It seemed a lively prosperous village. It was even possible Noel was here, or had passed through. She frowned. But if so, why? And where was he now?

If she found him, could she ever forgive him for leaving and not coming back, not telling her his reasons, and not communicating with her for so long? If he were alive and well, would he want her forgiveness? It no longer mattered. All she wanted now was an answer; an end to the uncertainty and seclusion the situation had brought her. She smiled. All answers might be found here in gloriously glittering Brighton.

Pippa was up and dressed long before her grandmother stirred from her room. That was nothing new. Unless they were traveling on early in the morning, Grandmother stayed abed until noon. It was fashionable, or so she said. And Grandmother, for all her new flirtatious ways, was not a young woman anymore. But Pippa was, and she couldn't wait to be out and about.

After she'd hurriedly washed and dressed, Pippa, in a blue walking gown, with a shawl over her shoulders and a pert straw bonnet on her flaxen hair to prevent the newly risen sun from etching freckles on her nose, left the inn to take the morning air. Her maid accompanied her. The girl was as eager as she was to see the town. Pippa sighed with pleasure. This time was her own. Her outfit was proper, so she didn't worry about her appearance. Her maid was with her; so strange men wouldn't accost her. But neither did either of the two men she knew. She frowned after she stepped out the door to greet the new day. There wasn't a trace of the marquis or Sir Whitley to be seen, and they usually appeared with the dawn. At least, they appeared and then left to go riding together.

Both gentlemen had avoided her since yesterday, although whenever they saw her grandmother they were all smiles and gallantry. It wasn't as if they were rude to her, Pippa thought. They just made themselves least in sight when they spied her. She didn't blame them. What sort of female went from home looking for her lost fiancé, and then ended up in another fellow's arms? Certainly, the marquis didn't understand her. But then, neither did she, not anymore.

"We'll go for a short walk," Pippa told her maid. "If you get tired, let me know."

Anne giggled. "Thank you, but I'm from the county, miss, same as you. Not likely to get tired on a walk, are we?"

"No," Pippa agreed. "So. Now the question is, do we go left or right?"

She startled as she felt a sudden blast of warm air on her cheek and a snorting sound, as a pleasant male voice asked, "How about straight down the middle?"

She wheeled around and looked up. A huge gray horse stood at her side and looked at her with interest. Lord Montrose sat atop it and was smiling down at her as he held the horse still. He wore gray and black, and a high beaver hat sat at a cocky tilt on his dark head. He looked immaculate, as ever, at ease and amused, as always. Her breathing sped up, then slowed as she succeeded in concealing the sudden jolt of joy she felt at seeing him so unexpectedly.

"I've taken this fellow out for a run," he said, patting the horse. "Now, the least I can do is the same for you."

Her head went up, her nostrils flared. "I don't need a run, thank you," she said, smoothing her gloves for something to do instead of gaping at him.

He sketched a bow from the saddle. "Excuse me. Badly put. I meant to say, would you care to come for a ride with me?"

"I'm not dressed for riding as you can see," she said briskly.

"But you are," he said. "Not for riding a horse, of course; but perfectly for riding in a phaeton. There's one in the hotel's stable ready to be out and around the town, with room for you and me and your maid. I can show you Brighton and tell you its secrets before the noonday sun rouses your grandmother from her bed. Care to go with me?"

It was an irresistible offer for too many reasons

for Pippa to consider just now. She nodded. "That would be useful. I'd like that, yes. I know nothing about Brighton and am not likely to be here again."

"So stay here," he said. "Let me return this nag. I'll be back with the carriage and we'll be off."

Pippa stood waiting. The sun rose higher. It began to seem like a long time, but she couldn't be sure because she was so eager to be off. Still, as time went on, she became afraid he'd been making a jest of her. She'd wait, she vowed, just a little longer, and then stride off with her maid. He could catch up with her later, if indeed, he'd even meant there to be a "later" for them.

She was about to step off when a jaunty yellow high phaeton with blue trim rounded the corner with Montrose at the reins. A young tiger, a boy to hold the horse for his lordship when he stopped, was perched on the back axle. The phaeton had two seats, and the boy helped the maid clamber in the back as Lord Montrose extended a hand to Pippa so she could climb onto the driver's seat with him.

She settled herself and looked at him quizzically. He still wore a dark jacket, but it was a different one, and his hair was obviously damp now, beneath a different high beaver hat.

"I washed and changed," he said in explanation to her curious look. "Hurriedly to be sure, but thoroughly. I love to ride, but will not put up with smelling like a horse."

"And so that's why you're late?" she asked.

He smiled. "Wouldn't you rather I be a jot late and smelling like a rose . . . or rather, a lavender bush?"

She blinked.

"Of course," he went on, as he picked up the reins, "Bonaparte prefers violets, and wears Seven-Eleven, while our Prince enjoys something sweeter and muskier, but one's scent is not political, or shouldn't be, don't you think?"

He was, she realized, no matter his preference for kisses from females, still a consummate fop. And she oughtn't to forget it for a moment. Curiously, it both calmed and disappointed her.

"You smell like spring rain," he went on, "with a touch of lilac. Or is the wind blowing from the direction of those magnificent lilacs there by the corner house?"

"I don't remember what I bathed with this morning, or put on after," she snapped. This wasn't true. She used fine French lilac soap, but she wouldn't give him the satisfaction of knowing it. He knew too much already. Or did he? She'd had little time to talk with him recently; first, because she'd felt so shy with him after that kiss, and then because they'd never been alone after that until now.

"Have you had any communications with anyone who saw Noel?" she asked now, because her maid was too far back to hear what they said over the sounds of the horse and carriage coursing over the cobbles.

He laughed. "So soon? No, not even I'm that efficient. But I've sent out my card to everyone who matters so I've hopes of going on polite visits and hearing something new soon enough."

"Can you think of any reason why he'd have gone to Brighton in particular?" she asked anxiously. "You never really said. I know grandmother and I have followed you like ducklings, but why exactly are we here?"

"Because you wouldn't go home," he said pleasantly.

Her smile was tight. "That's not what I meant and you know it," she said.

He shrugged.

"Then, I'll ask a simpler question that won't bore you. Why did my grandfather recommend you?" she asked.

"I'm never bored with you," he said. "That's part of the problem. But good," he added, slanting a dark glance at her. "Why didn't you ask that days ago?"

She was still for a moment. "I'm used to following my grandfather's instructions, I suppose. Now I think I ought not to have gone off so blindly. Why did he send us to you?"

"Your grandfather didn't ask me. He knew better. I fact, he asked me nothing."

She sat up straight, her eyes wide.

"He couldn't," Maxwell said, "I've not had the pleasure of meeting him. Don't look so shocked. And don't leap out of the carriage. He asked a mutual friend to recommend someone. I am that someone. And yes, I've tracked down missing persons before. The difference is that this time the missing person doesn't want to be found. Or so I'm coming to believe. Can you think of any reason for that?"

She shook her head. "None. I told you, he was eager to marry me. When he said he had some matters to take care of before we could marry, I never doubted him."

"Did you love him that much?"

She looked down. "I think I told you that too. I don't know. Not anymore."

"Abandonment can harden the heart," he said blandly.

"Well, it's that, and that I began to realize I'd been alone too long when I met him. I mean, not exposed to eligible gentlemen. So who knows how I might have felt had I more suitors? That's as may be. I have to know, why would Noel come to Brighton? . . . if he did."

"Why would he go to Bath?" he asked as answer. "Those people I spoke with lead me to believe he did both. Brighton is the closest city to Dieppe, across the channel. Had he relatives or friends in France?"

"You should have asked that before," she answered testily.

He smiled. "Good parry. So I should have, and so I did. I merely didn't ask you because I thought he never told you the truth about himself."

"Well, he mightn't have, I suppose, but he never mentioned any desire to leave England or any relatives"—her voice dwindled—"anywhere."

They drove on in silence for a few minutes. The sea breeze couldn't dispel the growing warmth of the day. Pippa removed her hat, raised her head, closed her eyes, and let the light breeze play with her hair. She thought he might be looking at her, and was glad her eyes were closed. He was maddeningly attractive, even though she'd never fancied such a man of Fashion before. She'd never met one before, actually. It might have been the fact that all the things he considered essential to his wardrobe, all the airs and graces he affected were so exquisite and fine that they seemed feminine, and because that aspect of him conflicted so strongly with the powerful masculine appeal that emanated from the man.

"Won't your nose turn pink?" Maxwell asked, cutting into her reverie.

She smiled. Of course a fop would think of that. But she reveled in the way the wind teased at her hair so that it slid from its restraints and grazed her cheeks as silken streamers. And the sunlight on her face felt like a caress. "Powder can conceal it," she murmured as she stared into the scarlet patterns the sunlight made on her inner eyelids. "Or a concoction of crushed cucumber might do it. I really don't care. I've had much more powder and facial cream than sunshine lately."

He chuckled. Or clucked his tongue at her, or the horse. She didn't care. But soon she lowered her head and looked sidewise at him again.

"My lord?" she said so softly he had to incline his head toward her.

"That . . . incident, the other night," she went on, avoiding his eyes, "was very wrong on my part, as well as yours."

He sighed.

"I know," she said. "We've discussed it, but I can't stop regretting it. I should have known better. I ask again, can we disregard it?"

"I don't regret it," he said. "Rather the reverse. But if you like, we can resolve not to repeat it. It doesn't make me think less of you, by the by. In fact, had you not succumbed to my attentions, I'd think less of you. At least, I would think you weren't precisely human."

Her eyes snapped open and she sat up upright again. "Well, if that doesn't beat all! You think you're that irresistible?"

"No," he said, considering. "I know it."

They fell silent. The next time they spoke was when he pointed out a crew of laborers swarming around a huge domed building by the sea. "There," he said, "is our prince's monstrous big erection. Or part of it."

"My grandmother," she said through gritted teeth, "is not herself these days. Or rather, if she is, it's a self I don't know. But though that might have been said in her youth, deep down she knew it wouldn't be taken the same way today and was moreover outrageous, and she said it for that reason."

"I know," he said more gently. "Is her condition worsening?"

"I don't know," Pippa admitted. "I never saw her like this before. She's happy and healthy, but bawdy and irrepressible."

"She may only be enjoying masculine attentions after so long without them. Your grandfather may have been enchanted and attracted by her liveliness when she was young, but I take it he keeps to himself most of the time these days?"

"Yes, to his books and researches and his visitors," Pippa said.

"And as to why your fiancé visited with him?"

"They spoke politics. Noel was researching a paper he wanted to write for the *Gentleman's Magazine*. Grandfather is a known scholar. They both were fascinated by Bonaparte."

Nothing in Maxwell's expression changed but she got the feeling he was intensely interested.

"In what way?"

"Grandfather said that when a great man arises, he stirs other men to greatness too, and the world becomes a more interesting place."

"More interesting, and more lethal in this case. Was your grandfather an admirer of Napoleon? Was Noel? Don't look so shocked, many loyal Englishmen do admire him."

"No, in fact, the reverse," she said. "Noel thought he was a great evil, and Grandfather said he was like Alexander the Great or Attila the Hun in that his greatness lay in his ability to change the world, not in his honorable intentions."

"Bonaparte's only intentions are to better himself," Maxwell said, turning his attention back to the road. "When the world is in chaos men turn to leaders. Some are born to lead but have the bad luck to be born in peaceful times. The little general was born lucky."

She shivered. "I hope we are not that lucky on this side of the channel."

She gasped as they rounded a curve in the road and she saw a long building topped with glittering golden domes and copulas. "That is beautiful," she said. "I see why they . . . called it as they did."

"It is large," Maxwell agreed. "And rather shocking, to be sure. But that's not where our prince lives. It's his new stables."

"Oh," she said sadly. "Then I can see why he's mocked. It's something out of an Arabian tale, beautiful, but quite out of place here in England. He built it for horses? With poverty being so widespread? No wonder there are those who think Bonaparte's the better man. I don't know if he actually helps the poor in France, but at least he says he will."

"They already helped themselves. He feeds

their greedy intentions. But surely you know females aren't supposed to be interested in politics," he commented.

She lifted her nose, and tried to stare down its inconsiderable length at him. "That," she said, "is something I was lucky enough not to be taught. My grandfather admires wit and brain in a woman." She paused and looked down at her gloves. "My grandmother had that."

"And still does," Maxwell said. "I tell you what, my dear," he added, adopting his bored, amused tones again. "I've an invitation to a soiree at our prince's incomplete pavilion. I do enjoy a good party, but it will also be in the nature of work for me. It's a fine place to hear gossip, since our prince is here. Should you like to come with me? With your grandmother too, of course, and Whitney. There should be no scandal about an engaged lady going out for an evening with her grandmother and a few of her grandmother's frivolous escorts. Everyone who comes to Brighton longs to be asked to see the latest treasures being installed in the Pavilion."

"I'd like that," she said eagerly. "Will I have a chance to meet him?"

"Our prince? Of course."

"I'd like that very much," she said. "So will

Grandmother. Wait until Grandfather hears about it!"

"They are your sun and moon, aren't they?" he asked curiously.

She nodded.

"Then why were you so eager to leave them?"

She held up her head. The sunlight glinted off her hair, making it shine as brightly as the domes they were driving past. "I'm four and twenty now. Noel made me realize time was passing," she said. "And that I hadn't yet lived for myself."

He nodded, and abruptly changed the subject. "Now would you like to see the bathing machines by the sea? Should you like to get out and walk on the strand by the sea for a bit as well?"

"I would," she said, plopping her bonnet on her head again and hurriedly tying its strings. "That would be wonderful."

"It would be a way of living for yourself," he said, "without the encumbrance of a fiancé."

She sobered. She looked at him and her expression was such that the humor in his dark, knowing eyes faded. She thought that he must have forgotten their incident in the night. Nothing in his eyes or his affect showed sensual awareness of her. He must have been testing her or himself that night. Whatever had spurred his desire for her, it was gone now. Well and good she thought, with disappointment she steadfastly ignored, she could speak to him honestly without that tug of attraction cluttering up her mind.

"I'm not encumbered now, true," she said. "This whole journey was to find out why. But now I see there's more to it than that and more to life than I knew. Noel awakened me. When he left and didn't return I was crushed and felt outcast and shamed. Now I'm grateful, whatever reasons he had. Now I want to see it all for myself."

"But a female isn't free in our world if she has no husband," he said. "So you yourself said."

"I was wrong," she retorted. "Just look at me. I am free. Maybe it's better to be a disgraced lady than an obedient one. How much scandal can one female bear? I think that if it doesn't bother her, there's no limit. If I am whispered about when I did nothing wrong, then there's little else I can do that's worse, I think. And since I was only disgraced because someone else acted badly I begin to wonder what exactly is good and bad, and if it matters at all, at least to me."

"I didn't mean to start a revolution," he said with a wry smile. "I begin to think that you ought never to have come to Brighton at all."

"Revolutions are caused by unhappiness and

desperation," she said, staring straight ahead. "That's what Grandfather says. And I was suffering from both."

"And now?" he asked quizzically.

"And now," she said with defiance, "we shall see, shall we?"

"So," he said, "we shall. But remember, your time is limited. This is all to pass that time until we can find out what happened to your errant fiancé. And when we do, no matter what you decide, whether you take him up or toss him away, you can't go capering off all over the world by yourself again."

She turned to him and smiled. "Why not? Who can say? I've only just begun."

Chapter 8

After much thought and trying on and casting off, Pippa finally decided on a dark blue gown with a filmy silver overskirt to match the colors of the moonlight shadows. Her hair was sleeked and pulled tight to a tumble of curls high on the back of her head. A single strand pearl necklace glowed at her throat. She stared into the looking glass and felt she lacked something. She had little color herself, her lips were pink, her hair light. The effect was elegant, she hoped, and she couldn't find a fault in her complexion or attire. But she thought she looked perhaps a bit too subtle for such a night of magnificence.

She badly needed a touch of color. But she'd not dare wear gold, red, or any vibrant jewel colors because although bright colors might liven her appearance, they also might make her harmonize with the prince's lavish Pavilion. She'd heard it was furnished in the latest Chinoiserie style, all dragon red and glittering gold; a gleaming symphony of exotic colors. She wanted to make an impression, after all, not fade into the wallpapers.

Of course, she didn't want to make a spectacle of herself either, she hurriedly reminded herself. Fine thing that would be, to be seen dressed like a doxie, dancing the night away, lost in gaiety, when anyone might find out she didn't know what was happening to her lost fiancé. So she guessed she was correctly dressed. Even so, she felt a bit flat.

She hadn't seen the marquis or Sir Whitney for days. But this morning she'd gotten a note from Maxwell saying that he might have something to tell them this very night. The thought of possible news of her missing fiancé wasn't what she was dwelling on now. The fact that she was going to a soiree at the Royal Pavilion amidst the famous and infamous of English society and might meet the Prince of Wales himself occupied her mind too much.

"You look like a moon princess," her maid cooed. "Cool and lovely."

"Thank you," Pippa commented absently as she turned to one side and pulled in her stomach in. She looked at herself up and down, backward and forward in the glass.

Pity, Pippa thought, that she couldn't pull in her impudent, jutting rear and full bosom so she could look even more like a Greek statue, as was the mode. At least she'd do. Again, she wished she had fashionable inky black hair and long-lashed dark sultry eyes. But that would make her a twin to a certain gentleman and she certainly didn't want that. After all, opposites attracted. She blinked. She certainly didn't want to attract him.

Liar, she thought, and so stopped thinking about it, picked up a blue silk fan, a silvery shawl, and went to fetch her grandmother.

Pippa took a few steps down the hall, delighting in the feeling of her whisper-thin overskirt floating around her. Then she stopped and listened. Laughter was coming from belowstairs: her grandmother's new high-pitched giggles, and the rich sound of masculine merriment accompanying it. Pippa wasn't a woman who cursed, but what she was thinking might have shocked even the new, jolly care-for-nothing grandmother she found herself with.

She tried to glide slowly down the stairs to make an entrance. She could have tumbled down the length of it, she thought sourly. No one paid attention. There was her grandmother, looking like a merry little elf, swathed in yards of scarlet and gold. She wore a golden necklace and more rings and bracelets than Pippa could count. She had scarlet feathers in her bright hair. Garish as it was, it suited her. Her round cheeks were flushed, her eyes sparkled. The flush and sparkle had obviously been enhanced by the subtle use of paint and brush. But the lady was vibrant and looked adorable.

The gentlemen were in the height of formal fashion, with no jewels or fobs or glimpses of bright waistcoats to ruin the stark black and white of their attire. But they didn't look funereal. Maxwell wore a single signet ring on his slender hand. His friend had a simple pearl stickpin on his high white cravat.

They all looked up as Pippa came near. Her grandmother lifted a bejeweled hand and waggled a few fingers at her. The gentlemen bowed, and then turned back to Lady Carstairs again.

Many things had happened to Pippa in the last year. She'd been proposed to and become engaged, had a celebration to honor her engagement, had planned a wedding, and then she'd been left in the lurch. Since then, people had begun to look at her, and then away, so as not to seem to be staring at her. She'd hated it, but had gotten used to it. But she'd never been roundly, utterly, completely ignored before.

"You look lovely, Pippa," Lady Carstairs finally said as her granddaughter drew near.

"Cool and collected. You'll do," Maxwell commented.

Pippa was silent as the moon itself as she got into a coach with her grandmother and the two gentlemen. She was so angry she dared not speak. It hardly mattered. The trio in the coach with her were laughing and talking so much they didn't notice.

Then she began to feel sorry for herself; abandoned by her would-be lover, ignored by her once doting grandmother, and absolutely invisible to the striking gentlemen opposite her in the coach. And yet all was as it should be. She was supposed to be grieving for her lost fiancé, not out for a night of dazzling the populace. That was true but was small comfort to her. There was nothing that said an abandoned fiancée couldn't be admired, or even noticed.

Soon enough she heard the distant assurance of the sea on the shore, and saw flaming torches and lights outside the windows of the coach. Their carriage waited in line, stopped in a drive that was illuminated by standing torches and linkboys holding torches as they escorted guests. They were in front of the Royal Pavilion, which itself was lit from every window. It seemed fantastical, a structure made of incandescent domes and cupolas in the darkness of the surrounding night.

So it was as well that she was both sad and angry, Pippa realized as she took Sir Whitney's gloved hand and stepped down to the pavement. She thought she'd be a little country mouse, dazzled and unsure, afraid to the point of mute timidity tonight. Instead, it seemed nothing, not even all this richness and glory, could faze her. She drifted down the drive in the wake of her grandmother and Maxwell and entered the Royal Pavilion, calm as a clam, cool as an oyster, and as seething with anger as a pot that was cooking either one of those cold-blooded creatures.

The interior of the place was just as she'd imagined. Rich Eastern colors decorated the carpets, walls, and ceilings in the great front salon. It was luxurious, rich and fantastical looking, like a page from a tale of Arabian nights. And yet, impossible as it seemed, Pippa had heard this wondrous place still didn't suit the Prince of Wales. He wanted his summer palace to be absolutely glorious and even more fabulous, so had contracted with his architect to build him something even more glamorous.

The guests at the soiree were as magnificently got up as the Pavilion. The women wore all the bright colors their prince admired, with matching jewels, feathers, and flowers at their necks and breasts and in their hair. Pippa felt wan and lost, like a ghost, not a moon princess, as she stepped inside with her party and waited to be announced. Even though the ceiling was high as a cathedral, the noise from the crowd was deafening. The company she saw was composed of bright chattering people of all ages.

They were greeted even before their cards were read aloud to the company.

"By gad!" a bald old gentleman cried out as he approached them, his two arms outstretched. "My teeth are gone, and so's my hearing, but these old eyes can spy a beauty every time."

Pippa hid a smile as he came nearer.

"If it ain't Poppy herself," the old fellow said with gusto as he took Lady Carstairs's hand. "And lookin' even finer than she did a dog's age ago. How are you, my lovely? And where's that bear of a husband? Don't want him blackening my eyes because of what they see."

Pippa's grandmother giggled as the old fellow bent to kiss her bejeweled hand. "Musgrave, you rogue," she said archly. "Talk about not changing! I'd have known you anywhere."

"Duke of Weedon now, Poppy," he said, thrusting out his thin chest. "Castle, acres, estates, and all. I'd have tried harder to make a match with you if I'd had the title then. But I suppose it would've done no good. You had your man, and what a fellow he turned out to be. Famous. Famous everywhere. Beats a duke any day. Where's he now?"

"At home," Lady Carstairs said. "I'm here with my granddaughter tonight."

The old man turned his eyes toward Pippa for the first time. An almost clownish expression of sorrow appeared on his lined and age-spotted face. He took Pippa's hand and patted it. "I'm sorry for you, sweetheart," he said. "Fella must have lost his mind, leaving a pretty bit like you in the lurch. Hey, Poppy," he said, turning to her grandmother again. "That means you and I can have a waltz together again tonight, hey what?"

Lady Carstairs tittered and looked up at her two escorts from under her painted lashes. "Of course you might," she said, "if there is to be dancing."

"I'll talk to our royal host," the duke said. "He's got enough room here for a dozen cotillions. So, if he agrees, you'll dance with me?"

Lady Carstairs turned her head and winked at Maxwell. "If my escorts tonight agree that you may."

"Demmed if you didn't always set the boys to wrangling," the duke said. "But I have precedence so now they'll have to let me take you into the dance first, eh what, my lords?"

Maxwell and Whitney bowed.

"But first let's go in and find some old friends," the duke said, taking Lady Carstairs's arm. The others let the ancient duke lead her into the main salon. They followed as the master of ceremonies hastily announced them. That caused a stir. The older guests at the soiree converged on Lady Carstairs and the duke. Some of the younger ladies and gentlemen immediately made their way to her two noble former escorts. And Pippa stopped where she was, behind her grandmother. She stood alone, feeling out of place, which was odd, she thought, since she also seemed to be invisible.

Sir Whitney disappeared into the crowd.

"I'll be making inquiries," Maxwell told Pippa softly. Then he left her, stopping to have a word with a soberly dressed gentleman before he was gone and into the colorful and clamorous gathering.

The neatly dressed gentleman sauntered over to Pippa. He wasn't precisely handsome but, rather, neat and self-assured. He bowed. "Miss Carstairs," he said in a cool voice. "Allow me to hope that my friend Lord Montrose helps you discover the whereabouts of your errant fiancé."

"Thank you," she said, casting down her gaze, horrified to discover that her reputation had preceded her everywhere.

He chuckled. "Wars may come and peace may go, but withal, gossip remains Britain's leading interest," he said. "Never fear. Like all fresh produce, nothing withers faster."

She was searching for something to say when she noticed that the crowd around them had fallen silent, avidly listening to them.

"Oh that," he said, waving his slender white hand. "My audience. I am Brummell, by the way."

Her eyes widened. The great George "Beau" Brummell, arbiter of Fashion, master of the cutting bon mot, advisor and bosom beaux to the prince himself? This was an unlooked-for honor. She couldn't have spoken if someone had pointed a knife at her and ordered her to.

"You'll survive this," he added in soft tones. "You have Montrose to ensure it, I will assist. Ah, here comes someone who will make them forget everything but him. Bow prettily, and keep smiling."

Pippa looked up and took in another quick breath. Guests were bowing at a pudgy gentleman as he passed through their midst, like tall grasses bending before a breeze. He wore a great-jeweled star on a golden chain on his wide breast. This must be the Prince of Wales himself. But surely it couldn't be. Her grandmother had called him beautiful. The man approaching them was nothing like. His bland face was decidedly plump. His hair was gold, but growing scarce, and he had a huge pillow of a stomach and hefty thighs that his long coat couldn't conceal.

"Ho, Brummell!" he called in a plummy voice. "I arrive!"

Brummell bowed. "As I see, sir."

"You've cornered a pretty pigeon," the Prince said. "But I've spied a lovely partridge. Lady Carstairs," he said, bending slightly over Pippa's grandmother's hand, "it's been years, but you grow lovelier."

"As do you, Your Grace," Lady Carstairs said, beaming. "You haven't changed at all. Pray tell me your secret."

The prince beamed.

"But first," Pippa's grandmother went on, her arm tucked into His Royal Highness's, "may I present my granddaughter, Phillipa?"

"You may," the prince said. He looked at Phillipa, pity clear to see in his mild blue eyes. "Pretty little creature. Forget him, my dear, as he forgot you. Come explore my little summerhouse, surely that will make you forget your cares, as it does for me."

"Smile and smile and smile, whatever happens," Mr. Brummell said into Pippa's ear as he put her arm on his, and they followed their host farther into the Pavilion.

At least afterward she could say that she saw the Prince's pavilion when it was just begun, although to tell the truth, Pippa realized she'd have to make up much of it. The cunning sculptures and artworks, the paintings and tables and chairs, the beds and sofas and ornate ceilings were a blur in her mind because she could only keep thinking, "I am here! In the Royal Pavilion, with the Prince of Wales! With the great Brummell himself, as well!"

There were many rooms and artworks to be seen. But in time, the little parade returned to where they had begun.

Brummel bowed to Pippa. "Thank you for your company," he said simply, and left.

The prince patted Lady Carstairs's hand again. "That thief Carstairs snatched you up before I could speak for you."

"You were only a boy," Lady Carstairs said with a twinkling smile.

"With an eye for a beautiful lady," he said and sketched a bow.

He turned, and nodding at Pippa, he too left,

following Brummel, but not before Pippa couldn't help letting out a small yelp. She spun around, but the Prince was already fading into the crowd converging on him. Pippa glowered after the vanishing prince, wishing she could rub her rear. It hurt.

"Our prince admires you," Maxwell said, laughter in his voice as he sauntered to her side.

"He pinched me," Pippa whispered in fury. "I know it was him. Mr. Brummel had already left."

"Brummel wouldn't do such a thing," Maxwell said. "It might ruin his manicure. Our prince is known for it. It's his seal of approval. The only reason he didn't pinch your grandmother is that he's too clever. He knew he'd be up against corsets as tight as the one he wears."

She smiled and absently rubbed the stinging spot on her rear.

"Why do gentlemen do that?" she asked softly. "They pinch a lady's cheek and a housemaid's rear. But where's the fun in it? A pinch is not a caress. Surely they can't feel anything by doing that?"

He took her hand in his, and began to walk with her. "It gets them noticed by the lady or the maid, I suppose," he said. "And it also tells their intent. But you've got it wrong, whatever their titles, gentlemen don't pinch ladies or serving maids' rears or any other tender parts."

She nodded, relaxing as they strolled away.

"I've news," he said.

She stiffened and stopped, staring up into his eyes.

"Not here," he said.

They walked toward a dimly lit side room. Maxwell nodded at a footman standing at the entrance. The footman bowed and stepped aside. The room was fashioned as a library, with thick scarlet-patterned draperies at the window, a huge hearth with an ornately carved marble mantel on one wall and rows of bookcases on the other. The bookcases were woefully short of volumes, but the hearth was blazing. He led her to a corner of the room where they weren't visible from the doorway.

"What news?" Pippa asked eagerly when they stopped there.

"I found out about Ned Norwich," Maxwell said.

She stared at him.

"And Norman Newell," he persisted. "Now you can go home. I must leave you and go to London to find Nicholas Newman." He smiled down at her expression. "I've every reason to believe that they are all your lost Noel Nicholson. One, because adventurers who use false names usually stay with those that are closest to their own names, so they're less likely to forget who they are and more likely to know when their name is called aloud. And two, because the description fits. I'm sorry to say that it's possible your fiancé may well be an informant for our enemies. And now more people than you and your grandfather are interested in finding him. Since Whitley and I both occasionally work for those people we must stay on his trail wherever it leads us."

"You think he's a spy," she said flatly.

"I know he's a liar," he answered calmly.

She took a long breath. "Then when do we leave?"

"Oh no," he said softly. "We do not. This is where we part, sweet. We'll meet again. When it's over with I'll come to you to brag and show my abilities—all my abilities—to you. But I can't have you coming to London with me. I have enough to do finding Noel. Watching over you as well in such a hotbed of opportunities for misadventure is too much even for me."

She began to protest.

"Watching over you," he said, holding up one finger, "and your increasingly adorable grandmother, that is to say."

She chewed her lower lip, frantically searching for an argument that might move him.

"Ah, don't mistreat your lips so," he said, touching her mouth with his finger. "There's a much better use for them."

He lowered his head, and paused. She knew that if she didn't want to be kissed she could simply move away. What was he playing at now? She didn't care. She wanted his kiss. She put her head up, parted her lips, and closed her eyes.

His kiss was gentle, at first, seeking, rather than demanding. She put her hands against his chest, so she could change her mind in a moment if she felt she had to. But his lips felt so soft against her own, his kiss was so sweet, and his lean chest so warm against her hands that she leaned into his kiss, and sighed with pleasure. His tongue touched hers, and the excitement and sweetness of it overwhelmed her. She felt her body puckering everywhere, her only wish was to get even closer to this strange, elegant male who spoke so lightly and yet could make her feel such deeply thrilling things.

One of his hands held the back of her head gently as his other slid down the soft material of her gown and gently cupped her rear so he could pull her even closer. She knew she ought to protest, but she couldn't think to speak. His scent was deliciously intriguing: a mixture of good soap and spice, and a fascinating aura of his own. She forgot she ever wanted to breathe. She was held close and yet lightly. She couldn't pull her hands from his chest even though she wanted to raise them so could feel the silkiness of his clean, softly scented hair.

She'd been kissed before. But never like this before, never with such gentle passion, and never had she been so inflamed with yearning so quickly, so completely. She forgot where she was and only allowed this rare pleasure to rule her. She let him take the lead, wherever it lead them, and followed eagerly.

"Oh my," her grandmother's voice said.

Pippa turned to see their audience: her grandmother and Sir Whitley.

Maxwell let Pippa go and lightly stepped away. She could only blink, as though coming awake from a strange, deep dream. After a scant second he spoke, but only to her. "And so this is good-bye," Maxwell told her as he took both her hands in both of his.

Then he turned to her grandmother. "I hope you'll forgive me for what looks like my taking advantage as I said good-bye to your granddaughter," he said earnestly, "but it's difficult to say good-bye to her."

"Not for some men," Lady Carstairs said waggishly. "That's why you're here. I forgive you of course, if you were saying good-bye," she added archly. "But I can't imagine why you were."

Pippa tried to gather her wits. Her only thought was a bitter one. Grandmother was right. This proved he was absolutely a liar, because of course he knew no man ever seemed to have any difficulty in saying good-bye to her.

"But why should you say good-bye?" her grandmother asked. She clapped her heavily ringed hands together. "Don't tell me! How exciting. There will be a wedding after all. You've found her Noel for her!"

"That I have not," Maxwell said. "But I know where he is now, and must go find him."

"Where?" Lady Carstairs asked.

"London," he said.

She laughed with delight. "Why, that's wonderful. Exactly where I want to go next. Won't my husband be pleased? We have so many friends in London. They'll be fighting amongst each other to put us up. It's been so long since I've visited them, what a delight. Pippa, my dear, you will adore London! You were too young to appreciate it the only time we took you there. Oh, wonderful."

For the first time since she'd met him, Pippa saw that Maxwell looked trapped. "But, my lady," he said quickly, the dumbfounded expression leaving his face in a heartbeat, "he travels fastest who travels alone, and I must find Noel before he discovers I'm on his traces. If he even sees a glimpse of Pippa or you he'll know what's happening, and will take to his heels again."

"Ha!" Lady Carstairs said. "Of course he would. So we shan't advertise our arrival. We'll arrive by night. We won't give out cards when we do, as we usually would. We'll stay in a hotel under an assumed name and not go very far until it is safe to do so. I'll write to my husband and let him take care of it for us. And when you have wicked Noel in your clutches, we can discover what he was thinking at last. Then, whatever the outcome, we can celebrate. Why, we might even lure my dear husband out of his sanctuary to join us. When do we leave? Ah, what a foolish question, first thing in the morning, of course. Well then, I'll just go back to the inn, scratch out a letter to my husband, and we'll be ready to leave at sunup. What fun!"

Pippa stood wide-eyed. Maxwell seemed at a loss for words. And his friend's face was unreadable.

"But my lady," Maxwell began to say, "what of your friends here? . . . The duke?"

"Oh, I'll have bundles more friends in London," Lady Carstairs said dismissively. "Everyone's going there now that spring is here, and the last of the Season is upon us. And the duke? Musgrave or whatever he's calling himself now? That silly old boy? He's just as married as I am, and to a lady who would knock him silly if he dared a thing with any other woman. As I would, if it were me," she added.

"But surely you haven't seen half your friends here yet," Maxwell protested. "After all, our prince is in residence. Think of all the fetes and parties there will be here."

"And think of how many more in London. That's all everyone is talking about," Lady Carstairs said. "The prince will likely remove there soon as well. What good fortune for us! Can you call for our coach, my lord? I am so excited. Come along, Pippa," she said. "We'll make our excuses, say you've a headache, and say our farewells. But no more personal leave-takings for Lord Montrose, mind," she added, shaking a finger at the frozen couple. "For this isn't to be a good-bye to him, after all."

Now it was Maxwell's face that was unreadable. Pippa's expression was still one of absolute shock.

Chapter 9

"What were you thinking?" Whitley asked.

Maxwell sat with his head in his hands. "I wasn't," he said in a muffled voice.

"I see," his friend said.

Maxwell lifted his head. "No, you don't. I wanted to kiss the chit. I did. Most satisfactorily. That's all it was. And yes, I know it was wrong, but I thought it was good-bye. It became more than that, but I didn't mean it to be. I thought she wouldn't mind and indeed, she didn't. I thought we were alone too. I may have put my head in a marital noose for it, but that's all it was."

They sat in Whitley's dimly lit library in his old house at Brighton.

"It won't mean a marriage," his friend said. "Not unless you want it to. Lady Carstairs obviously didn't think it meant a thing. As for the younger lady, who knows? But she doesn't seem the sort to rope you in if you don't want her to. Do you?"

"The elder lady has clearly lost her wits," Maxwell said with an expression of distaste. "So it was an especially heinous thing for me to do, presuming upon the younger one when she had no protector. For what it's worth, I don't think she'll try to make a proposal out of it either. But I behaved badly and I feel badly for it. Although," he said, picking up his head, "I feel even worse about having them come with me to London."

"Because you don't think you can keep your hands off her?" his friend asked curiously.

"Because they'll be more trouble than they're worth."

"You don't want her, then?"

Maxwell looked frustrated. "Are you mad too? Phillipa Carstairs? How can I want her? The lady is already betrothed, remember? For all we know she may love her absent fiancé. She could be in league with him and knee-deep in whatever he's doing. Clearly she has her wits and to spare, but she may not have a moral in her entire immortal soul. I don't know. How can I think of tying myself up with someone like that even for a moment? It was not only badly done of me, but a bad mistake. She has fire and desire aplenty. Is it for me? Or is she just a fickle wench? Or is it something worse? Maybe he left her for good reason.

"I can't afford to find that out by getting embroiled with her physically or mentally," Maxwell went on. "I have to find her Noel for her and then, who knows? But for now, we've got to get them to go home. Correction," he said shaking his dark head. "I have got to get them to go home without insulting or harming them. You've done enough, and you planned to stay here when I went on. So, I'm the one who's on my way to London."

His friend shrugged. "Then just leave tonight. I'll know nothing in the morning, nor will anyone else. Go to London. It's a big city. The ladies will never find you if you don't want to be found. They might even decide to go home once you've left. The least I can do is see them safely there, and I will. Don't worry about it. Go. Let them find an empty room and an empty stall at dawn."

Maxwell looked interested, then crestfallen. He knotted his hands together, hung them between his knees and scowled down at them. "That's craven. It's tempting too, but that's not me. I wish it could be, but it isn't. Old Carstairs may still have his wits. He was brilliant and a good friend to the Crown, a rare source of information in his time. We owe him something. And moreover, I promised to find the girl's affianced. My word is good, and apart from that, I think I will find the wretch."

"So let them go to London with you," his friend said, "and leave them there while you get to work. Make sure they're snugly housed; hire some lads to protect them, and then do your best to find the rascal who left her. But when you do see Miss Phillipa, you have to keep your hands off her. Do you think you can do that?"

Maxwell looked at his friend with disgust. "I'm not a randy boy. I may have made one misstep—well, maybe, two," he admitted. "But I was raised a gentleman. I have control over my emotions as well as my privy parts. So does she, or so I thought. There it is. I don't know why she's so accommodating to me. In truth, I grow daily more intrigued with the whole puzzle of the delicious Miss Carstairs and her errant lover."

His friend look bemused. "I thought it was your father who was the susceptible one. I've known you for years, and never saw you react to a female the way you do to Miss Carstairs."

"Nor have I," Maxwell admitted, rising and beginning to pace. "But the difference is that I learned from my father. He wed wisely and well. At least he did when he wed his first and second wives. Nevertheless, his luck didn't go well. There's not always a happily ever after. I don't want to go through such soul-searing misery as he did when my mother died, and then again when my step-mother did after that. No, I wouldn't risk such heartbreak unless there was a damned good reason for trying for happiness. There's no avoiding chance and fate so I have to be absolutely sure before I make any vows. I'm not ready to do so, far from it.

"I've known many women; you know that," he added. "Not more than most men of my age and class, but not less either. I'm not proud of it, but neither am I ashamed. In every case I knew what I was after, and how important it was to me. In all cases, it was never that important. I also know how important it was to the female in question. All my amours were worldly, and if not wise, then clever and sure of their paths in life. I think that the fact that I don't know much about Phillipa Carstairs is half her allure. I hope it is. I hadn't planned to become attached to anyone for a few years yet, if ever."

"Love has no plan, and luck and fate doesn't care about plans," his friend murmured.

"Very wise, aren't you?" Maxwell asked, sending his friend a glinting glance. "And very much a bachelor. I'll gloat when you become snared, believe me." He drew in a deep breath. "Luckily, I'm not. Yet. Craving a kiss from a lady doesn't constitute grounds for marriage, at least, not for me. Very well. I'll let them tag along to London with me. Lady Carstairs grows more foolish by the day. Soon she may need a keeper and her granddaughter is certainly too young to qualify as one. I'll hire on guards to watch over them wherever they stay, and some sensible female to go around Town with them. That way I can ensure that nothing untoward happens to either of them. And on that score, be sure I'll avoid any time alone with her," Maxwell went on. He suddenly grinned. "By that, I mean either lady."

"Very good, if you can."

"I can until I find Noel No-name, and I will. Then all will become clear."

They sat and talked long into the night, until the blazing fire in the hearth turned to sighing embers. Then they parted and went to their separate chambers. Whitley went to bed and then to sleep. Eventually, so did Maxwell, but only after promising himself that he'd ignore all intrusive thoughts of Pippa: her mouth, her scent, her silken, shapely body, even if she floated into his bed naked as the dawn. Which she did, when he finally fell asleep.

He didn't sleep well, or for very long, that night.

* * *

Pippa couldn't get to sleep in her bed at the inn. She tossed and turned. She damned herself, and then Maxwell. She relived the kiss. She squirmed and twisted to find a more comfortable position. There was none that night. There was only a hard bed of truth.

She remembered how good it had felt to be locked in Maxwell's arms, against his strong lithe body. How odd that such a fop could become so irresistible. How strange that he wanted her. But that was clear. It wasn't just another of his poses. She knew enough about men to know when a fellow was honestly interested. How could she not, when he'd held her so close? Knowing that his body didn't lie about his interest in her had thrilled her.

She slammed her eyes shut, thinking of how that hadn't deterred her ardor, remembering what a shameless partner she'd been to his advances. She sat up, pounded her pillow, and flopped down again, wishing she were home so she could walk out into the night until the soaking dew restored her sanity.

Why had he kissed her? He knew she was engaged to be married to another man. That was the whole reason they'd met in the first place. There was nothing in it for him unless he thought she was a wanton. She shivered. Was she? She hadn't thought so. Then why had she let Maxwell embrace her, given him such cooperation, and wanted more? Was she catching whatever malady was stealing her grandmother's sense away?

Noel's kisses had never moved her half so much. No man's had. She realized with shame and embarrassment that every time she thought of Noel, his face became more like Maxwell's in her mind. She was going to London to find Noel, but now she wasn't sure that she'd want him if she did. Maxwell was so much more alive and appealing.

Pippa groaned. But the truth of it was that she'd never met a man like Maxwell, and the curse of it was that she wanted him. And she couldn't have him. At least not now, or ever, if she continued to behave as she'd done. He excited and interested her. That wasn't any excuse for making such a thorough fool of herself. She didn't know him. His kissing her meant he was a villain or an opportunist or a cad. But the slightest touch of his mouth had stolen her wits.

His expression when her grandmother had walked in!—he'd looked as startled and appalled as she'd been. How could she face him again? How could she not? That voice, that scent, that face . . .

She finally fell asleep, but never for very long, not that night.

Pippa was hollow-eyed and lethargic when she faced her grandmother in the morning. It was a dull day, coming after a heavily misting night. Even the daffodils in the inn yard hung their bright heads and dripped translucent tears. But Pippa's grandmother was up and dressed, bustling around her room, instructing her maid as to how to finish the packing. She was wearing a handsome black-and-white striped traveling gown. Her neck was hung with several sparkling necklaces. She was humming, bright-eyed, merry as a bird on a budding tree.

Pippa yawned. "How do you do it, Grandmother?" she asked as she sank into a chair by the window.

"Do what?" her grandmother answered absently.

"Wake up so cheerful and lively at this hour?" Pippa frowned as another thought occurred to her. Her voice was lower and she watched her grandmother carefully as she added, "You never used to be so ebullient when we were back home: morning, noon, or night."

"What was there to be ebullient about, except for

having lived through another night?" Lady Carstairs asked as answer. "You may go now, Nancy," she told her maid. "We'll be down directly."

After the maid had left, closing the door behind her, Lady Carstairs looked at her granddaughter shrewdly. "You worry about me, don't you? In truth," she sighed, "so do I. Or so I did. I don't any longer because how can I fret when I feel so fine? I seem to have a new lease on life. I feel different: younger, happier, free again. If old age has changed me then I don't care if it's a weird solace. If it is some malady, I wish I'd had it earlier. I feel a weight off my heart. And I still love your grandfather, my dear. Who would not? But now I see I'd shrunken to his shadow because of living so many years in the countryside with him, alone except for you and friends I'd think were my inferiors had we lived in London or any of the great cities that we did before you came to us. Now I feel reborn. It is grand. And if feeling young means being silly sometimes, less worried, more carefree, so be it."

"So you know . . . ?" Pippa began to ask.

"That I am behaving in a different way? I know," her grandmother said, smiling. "At first, I admit, it worried me. No more. Look at me. Now I laugh a great deal. I flirt with handsome young gentlemen who humor me, and older ones who actually think I might dally with them. And who knows? I might. I am not the person who left home with you. Yet I'm pleased about it, Pippa. If losing my wits means gaining happiness, what of it? I'm too old to care what people think of me. Your grandfather wouldn't notice even if he would care. He hasn't noticed me in years. I'm happy, my love."

Pippa thought a moment, looking for another way into her grandmother's mind. The grandmother she'd known would have cared a great deal about behaving as she did now. "Isn't all this traveling a trial for you?" she asked to keep her talking sensibly.

"It is odd," Lady Carstairs said thoughtfully, suddenly looked older and more like the sober lady Pippa knew. "Curiously, I find that so long as I keep moving onward, I keep growing happier. The less time I have to think, the more contented I am with myself. It seems to be that way for you too," she added, eyeing Pippa.

"You're blooming for the first time since your Noel left," Lady Carstairs said. "In fact, you didn't glow like this when he was with you. It's because you've taken quite a fancy to the marquis, haven't you? And who can blame you? He's more handsome and far cleverer than your Noel ever was. There's something about him that one seldom sees in a male, and yet often dreams about. And you may meet even more exciting men in London. I know I will," she said, and giggled in a girlish manner, as if she'd never voiced the reasonable things that she'd just said.

"Grandmother," Pippa said desperately. "Sometimes I think I'm losing you, and I'm afraid."

"Pippa, my love, sometimes I think I'm losing me too, but I'm glad of it," her grandmother said. "Now, are you going to travel in that gloomy gray gown? Pray do not. It makes you fade away. It makes me sad. We don't want that, do we? Go back to your room and change. Wear something bright: pink or yellow or saffron. Something with flowers or stripes, cheerful attire to chase the megrims, bring out your beauty, and lure the gentlemen. I'd dislike my being the only beauty in our coach, wouldn't you?"

When it was time to leave the inn, Pippa was wearing a saffron-colored gown and a red cape with a hood to draw up against the weather. She followed her grandmother, who hung on Lord Whitley's arm, chattering to him as they walked toward the traveling coach.

"Oh, what a bouncer!" Lady Carstairs trilled as she mock-swatted at the tall gentleman. "Looking forward to dancing with me! I don't think so. I doubt we'll ever clap eyes on you again. But it was nicely said. Thank you for the thought, and for all your kindnesses to us."

He disengaged his arm and bowed. "It was a pleasure, my lady. I do indeed hope that we will meet again one day."

"As do I," the lady said. "Now where's that rascal, Montrose? We haven't seen him yet today. Does he mean to send us on our own? Not well done of him, I'd say."

"He'll be here," Whitley said. "Ah, as I said. Here he comes. No need to fret, my lady. He's a man of his word."

Maxwell came strolling out of the inn, dressed in riding clothes. He bowed to them and spoke in a bored, fastidious drawl. "I breakfasted in my room, so that I could oversee my valet and be sure everything I needed was in my bags. It's tiresome to discover you've left a brush or a fingernail clipper along the way when you need one. I'll ride on beside your coach, ladies, along with the footmen, to see you safe until our next stop."

He handed Lady Carstairs up into the carriage, as Pippa and his friend stood and watched. Once Pippa's grandmother announced she was comfortably settled inside, Maxwell offered his hand to Pippa.

She looked up into his face. "I'm sorry," she said in a soft voice. "It won't happen again."

He didn't pretend to not know what she meant. He laughed. "You've stolen my speech. You've no need to be sorry. Allow me to apologize for my actions. I'll see you at the next stopover."

Pippa got into the coach, and once seated, looked back out the window. Maxwell and Whitley were saying their good-byes, and they looked serious and somber. She wished she could speak with Maxwell that way too, without the requisite flirting and coyness and nonsense that must go on between an eligible male and female when they have a conversation. She wished he would consider her a friend. She needed one. She sat back, impressed by her new thought. She could be that. If he could act the fop when he surely wasn't one, she could stop all the foolishness involved with being a well-bred lady, and act more like a well-bred gentleman. And so she would. It would be easier for both of them.

"Handsome as he can stare," her grandmother commented from the opposite seat as she watched the direction of her granddaughter's gaze. "Now, aren't you glad you wore something livelier this morning?"

"He didn't notice, I'm sure," Pippa said.

Her grandmother snorted. She closed her eyes,

and folded her hands in her lap, preparing to catch up on her lost sleep.

But Pippa kept her eyes wide open. She would speak with all the reason and sensibility that her grandmother had been so glad to be rid of. She knew no other way she could cope with Lord Maxwell. If she couldn't be his lover, and didn't want to be a flirt, then she could certainly become a friend. It would be a new thing for her and for all she knew, for him too.

"All in gold and red, fresh and fragrant as a dewy rose," Whitley was saying to his friend. "Can you resist her?"

"I can, I will, I'll certainly try," Maxwell said. "But help me here."

Whitley looked at him curiously.

"Pray that I find her damned Noel for her before much more time passes," Maxwell said.

Chapter 10

"Isn't London grand?" Lady Carstairs sighed, looking out her hotel window.

"It certainly looks that way from here," Pippa answered carefully.

It wasn't the right time to remind her grandmother that they'd been in London for three entire days and had gone nowhere except for a daily walk around their street. When they did go out, they wore hoods or poke bonnets that shadowed their faces. The only saving grace for Pippa was that it had rained the entire time. She thought that if the sun were out she'd have tossed her bonnet away and literally run mad; dashing into the nearby park just to feel the light and air on her face, because at last they were in London, and yet they were still indoors, in seclusion.

But now the sun was peeking through gray clouds that were shredding overhead.

"We had some sort of social life at home, but nothing like the one we'll have in London," Lady Carstairs said happily. "You've been to parties, soirees, teas, and morning calls, all with the best people in our district, to be sure. But that's like saying you've seen the sea, when all you've ever seen is a pond. We'll go to those as well as masquerades, musicales, fetes, and festivals, the theater, and the opera. It will be wonderful. And tomorrow night!" she said with rapture, "we go to a grand ball. I haven't been to one in ages."

Her lined face suddenly grew comically sad. "Good heavens! Ages? I'm right. It has been an age. You never went to a grand ball with me when we were here last, did you? Well, don't fret. Tomorrow, at last, is our night. I shall wear my new gold silk. And you?"

Pippa looked up in surprise and trepidation. She'd gotten used to her grandmother's strange new attitude. There were no gentlemen for Lady Carstairs to flirt with, so that, at least, had stopped. Even if she were half out of her wits, Lady Carstairs had told Pippa, albeit reluctantly, when the men who worked at their hotel smiled at them, "No decent lady would flirt with a footman or a butler, a waiter or a tradesman—at least, not in plain view." Her grandmother might be half unhinged,

Pippa thought with relief, but not wholly so. She wasn't yet lost to all reason.

They hadn't heard from the marquis. There were no other gentlemen on the scene and so the ladies still had to avoid the public eye lest the sight of them caused Noel, or those who might be holding him captive, to flee. These days she and her grandmother were, Pippa thought disconsolately, like members of a strange new order of nuns.

But that didn't mean that her grandmother had reverted to her normal self. When she spoke to Pippa she talked more about her yesterdays than their present days. Sometimes she talked about what they would do in London, plans of such grandiosity that Pippa doubted they could ever be achieved. Other times she stayed in her room and avoided Pippa altogether. Yet now she was excited about going to an imaginary ball tomorrow night? This was worrisome. Her grandmother had clearly finally mistaken fantasy for reality.

Pippa put down her book, rose from the chair she'd been sitting in, and went to her grandmother's side. "Won't it be better to wait until we have an invitation?" she asked gently.

"But we do, silly chit," her grandmother said affectionately. "I showed it to you the other day."

Pippa's face grew ashen and her heart felt cold.

She would certainly have remembered an invitation to a ball. But there had been no such thing. So far as they knew, they were still supposed to stay out of sight, unless they received a message from the marquis. That, she would never have forgotten.

What her grandmother said was then true madness. Pippa didn't want to argue with her. But someone had to talk sense to Lady Carstairs, and soon. Who could she turn to? Her grandfather was many days travel away from them, at home. She had an address for the marquis here in London in case of emergency. This was truly such, but she had no guarantee he was there. What was she to do? Let her grandmother get herself up in golden silk and diamonds, and then hold her down physically to keep her from going to an imaginary ball?

"I think we ought to go have a new gown made up for you," Lady Carstairs mused.

"Yes, an excellent idea," Pippa said as calmly as she could. Whatever Maxwell had said, keeping hidden hadn't been good for her grandmother. Let them be recognized if must be. Noel's welfare wasn't as much of a concern to her now as her grandmother's well-being was. Fresh air, sunlight, and a change of scene might help clear her mind.

"Wonderful," Pippa said with false enthusiasm.

"But do you know of a good seamstress?"

"Seamstress?" Lady Carstairs said with a sneer. "Pah! We shall go to a modiste. We're in Society now, my dear. Now, in my day, it was Madame du Claire. Every modiste has a French name, you see, otherwise they would have no trade. The Franchise may be wicked, but no one knows fashion as they do. Of course, many of the modistes in London are plain dressmakers from England who use French names. But they aspire to Fashion and the best way to achieve a reputation for it."

"How can we find the right one?" Pippa asked. "Shall we ride to the best districts and look for signs?" She hoped hours of riding in a coach, up and down the streets of London, might somehow clear her grandmother's mind.

"Searching for street signs? Peeping into windows? Perhaps asking well-dressed females in the street?" her grandmother asked playfully. "Ho!" she hooted. "No need! No valued modiste has a street sign. They don't encourage the rabble. But I read all the latest magazines, and hear that Madame Berthon is the latest one that anyone of any merit goes to have a gown made up. We shall have you fitted and insist on a quick resolution, and be damned to the cost!" She beamed at Pippa. "My granddaughter shall outshine them all. I couldn't take you to London for your come-out, my love. But I'll make it all up to you now."

The lady turned from the window. "Now, change your gown, Pippa, as I shall mine. Wear something striking. We can't go to Madame Berthon looking no account. I may want a few gowns made up too. And so the better we dress, the better we shall be dressed." She tittered at her own jest, and shooed Pippa off to her rooms.

The first thing Pippa did when she got to her rooms was to sit and scrawl a note and then ring for a footman so she could have it sent to Maxwell. The second thing she did was raise her eyes to the ceiling and utter a brief prayer. And then, with her maid's help, she got dressed.

Her grandmother had been right about one thing. It was impossible to know that the shop was that of a modiste. There was nothing in the window but a swath of rich-looking cloth draped over a chair. Still, Lady Carstairs stepped out of their carriage with certainty. Pippa and the ladies' two maids followed less confidently.

A bell chimed when they entered the shop. Inside, it was quiet, slightly perfumed, and as well furnished as any lady's sitting room. The red curtain that acted as a partition to another room was the only thing that was different. Indeed, Pippa thought, Madame herself didn't look like a tradeswoman. She was a tall, thin, well-dressed young woman who came through the drapery to greet them in a ridiculously heavy French accent. Then she looked at them with inquiry.

"I am Lady Carstairs," said the elder woman with all of her former gravity. "This is my granddaughter, Phillipa. We are newly come from the countryside. She is to go into Society. We need a magnificent gown for a grand ball, for tomorrow night. No need to fling your hands in the air, Madame, I know your time is important to you, but it is of the essence for us. I also know that will be expensive. I will pay for it. Now, what do you suggest?"

"Helas!" Madame said with obvious sorrow. "Zees I cannot do, not for any money, my lady. I am rushed off my feets. I can give you zee name of another fine modiste in London. But it cannot be me."

Pippa stood and looked around as the two women argued. She thought that the modiste meant what she said, but whatever mental state she was in, her grandmother never took no for an answer. Pippa turned as the bell sounded gently again and the door to the salon swung open. Her mouth almost did as well.

Maxwell stood for a moment, poised in the entryway. He wore a long fitted tan jacket; there was a glimpse of a golden waistcoat beneath it. His highly shined brown boots came up to his knees, and didn't obscure the sight of the smooth buckskin unmentionables that showed off his well-muscled thighs. His neckcloth was dazzling white, tied in a casual knot that was clearly the work of a superior valet's art. Maxwell swept off his high beaver hat as he bowed to the women in the shop.

"Ladies," he said in his cool voice, "I bid you a good day, but see it's not necessary. Never have I seen any of you in finer fettle."

Pippa couldn't tell who was blushing and tittering more, her grandmother or the modiste. She realized he was in his highest aristocratic and foppish mode, the affect she especially disliked. Obviously not everyone did. She noticed that at the sound of his voice there was a sudden excited murmuring of lighter voices from behind the drapery, as it was drawn back a few inches to show several lovely young women's faces peering out at them. The modiste's models were watching the new arrival too.

"Ordering up new gowns, Lady Carstairs?" he asked as he sauntered into the room. "But why? You always look splendid."

The lady smiled. "Not for me, my lord. But for my Phillipa, who hasn't a new gown in her wardrobe. And with the ball coming up tomorrow night, I felt it was necessary to get one at all speed. But Madame Berthon tells me that's impossible. What am I to do?"

"Impossible?" he asked, putting one hand over his heart and looking at the modiste. "I am staggered. Surely, nothing is impossible to you, Madame."

The modiste straightened. "But of course not. *Vraiment!* But I did not know the ladies were friends of yours, my lord," she added, her French accent becoming replaced with a Londoner's. "Because nothing is impossible for you. I have other clients whose gowns are almost finished. They will be delayed while the young lady chooses the one she wants. *Tant pis!*" she added, shrugging her shoulders. "What am I to do? Only the best I can for them, and better than that for you."

Everyone in the room and behind the curtain, except for Pippa, smiled.

"Just as I hoped," he said, bowing. "You continue to astonish and delight me, Madame. Now, if I may have a word with the young lady before she begins to try on your creations? I shall only offer her a bit of advice," he told Pippa's grandmother. "The same, I think, that you would do. But I am considered somewhat of an expert on fashion in certain circles. And I know how obstinate the young lady can be."

They exchanged conspiratorial smiles, and Pippa clenched her teeth. Her grandmother and Madame Berthon began to talk of colors and cuts.

"She thinks," Pippa whispered through those clenched teeth when she came to his side, "that we are invited to a grand ball tomorrow night. I sent for you because I didn't know what else to do. We haven't seen anyone or gone anywhere because you told us not to. I confess I'm a bit frightened. She never imagined things on such a large scale before. What am I to do?"

"This ball is the reason you sent such a frantic note to me?"

"What else could I do?" Pippa asked.

"You could believe her. She did get an invitation. I arranged to have it sent. I imagine she forgot to show it to you. A minor oversight and surely not senility. Are any other changes in her behavior worrying you?"

Pippa scowled, but relaxed. "No. But you might have had one sent to me too."

"So I might have," he said imperturbably. "Now I want a word with Madame, and I'll say my farewell to you until tomorrow evening when I come to call for you."

"But wait!" she asked. "Why do you suddenly want us to burst into Society? I thought you wanted us hiding so Noel's captors don't know we're here."

"Or Noel does," he corrected her. "No need any longer. He isn't a prisoner in London, that much I now know. Apart from that, he's either fled or still here for his own purposes. And if you go to the ball, and he is here, I'll wager he'll manage to find you."

Pippa held her breath. "Truly?" she asked.

He grinned and touched the tip of her nose with one gloved finger.

"Truly," he said, and ambled off to have a word with the waiting modiste. "If I may have a look at the gowns in question?" he asked her.

"But of course," she said, and sweeping back the curtain that served as a partition, exposing several beautiful young women in the process, she invited him into her back rooms.

"No," Pippa said, moving this way and that on the platform in Madame's back room. Three mirrors surrounded her. She said no to each one in turn as she turned. "It's beautiful, Madame," she went on. "Exquisite, actually. The cut and cling, the fit and fashion, are perfect. But scarlet? For me? I'm overpowered by it. My hair is too light, my face too pale, the color shouts and I'm afraid I only whisper. For a dark-haired lady, or one with brown hair, certainly. But me?"

She didn't mention how shocked she was by the astonishing curves—the soft scarlet material that had been pinned to her clung to her. They were curves she knew she had but never put on such public view. They were astonishing. Even she was impressed by her own high breasts, rounded hips, and flat abdomen. Impressed, and she secretly admitted, a little stirred. The color was vivid and compelling. She'd never guessed she could look so wanton, so seductive, so unlike the self she recognized. She was flattered and strangely envious of this other Pippa. But she knew it wasn't her.

"It is you," the modiste insisted.

A babble of high voices agreed; Madame's covey of beautiful young models had been watching the fitting.

"A dab of soot on your lashes," one model volunteered, "and a skim of it on your brows will make your eyes wicked bright."

"A brush of color on your cheeks will help too," another sighed.

"And your lips touched with red," Madame agreed. "Not heavy maquillage, but just a soupçon of color. Don't you agree, Lady Carstairs?"

"I do," the lady said as solemnly as if she were being married. And then she added, as though she were a fixture of London Society, "It is what I myself do for grand affairs."

"The gown suits her as it is, my lady," Madame went on. "And with the right hairstyle, a rope of garnets, and a dab of color, no one at the ball can touch her."

"Except for his lordship," another model said with a giggle.

"Not garnets," Lady Carstairs said, rising from the chair she'd been sitting in. "I have rubies for her."

The models sighed.

"My own maid will know how to brighten up her face," the lady went on. "And furthermore," she sternly turned to the model who had dared mention Maxwell and touching, "the marquis will not touch her. He apologized for last time and said he wouldn't do that again."

"Oh, my lady," the model protested, as the other models looked at each other round-eyed, and Pippa bit her lip, "I only meant that not even he could be as fashionable as she will look."

"That," Lady Carstairs said grandly, "is debatable."

Pippa gave up. Her grandmother's mind was set as though in stone. Though she acted strangely sometimes these days, that hadn't changed. The battle was lost. Pippa would have to be a scarlet lady tomorrow night. And yet deep down in her heart where she seldom dared look these days, there was a portion of her soul that was thrilled to have been defeated over all her protests. A part that was, she discovered, simply ecstatic about it.

A web of faceted rubies glanced occasional fire where they lay on Pippa's white breast. The dazzling scarlet gown tamed them to burning embers. Her fair hair was dressed high and coaxed into ringlets at the back of her head. She wore a light underdress but could still clearly see the swell of her breasts. She colored when she realized the chill of the room sent a chill up her spine, and when that happened she could clearly see the tips of her breasts rise and pucker. But when she protested, everyone insisted that was the style, so she vowed to try to stay warm tonight.

Her skin was white and clear at her neck and breast although she thought there was far too much of it on show. But her face wore dabs of this and finger strokes of that. The cosmetics livened her looks just as much as Madame Berthon's models had vowed it would. When grandmother's maid was finally done, Pippa looked into the mirror and thought she looked like an illustration of Delilah from an old bible, or a religious tract warning against the ploys of wicked temptresses.

Curiously, she didn't feel embarrassed, mostly because she didn't recognize herself. It was like wearing a costume. She felt deliciously wicked, even excited, by the glamorous creature she saw in the glass.

"Well done," her grandmother pronounced when she saw the result of the day's work.

"You look wonderfully well too," Pippa said, and meant it. Her round little grandmamma seemed to have grown in stature. She certainly appeared to take up more space in the room, because of how she captured the eye. It would be harder to ignore the sun in a clear noonday sky. She glowed in golden swathes of silk, diamonds twinkled in her hair, there was gold at her ears, and a heavy gold necklace echoed the Midas look. Best of all for Pippa, the lady gleamed so much that she made Pippa look decidedly modest in her shade.

"Now," Lady Carstairs said triumphantly, "we shall give them something to talk about at last."

That made Pippa anxious again. But then she realized she wouldn't know anyone at the ball, except for her grandmother and Maxwell. She reveled in thinking about the look on his face when he beheld her tonight. And if Noel did turn up, she loved the thought of how chagrined and shocked he'd be at her magnificence. Because if he didn't have an excuse for his deserting her, and a magnificent one at that, he'd never forget how sure of herself she looked, how fashionable and exquisite she'd be as she broke their engagement and said farewell to him forever. She hoped it would break his heart. If, she reminded herself, his heart hadn't already broke, for her, during his time away.

They received a message that said that the marquis awaited them in the hotel's front salon.

Pippa snatched up her wrap and, behind her grandmother made her way majestically down the stairs.

Maxwell was immaculate in black and white, his hose was white, his pantaloons black, his jacket black, and his linen and neckcloth as white as the piratical smile he showed when he saw them. Pippa was sure that no man in London could look as severe and as handsome, as amused and as cool as he did. He bowed to them.

"Good evening, ladies," he said with a crooked

smile, looking from one to the other. "Well done! No one can miss seeing you tonight."

Then he saw them into the carriage he'd hired.

As Pippa got into the carriage, her skirts making whispery sounds as they slid around her ankles, she felt much less seductive and far less magnificent. In fact, she had to control an urge to rush back upstairs, wash her face, and put on a different gown. Because now she felt overdone, and more uncomfortable by the minute.

Doubt had lodged in her mind, splashing on her high spirits like a glass of punch spilled on her silken gown. She was still wondering if what he'd said was a compliment or not. It would only take a word from him to make her newfound grandeur seem tawdry. She wondered if he'd said that word.

Chapter 11

"It's impossible to be a wallflower in scarlet," Pippa managed to say, laughing. She was short of breath from dancing so much; the exertion had turned her cheeks pinker than any cosmetic could have done, and her eyes sparkled and would have even without the dabs of kohl to make them seem brighter. "Why even a Gorgon would be asked to dance if she wore red," she said, as the pattern of the dance whirled her away from Maxwell again.

It seemed she hadn't stopped prancing since she got to the ball. The thought of a grand London ball had daunted her, but from the moment she stepped down the grand gilded staircase and into the crowd of guests, she was sought after, and she danced set after set.

No one spoke about her engagement, no one whispered about her fiancé deserting her; there were no speculative, sad, or pitying looks sent her way. It was as though no one knew her, and she thanked whatever had ensured that. Tonight she was just a lady in red, dancing the night away.

She danced a quadrille, a minuet, a few polkas because the many military gentlemen in attendance seemed to fancy them the most, and was asked into several sets of country dances as well. She couldn't count her partners. It seemed to her that every one of them was handsome, well dressed, charming, and polite. And yet, in spite of the impressive London mansion she found herself in, and the glorious clothing of the company, she was as comfortable as if she was at a party at home. And she'd never felt so wondrously pretty and absolutely dazzled.

Since no one knew who she was, she didn't doubt it was the scarlet gown that had given her such popularity. She saw many more beautiful and beautifully dressed ladies than herself, and some were without partners at the sidelines. And yet and still, she told herself, however eye-catching, it was only a gown. Still, here she was, feeling as though she was the belle of the ball.

She thought the fact that no one teased her about her aborted wedding or her abandonment might have been because of her grandmother's machinations. Pippa had been shocked at the evidence of Lady Carstairs's popularity. It was just as she'd said, though Pippa never would have believed it. Grandmother did have dozens of friends here who obviously rejoiced at seeing her again. Lady Carstairs had been swept away by a crowd of her old friends the moment she set foot in the ballroom. No wonder she'd been so insistent on coming to London. She was gloriously at home here.

And, Pippa thought, her own present popularity could have been the influence of the lofty Lord Montrose who had disappeared when they came to the ball and had just reappeared again.

She didn't care. This was a time to remember. She suddenly understood why Grandmother had become so staid and sensible when she was at home, yet had passed all her time laughing since they'd left there. She wasn't losing her mind; she was regaining her joy in life. Grandmother had been terribly suppressed at home. Pippa had never suspected it and doubted that grandfather even noticed. This was the life her grandmother had obviously been secretly yearning for. And why not? Pippa understood at last. She too was rejoicing in it every bit as much as her grandmother was.

Or at least she was until Maxwell took her hand for the next turn of the dance and whispered,

"Come with me when the music stops. I've a surprise for you."

She didn't know why she felt so much apprehension at his simple request. But she was suddenly very afraid. The surprises he'd given her before had always been unannounced. He'd never cautioned her about a sudden kiss or a breathtaking embrace. But now, he warned her. However much she might yearn for him to attempt lovemaking, she had to restrain him, and herself. He wanted to see her alone. It must be for something she had to steel herself for.

The music came to an end; Pippa bowed to her last partner and took Maxwell's arm as he came to her. There was grumbling from her other partners as she left the dance floor, and a few hoots at Maxwell for escaping with her.

"Spoilsport!" one of her dancing partners shouted at Maxwell.

"Old friend of the family," he told them calmly.

"Lucky dog," another fellow said. "Bring her back soon."

That delighted Pippa. She held her head higher as she walked on. Whatever the surprise was, she felt she could face it. So much as she wanted Maxwell's kisses, she knew she could deny them and herself.

But when they got to a back chamber off the

dining room, an obviously unused salon in the great house, she looked at Maxwell in puzzlement. This room wasn't meant for a lover's meeting.

Three men stood there. Two looked like stolid older men from the working class. They stood on either side of a younger man, a gentleman dressed in finery for the ball. The young gentleman look terrified, and that might have been what made him look shrunken. But he wouldn't be very tall under any circumstances. He was in his third decade, Pippa guessed. He had dark curly hair and a terrified expression. That was the only thing that distinguished him, because otherwise he was unexceptional.

Pippa heard a stir and turned to see her grandmother being escorted into the room by a serious gentleman who bore the look of someone of importance. He looked from Lady Carstairs to Pippa.

"Well?" Maxwell finally said as he too gazed at Pippa.

"Well, what?" she asked in confusion.

"Do you know him?" Maxwell prodded. "Remember that disguises can be devilish to penetrate."

She frowned at him. "Am I supposed to do that, and know him?"

"Is he, or is he not, your long lost Noel Nicholson?" the other gentleman asked impatiently.

Pippa's answer was a peal of relieved laughter.

"Absolutely not, Lord Talwin!" her grandmother thundered. "This fellow is younger, shorter, thinner. That cannot be changed so easily."

"He's not Noel," Pippa said, sobering. "What made you think he was?"

"He said so," Maxwell said with a scowl.

Pippa gazed at the man, who quickly bowed, and holding his hands tightly in front of himself, said in a rush, "So I did Ma'am, but the gentleman I met gave me these clothes and some coins, and promised me more if I came to this ball on his card of invitation. I didn't mean any harm, but times have been hard and I looked forward to some gaiety. So I came, and before I could so much as show my nose to the company these fellows grabbed me and took me here."

"Do you know the gentleman whose card you used?" Maxwell demanded.

"Not likely," the young man said sadly. "I'm a clerk at Johnstone Brothers, fine fabrics. I never even see the customers. And he was a gent. We met in a tavern. I was surprised when he spoke to me, but he said as to there might be some money in it for me too, and that he'd pay me some right off, and the rest after if I'd did him a favor. He said as to how he had to leave Town immediately. And because hosts and hostesses never get to see everyone they invite to a ball with such a crowd, and he didn't want to anger them by turning down their invitation, so if I went and gave his card, they'd see it after the ball and think he came." He took in a deep breath, and fortified, added, "I never saw him before, or since, I swear to it."

"And so how did you expect to get the rest of the money he promised?" Maxwell asked smoothly.

The fellow looked down at his clasped hands. "He said he'd send it to my rooming house." He picked up his head and cried out in despair, "So he tricked me? And he a gentleman to the manner born?"

"Not a gentleman," Maxwell corrected him, "to whatever manner born. And you don't know these ladies?"

The wretched-looking fellow glanced from Pippa to her grandmother. "How could I, sir? Never seen them before. I swear, I didn't think doing this would lead to any trouble. I'm a peaceable man."

"We shall see," Maxwell said ominously, all his foppish aspect gone. He turned to Pippa. "Please return to the ball with your grandmother and Lord Talwin. I'll speak with you later."

Pippa nodded. "But what of this poor fellow?" she asked him in a soft voice. "It seems to me that he was as taken in as I once was. Please be gentle with him."

"Like you," Maxwell said sternly, "if he's innocent, he has nothing to fear."

Pippa thought about that on the way back to the ball. Did he now doubt her innocence in the matter of her missing fiancé? What had Noel been up to? When the music struck up for a new quadrille, she danced again, and laughed with her many partners, but her joy in the night had vanished.

There was a pause in the music as the musicians rested, and servants began to ready the guests' dinner in the dining chamber adjoining the ballroom. The scents of various delicacies being set out wafted through the air into the ballroom. Pippa went to the sidelines to pick up her shawl and look for her grandmother. Almost immediately a servant found her, bowed, and handed her a note. She read it, and crushed it in her hand. Then she strolled toward the lady's withdrawing room. She never got there. When she thought no one was watching, she nipped out to the terrace behind the great house.

She breathed easier when she was there, and looked around. She wasn't alone, far from it. That was comforting. It wouldn't look as though she'd gone out for a secret tryst. Half the attendees at the ball seemed to have also gone out for a gulp of fresh air. But there was room for all. The terrace was long and ringed the back of the house, the gardens were deep, and the night profound, so everyone could find a private space if they wanted one.

Torches threw sporadic flares of light over the terrace, and lanterns bobbed in the garden, making little bright circles. The scents from the spring garden were more delicious to Pippa than the smells inside the house had been.

Pippa wasn't hungry. She was anxious.

"Ah, you are prompt," a deep, familiar voice said.

Maxwell was leaning against a side of the house, completely covered in shadow. "Don't worry," he said, a smile in his voice as she hesitated where she stood. "Scarlet looks black in the darkness. To be even safer, throw your shawl over your shoulders so your skin doesn't gleam in the light. Then come here, to me. We must talk. In fact, come with me. We may be interrupted where we stand, and I've important things to say."

He took her hand and led her down the garden stairs. Down the garden path, fittingly enough, she thought, promising herself she wouldn't commit folly this time. If he was angling to kiss her, she could deal with that. Her newfound popularity tonight had done wonders for her self-esteem. A young woman who fell into a gentleman's arms every time he opened them to her would be a fool. And she was never that. This fellow had too many women dancing favors on him as it was. She may have been dancing earlier this evening, but she hadn't been blind. He'd never lacked for adoring partners staring up into his dark eyes. The only thing worrying her now was what he'd found out about Noel. Had she been a fool there as well?

"I've found out some more things about your fiancé," he told her in a soft voice as they strolled down the crushed shell garden path. "We've been on his trail, all right, but he eludes us every time. He's been traveling around the country, getting cash where he can and moving on as though the fiends of hell were pursuing him. I'm formidable, but I don't think that's why he's fleeing. Have you any idea of why he might fear a pursuer?"

She stopped and glowered at him. "Of course not!" she snapped. "I obviously had no idea he was . . . or rather, is whatever he's turning out to be, whatever that may be. I only knew Noel as a decent man, a scholar, honorable with me and sincere with my grandfather. If I'd a hint then of what's happening now I'd never have promised to marry him. And what's more, had my grandfather any idea, he wouldn't have considered his suit for a minute.

"I don't know how we could have been so taken in by him," she said slowly, taking a deep breath as they passed by a heavily flower-laden arbor. "In truth, although he was all kinds of good things, I suppose now, in looking back, that he wasn't that handsome or seductive or fascinating in any way. He was new to the area, but that couldn't have been all of it, could it? He must had had something, mustn't he have?" she asked plaintively, stopping to look at him again. "I mean, to take us all in the way he did. Oh. How selfish of me? What of the poor clerk? Is he in league with Noel, or only a poor dupe?"

"A dupe, and not so poor anymore. He's free, with the cash in pocket that Noel promised him. We aren't monsters. We paid him and let him go. Apart from being the decent thing to do, at least this way the poor fellow is more likely to send for us if Noel ever approaches him again."

"How charitable," Pippa commented.

"Tolerably so," Maxwell answered. "He did help us, because one thing is made clearer. Your Noel is a practiced seducer, and I don't mean just of females. He has a way of convincing people that what he's doing, whatever it is, is the right thing to do.

That talent is a gift to a rascal, whether he's planning to steal your jewels, run off with your wife, or swindle you out of your legacy. He could be a spy, a lothario, a thief, or a bigamist," he added. "He has all the talents he needed for any of those professions. It's what he actually is that interests the government, and where he is that influences your life. I mean to find out both things, and soon."

Maxwell paused by another arbor, this one of white roses. He reached into a waistcoat pocket, took out a small silvery implement, and snipped off a rose. He sniffed it. "It contrasts with your gown; even here there's enough light to see that. You can wear it in the ballroom. It doesn't smell half so alluring as you do, though. But wait," he said, applying the implement to the stem. "Roses have thorns, and you don't need any more. There," he said, bowing and offering her the flower. "Coals to Newcastle, I suppose. But a gesture of my appreciation of how you look tonight. So then: beauty to the most beautiful."

She took the flower, buried her nose in it, and was glad the night concealed her expression.

"Now I have to say good-bye again," he said softly.

Her head shot up. "Why?"

"Because I must find your Noel. He isn't in

London any longer. You must stay here and wait, like patient Griselda, or whatever her name was. I'll bring him to you."

"Not likely!" she exclaimed, standing tall as she could. "You thought that poor little man was Noel, didn't you? Ha! He was nothing like. That only proves you can't find him unless I'm there to identify him. You've been trying to be shut of me since I left home, but I tell you that is ridiculous. I'm the key to finding him; you can't get him without me. And I'm getting tired of all these attempts to jettison me, all these false farewells, because you know very well how important I am to your success."

"Tired of my farewells?" he asked, stepping close to her. He bent his head and put his lips on the side of her neck.

She shuddered, but didn't move. She could feel his smile as it blossomed.

"Why, Pippa," he whispered as he placed small, light kisses down her neck. "I really do think our good-byes are the best part of our arrangement. Cold, are you?" he asked as she shivered. "Mmm, I can easily warm you."

"I know you can," she said, stretching her neck upward. "But you know you shouldn't."

"But this is just a sweet farewell," he said softly as he put his arms around her.

He held her close, but lightly. Their bodies touched. She didn't move away and, scarcely realizing what she was doing, wrapped her arms around his neck. She wanted to be closer to him. He smelled better than the rose, his lips were softer than its petals, and though she wore scarlet, he was the one who blazed in the night. She thought he contained all the warmth in the world in his arms. She needed to be closer to it.

He smiled, and bent his head. "No shame attached at all in friends bidding each other a sweet farewell," he said as his mouth came closer to hers. "Nothing wrong with that, is there?" he asked in a husky voice.

He kissed her and she sighed into his mouth. His hands were warm on the silken softness of her gown; he cupped her breast as his mouth silently promised everything. His lips, warm and dry, then grazed against her neck, making her feel chilled and warmed at the same time. She relaxed though her senses awoke, her arms tightened around his neck as she threw back her head. She was utterly at his command—until he drew back to look at her face. Her eyes fluttered open, and then her gaze sharpened.

She lost her wits in his embrace, but they never went far. She'd heard what he'd said belatedly, through a blur of sensual arousal and deepening excitement. But she finally listened to what she'd heard.

"Where are you going?" she asked.

"To France," he said and bent to her again. He gently pulled her closer. It was, he thought, like trying to pull the rose arbor closer. She'd become wooden. "What?" he asked on a sigh.

"I can go to France," she said.

"Your grandmother would let you, I suppose," he said. "But I won't. It could be dangerous."

"We are at peace and have been since Amiens. That's almost a year," she said.

"Behold me shocked that it's lasted this long," he said.

"There are thousands of English persons in France now," she said. "I read the news sheets and the magazines."

"Unfortunately, yes, you do. But you don't know the news behind that news. I do," he said. "Napoleon will never be content with this peace nor, for that matter, will England. It's simply a regrouping, a gathering of forces and plans, and may be over at any moment. When the peace fails, which it will, what a lot of hostages France will have! And how nicely that will help finance their next attack on us. It will be more difficult to get an Englishman out of Paris than it was during the revolution. Heads will roll again, I fear. At least, that's what they will count on us remembering. As if we could forget," he muttered.

He faced her squarely, holding her shoulders. "You want to beggar your grandfather by having him ransom you and your grandmother? I wouldn't care for that even though I don't doubt she'd love the excitement of it. No," he said, shaking his head. "You stay here, I'll go. This time I'll find the right Noel if I have to chase him to China. I'll find him and return him to his homeland. And this time I don't have to grab any fellow at random. Seems our poor wronged clerk was also an impressively good artist. What do you think of this sketch? He says he can do even better, and I don't doubt he will when he's not shaking with fear."

He reached into his jacket and pulled out a paper. He unfolded it and held it up to a lantern's light.

Pippa gasped. It wasn't Noel to the life, but still and all, it certainly was Noel.

"Exactly," Maxwell said with satisfaction, folding the paper and putting it back in his jacket. "A good thing we have it too. And whether you believe me or not, it's good for you too. Putting a foot wrong in England is a very different matter than doing it abroad. My mother was a Frenchwoman, and I have relatives who survived the Revolution; I still have connections there."

"Jolly for you," she said, raising her chin. "My grandfather is world famous. He has correspondents everywhere. My grandmother and I will be treated like queens."

"You do remember how they treated their queens, do you?" he asked with too much amusement to suit her.

"Yes, I do," she snarled. "But I won't stay behind. I come into your arms too easily, I know that," she said, lowering her gaze. "And don't think I'm pleased with myself for it. I'm not. I've never done that before, and I must stop it now. You have a way of making me stop thinking, but I can change and I will. If you think I've been making a dead set at you, you may bury that thought. Your kisses are very fine, but a lady may enjoy them without being willing or even eager to share her life with you. Or even her bed," she added loftily, though she was sure her face was now the color of her gown.

"It's not entirely my fault either," she tried to say airily. "It may be that you and Noel are both in the business of seduction."

He took a step back. Even in the inconstant light, she could see his thin nostrils flare.

"Isn't that always the case?" she remarked to the rose she still held. "Tell a female that she kisses very well, and she's supposed to be flattered. Tell a male that he might make a business of it, and he's insulted."

"I never told you that," he said. "Nor would I."

She shot him a look that was best concealed by the darkness. "You're saying I don't kiss very well?"

"Oho," he said, coming close to her again, holding her around the waist so that their bodies touched. "Innocence indeed, you stepped right into that, did you?"

Before she could answer, he kissed her again, and then she couldn't answer.

"Even if this is your idea of farewell," she managed to say as he moved his head and gently tugged the puffed sleeve of her gown down and began brushing kisses across her shoulder and collarbone, "it isn't good-bye. I hope you realize that. I may not see you in France, but to France I shall go."

"So why," he asked softly, raising his head, "are you allowing me this splendid good-bye?"

"Why," a loud voice declared, "indeed?"

They sprang apart.

Lady Carstairs stood there, her gold gown glittering in the darkness like the flaming torch the angel flourished when he threw Adam and Eve out of Eden.

Pippa pulled up her gown. "He's going away again, Grandmother, and again, he insists we cannot go with him."

"Oh well," Lady Carstairs said. "I could understand your vexation in Bath, even in Brighton. But now that we are in London, my love, let him go. There's such fun to be had here, why should we depart?"

Pippa knew Maxwell wore a detestable smug smile. Even if she couldn't see it in the scant light she could imagine it. Again her grandmother had caught her in his embrace, and again, she hadn't defended her honor, raised an alarm, or seemed shocked. Pippa's breast rose and fell in a deep, resigned sigh. She supposed that aspect of her grandmother was gone forever. But she was fairly sure another one hadn't.

"Grandmamma," Pippa said, "he goes to Paris."

There was a shocked silence. Her grandmother's head went up like a hunting dog on a clear scent. "Paris?"

"Yes," Maxwell said. Then told Pippa, "Clever girl to have figured that bit."

"Where else were you going to hunt Noel?" Pippa asked sweetly. "Where would one expect to find a fellow escaping from England and looking for friends, if his past actions are any guide? Did you suppose he'd hurry to Provence? The forests of Anjou? Give me credit for some wit."

"Actually, I may have to go to those places too," Maxwell said. "It appears he also pursues an elusive prey."

"Paris," her grandmother said again, tasting the word. "Of course. Of course we shall go!" she cried. "That is where the world is now. How clever of Noel to have thought of it. I think much better of him now. But," she added, shaking a gloved forefinger at Maxwell, "I am not pleased that you constantly seek reasons to say good-bye to my granddaughter, my lord, and so fulsomely at that, when it's clear you're not leaving us."

"I am," he said staunchly.

"Perhaps," Lady Carstairs agreed amiably. "But we come with you."

Chapter 12

"She forgot one thing," Maxwell said as he leaned against the sloop's railing and watched the bustling dock.

"You think so?" His companion, a fair-haired and well-dressed young gentleman, looked at him curiously. "Seems to me like the dame has taken everything but her carpets. But then, you know her better than I do."

They both stared down at the wharf, where there seemed to be a parade passing through. Footmen, sailors, and all manner of menial servants were following the directions of a grand lady who was ordering them as they carried boxes onto the ferry bound for France.

"I have to," Maxwell commented. "But all I meant is that Lady Carstairs seems to have forgotten her trumpeter. She's done everything else but have fanfares blown at her departure to alert the immediate world to her leaving England, bound for Paris."

"Her poor granddaughter," the other gentleman said.

Maxwell looked at him sharply. "I detect more lust than sympathy in your tone, Cyril," he said. "The younger lady is humiliated, embarrassed, and apprehensive at this venture, as she should be if she has any sensibility. And she does. She is, after all, the reason for the journey. And that reason is predicated on her fiancé having left suddenly, without explanation. She was jilted, abandoned, and left in the most uncomfortable lurch. Is she engaged to marry? Can she become engaged to another now? So certainly she's anxious and her grandmother's behavior shocks her. But I'm the one who should comfort her. Hands and mind off Miss Phillipa Carstairs, if you please."

His companion threw both hands in the air. "Done. I'd no idea. She's replaced her errant fiancé already, has she? Caught, are you? Understandable. She's lovely. And an affair with a female who was about to trip down the aisle doesn't carry the same, shall we say, danger, as with one who doesn't know men. It's like a romantic association with a widow; there's no ruination in question. The lady is experienced and so cannot be compromised. Clever fellow."

Maxwell's answer was a well-placed right fist to Cyril's face. The gentleman tumbled to the deck, and Maxwell stood, fists up, bracing himself for another blow.

The scuffle on shipboard stole everyone's attention from Lady Carstairs's passing parade.

When the victim staggered upright, Maxwell dropped him with another fist to the chin.

The deckhands and sailors were fascinated, calling encouragement to the fallen gent. But the altercation didn't last long. When the gentleman got to his knees again, Maxwell offered him a hand that wasn't a fist and helped him to his feet. Then he offered him a clean handkerchief for his nose.

"Let's not squabble," Maxwell told him softly as his victim blotted his streaming nose. "Talwin sent you to see me off and report back to him, not to engage in a battle. My apologies. All is forgiven?"

Cyril nodded.

"Then, no harm done. Everyone will think we're just another pair of gentlemen brutes on our way to debauchery in Paris. But for the record, my friend, Miss Carstairs is honestly searching for her Noel. He must be something," he mused. "And I'm trying to be merely a help to her no matter how tempting she is. Furthermore, I've no idea of how intimate their engagement was before it was broken. Nor do I want to know. Understood?"

"Understood," Cyril echoed in a soggy voice from behind the handkerchief. "But not comprehended, if you get what I mean. She's a peach."

"That she is. But I promised to get that peach safely through her quest," Maxwell said. "I may do things for our cause while I'm about it, but that was something I gave my word on."

"So be it," the gentleman said. "Did you know you're being followed, by the way?"

"Tall dark fellow with a bad limp?" Maxwell asked. "Wearing shabby black clothing? Kept his face in his scarf and scuttled up the gangway, and disappeared into a cabin while we were disagreeing?"

"You noticed."

"Never saw a worse spy, which means he isn't one," Maxwell said. "Probably escaping a debtor or a shrew. But I'll keep an eye out."

"He could be pretending to be inept," his companion said.

"Aren't we all?" Maxwell asked wearily. He became aware of his companion's swollen eye becoming transfixed by something just behind him, and swung around prepared for the worst.

He wasn't prepared for the best thing he'd seen all morning.

Pippa smiled at him. She wore a cherry-colored cape and a petal pink bonnet over her golden hair, which gave her face a lovely glow. "Good morning," she said with a tiny dip of her bonnet. "Here we are, finally on our way. That is, if my grandmother is sure she's packed everything. I vow, the only thing she seems to have forgot to bring is a trumpeter."

Maxwell grinned. "My thoughts exactly. Miss Carstairs, may I present Lord Graves? An old friend come to see me off."

She dipped her head again. "Good morning," she said.

The gentleman bowed. "My great pleasure," he said. "But your grandmother doesn't need a trumpet to get everyone's attention if she has you by her side."

Pippa grinned. "I'm not in France yet and the compliments are already getting prettier. Thank you, my lord." She looked up at them with shining eyes. "France! I know I may sound provincial to you gentlemen, but the thought that I'm actually going to be in France soon is overwhelming to me. I never thought it would be possible in my lifetime."

"Neither did we. Just don't get too fond of the place," Maxwell said softly. "No one knows how long this peace will last. And, of course, if we find your Noel, you'll be on your way home again shortly thereafter, with or without him."

She grew serious. "Have you heard anything about him?"

He shook his head. "Too much and too little. Nothing to credit, at any rate. I didn't mean to get your hopes up, only to warn you that our stay in France may be limited by things we don't expect. But please remember whatever happens with the peace, and whatever we discover there, France is as far as we go."

"What?" a familiar voice cried. "But with the peace, what about Vienna? And Roma? Brussels? All the wonders of the Continent? I saw them on my honeymoon and want to see them again, and I think my granddaughter should too," Lady Carstairs exclaimed as she came puffing up beside them.

"Then she must travel with you and your esteemed husband someday, my lady," Maxwell said smoothly. "Perhaps on a second honeymoon for you, or a first one for her if we find her lost Noel. And yes, I agree, she certainly should see all those cosmopolitan capitals. Except now is not the best time to wade off England's shores. We go to France, and what I ought to have said is that France is as far as I go whether or not I find Noel. Our relations with Napoleon are balanced on the edge of a knife. It's too much of a risk to go farther. Were I you, my lady, I'd reconcile myself to that. I mean what I say, and I doubt your husband would allow you to go farther on your own or with newly hired help."

"Oh," Lady Carstairs said dismissively, waving one gloved hand, "why worry about that? He's so far and we're so near, what does it matter? It remains to be seen or heard." She laughed. "Come along, Pippa. We've engaged a small cabin for the duration." She turned and marched toward her cabin.

Pippa shot Maxwell a worried look and followed in her grandmother's wake.

"I no longer envy you," the gentleman told Maxwell as they watched them go.

"And I didn't even get to introduce you to the grand dame. But she's right," Maxwell said with a frown. "It no longer matters. Events move too fast now. Still, her husband should be alerted. I'm afraid the lady is no longer existing in the present. That reminds me, I must go now too. I've a compelling letter to dash off and send before we leave the dock. Old Carstairs must be told of the goings-on here. Oh, and watch your back, Cyril. We seem to have achieved a certain fame. Not only are we being watched by that odd lame fellow scuttling around the packet and disappearing whenever I look at him, but some of the sailors are watching us too hard, and some of the passengers are making too much of a show of not watching at all. Lord knows how many other weird characters are following us. I think I know many of them from old times, that's why their disguises are so absurd."

"I thought so too. The big lame fellow is Roché, don't you think? The size is right and I noticed that sometimes his limp is worse than other times."

Maxwell smiled. "Very likely it is Roché. He's the most inept spy I ever met, but somehow he finds out more than one would think. Could he possibly be intelligent? I've often wondered. What is the world coming to when we can't trust our old adversaries?"

"Coming back to war, I think," Cyril sighed. "Should I be following them now, do you think?"

"No. No point to it," Maxwell said. "We're going into their home arena. But I have to stay alert. Some of them mightn't be French. There's a bigger field of play these days. What I must do is remain calm and watchful, and do my best to get to France in one piece. It's only polite. As you know, the Frenchies like to dismember their well-born enemies themselves."

"How unforgiving. And you, half French. What would your mama say?"

"Maman knew and would approve. After all, she was clever enough to flee to England before she had to travel in two pieces. See you when I return, regards to Lord Talwin."

Her grandmother sat in their tiny cabin and composed notes to everyone she knew in France. From the look of the growing pile of missives, Pippa thought that must be the whole of the city of Paris. She threw on a light shawl and went out on deck again.

The deck was mostly deserted. Pippa imagined most of the passengers where getting ready to disembark. The land she could make out in the distance through the early mist in front of the ship must surely be France. She walked to the rail.

France! She was actually traveling to a new land. Excitement was bubbling up in her as fast as the rapidly running waters the packet was cleaving through. She hugged herself.

But then her shoulders slumped. Surely it was wrong to be so happy when she still didn't know where Noel was? And certainly it was wrong because, increasingly, she didn't care. There was only one man she thought about constantly. She hugged her shawl closer.

"Mal de mer?" a familiar voice asked from beside her.

"Oh no, I'm an excellent sailor," Pippa said without turning her head. "It's just that events have been moving so fast I'm a bit bemused."

She didn't look at him. She didn't dare. He was never far from her thoughts, and when he appeared in reality she found herself less and less able to deal with him.

"Second thoughts?" he persisted.

She nodded. "Now, when it's too late, of course, I admit I'm beginning to think this venture, on my part at least, was a little . . . hasty. I'm sure it will be educational. But I wonder if it was necessary."

He seemed surprised. "That's a great deal to admit. I'm impressed. Is it an apology, I wonder?"

She turned to face Maxwell. "Perhaps it is. The truth is that if grandmamma hadn't been so enthusiastic I mightn't have insisted on it " She frowned, and then looked up at him with sincerity. "I couldn't let her go on her own, because it wouldn't be safe for her. I don't really know her anymore. Is this how she really is, exposed after years of being cooped up? Or is it something more sinister?"

"You think she's a spy?" Maxwell asked with a smile.

She smiled back at him. "Of course. Don't you?"

He cocked his head to the side. "I mistrust the world. But not her."

"And me? Do you distrust me?"

"I don't know," he said seriously. "I do know that I mistrust myself with you."

The boat skipped as it crested a swell. It gave Maxwell the chance to reach out to steady Pippa. Once he had her in his arms, neither of them moved until Maxwell lowered his head to kiss her.

She didn't resist. She couldn't. Instead she kissed him back with her whole heart. She was pressed so close to him she didn't know if it was her own heart or his that she felt banging so loudly, pulsing throughout her body. His kiss stole her thoughts. He was warm and comforting, yet exciting and dangerous too. She wanted to be even closer to him and stay that way for a very long time. The ship, their journey, their plans no longer mattered. It was his mouth and their bodies that were her only concern—until she heard her grandmother's voice. Then she quickly dropped her arms from Maxwell and stepped back, red-faced.

"Déjà vu?" that lady said as she crossed the

deck to them with stately tread, like a ship breasting the waves, her maid in tow. "Or is the spell of France already at work? Ah me. Spring, France, and *l'amour.* I understand. But I cannot condone. This is not *comme il faut.* Phillipa, please leave. See that your luggage is in order."

Pink as a rose now, Pippa ducked her head. With one backward glance at Maxwell, she turned and hurried to her cabin.

"And as for you, my lord," Lady Carstairs told Maxwell, "let us please not repeat this scene."

"My lady," Maxwell said seriously, "I am entirely at fault. I lost my good sense, and I beg your pardon and promise it won't happen again."

"At least not in public, eh?" the lady answered with a wink. She turned and went back to her cabin, leaving Maxwell to stare after her. He was frowning.

Chapter 13

The first thing Lady Carstairs did when she arrived at her hotel in Paris was to denigrate the place.

"I'm used to so much better than this," she said in a loud voice as her granddaughter winced, because the hotel manager seemed to understand English.

But she and her maid, her granddaughter's maid, two footmen and hirelings from the dock waited with their cases at hand for Lady Carstairs decision as to whether to stay or not. Pippa had hoped for better too especially since the inns they had stopped in on the way from Dieppe had been decidedly inferior. She'd slept on top of her clothes to avoid coming in contact with grimy much-used sheets and pillows. And now, this hotel seemed little better than some of the noisome places they'd stopped at.

"There is no better accommodation to be found," Maxwell, who had accompanied them from the dock, said, as though reading her mind. "Paris is filled to the rooftops now that there is peace. And this place is clean and in a decent neighborhood."

The lady finally accepted the facts. She bid farewell to Maxwell, called to Pippa, sent her hirelings up with her bags, and went to her rooms.

The first thing she did when she got there and the extra servants had left was to change her entire attitude. She flung the latticed shutters in her chamber wide open, leaned out, breathed deeply, and smiled. Pippa was puzzled. The view from the room was not inspiring.

But her grandmother had her eyes shut in what looked like a kind of ecstasy. Her bountiful bosom grew even bigger as she stuck her curly blond head out the window and took another theatrically deep breath.

"Ah, la belle France," she said. "I remember it well. Come child, Paris in the springtime is something no romantic young filly should miss out on. Come breathe it in!"

Pippa went to her grandmother's side. The houses in this district were so packed together that the view from their window was of rooftops, chimneys, pigeons, and church steeples.

"Come," her grandmother insisted, "breathe it in. Fill your lungs. Paris in the spring! What a bouquet. Horse chestnuts in flower, roses, violets, lilacs, jasmine—all in bloom."

Pippa leaned out the window and took in a deep breath. Her eyes widened, her nose wrinkled, she sprang back, reached into a pocket for a handkerchief and covered her nose with it. "It actually hurts! All I smell is cat urine and smoke, stale wine, horse droppings, and . . . more urine," she said from behind the handkerchief. "This can't be what you remember. Perhaps later when we go for a walk we can go to a park and I'll know what you mean."

Her grandmother scowled. "Nonsense! Where's your nose? Stuck up so high in the air it doesn't work anymore? Where are your dreams of romance? I don't understand. Those are curious words coming from a girl who climbs a certain gentleman as though she was a draggletail slut trying to pay the rent every time my back is turned."

"Grandmother!" Pippa said, shocked. "Your language!"

"We weren't mealy-mouthed prisses when I was young," her grandmother said with a sniff.

"And besides," Pippa went on in agitation, "it isn't true. Those encounters weren't clandestine. I didn't seek him out, either. They may have got out of hand, but not for long. They were just a . . ." she faltered and went on, "a few accidental meetings with one gentleman."

"Whilst you are affianced to another!" her grandmother retorted triumphantly.

Pippa lowered her eyelashes.

"Nice goings-on however you say it, eh?" Lady Carstairs said. "I knew this journey might be difficult, but I never guessed what hot tail feathers you had until this trip, my girl. Is that why Noel beat a retreat?"

"GRANDMOTHER!" Pippa gasped.

"No more of this," her grandmother said, turning from the window. "Have your maid unpack for you, and be sure to dress nicely for dinner. There are dozens of my friends and acquaintances here in Paris and we may run into some of them. At any rate, even if we don't, I've sent word to all my old cronies and they'll surely come to visit, even this soon. They were always up for jollity. And everyone's in Paris now! What good times we had! Tomorrow, we'll go and look some of them up, no doubt in much nicer surroundings. In the meanwhile, rest so you can be bright as sunshine at dinner. I want to show you off."

The lady dropped a kiss on Pippa's forehead,

as though she'd never uttered one harsh word. As Pippa left she could hear her grandmother humming a pretty dance tune. She appeared to be her old self. But that self was new to Pippa.

Pippa went to her own chamber next door. Her maid was busy in the tiny dressing room, arranging clothing and cases. Pippa sank to the tilted bed and thought deeply. She was tired and confused, and a bit frightened.

She felt alone and in danger. The facts were plain. She'd rushed into things without thinking again. She doubted she'd find Noel in Paris and, in truth, realized that he was no longer foremost in her mind. In fact, she no longer cared if he showed up or not. Noel and she, all the promises he'd made and the future they'd planned, were definitely over. Whatever happened, this was so. She'd known it before ever setting foot on the packet to France.

But she couldn't have let her grandmother go abroad alone. Now she was in a difficult situation and didn't know whom to turn to.

She was in a strange land with an unsteady companion and a dangerous gentleman who she needed a chaperone to meet with. Because in truth, Pippa thought as she curled up on the lumpy cot with a sad sigh, she wasn't sure she had the good sense or sufficient self-control to chaperone herself any longer. She was weary and self-doubting. Pippa closed her eyes and welcomed sleep. A brief nap might clear her mind.

As she drifted off, between oblivion and wakefulness, she found herself wondering what she was worrying about, at least so far as the gentleman in question was concerned. Because she was four and twenty, and nominally engaged to be married to a man that the world knew had run from the altar rather than join her there. Even her grandmother doubted her honor. So what was she afraid of? Losing her reputation? Why? She had none. It was gone, if not when Noel had deserted her, then certainly now that she was fruitlessly pursuing him across the continent.

She thought about Lord Montrose. Maxwell. She shivered, although she didn't feel cold, not when she remembered his warmth, his scent, his voice. He was handsome and clever, and a true gentleman. It was also true that he threw out lures to her. She didn't have to take them. But she always did. She knew he'd never force her to anything. It was her own desires she feared.

Why? Was she afraid of losing her purity? Who would expect her to have any, after all?

That made her eyes open. It was true, though.

And also true that the stark truth of it made her feel a bit wicked. The fear she'd had before was being replaced by a giddy new sense of freedom. Who knew about her physical state, or her past with men? Who cared?

She closed her eyes again. It might have been a frightening thought at home. But here, warm and snug and safe from the world, lying in a new bed in a new land with no one to count on but no one to disappoint, it only bemused her.

Perhaps Paris in the spring did put a spell on visitors, she thought muzzily. And then she slept, with a tilted smile on her lips.

"No one is here!" Lady Carstairs trumpeted.

Some of the other diners in the hotel's crowded dining room looked up, and then back at their dinners.

"But grandmother," Pippa whispered, "every table is taken."

"No one who is anyone," her grandmother explained. She pushed her empty soup bowl away. "I heard everyone was here. But where?"

"Most of your friends were in London," Pippa said.

"Those feeble old creatures?" her grandmother said. "They're out of juice. I mean all the friends

I shared such jollity with last time I was in Paris, with your grandfather."

"How long ago was that?" Pippa asked quietly.

Her grandmother scowled. "It doesn't matter," she said abruptly. "I heard everyone was here, but here—they are not. Some are doubtless too old to travel, but not everyone is dead or decrepit. It's this bottom-of-the-barrel hotel. But never fear. Tomorrow we'll meet the crème de la crème. I've sent out notes. I'd hoped that tonight would be amusing, instead we're here with nothing to do. It's too bad you've put on such a lovely gown for no reason."

Pippa looked down at her light green gown. It was lovely, with puffed sleeves and tiny yellow flowers along the hemline. She knew she looked well in it, and didn't think wearing it was a waste. It made her feel cheerier.

"Surely Paris still knows how to amuse visitors," her grandmother said bitterly. "But where can two ladies safely go at any time, anywhere? To a dressmaker's, of course. But after that? Where's that Montrose when you really need him?"

"Aren't you in least tired?" Pippa asked curiously. Her nap had been brief, and she thought she could do with some hours of solid sleep before she took on a strange new city.

"Tired? At ten at the night in Paris? Where are your wits, child?"

"But I confess, I'm a bit weary," Pippa said. "I don't think I'd be at my best, especially at some grand fete. We just arrived, Grandmother. I'm happy to rest before going out on the Town."

"I suppose you've the right of it," her grandmother said grudgingly. "We could use some beauty sleep." She glanced up and broke out into smiles. "Aha! Perhaps we won't have to! There's Lord Montrose. He probably has fun in store for us."

Pippa looked up, and her heart sank. She'd told her grandmother the truth. She was still a bit groggy from her brief nap and tired from traveling since sunup. But Maxwell was making his way through the dining parlor, weaving around tables toward them. He looked immaculate, well rested, and wore correct black-and-white evening wear. That meant he might have someplace to escort them to tonight.

"Ladies," he said when he got to their table. He bowed. A waiter hurried with a chair for him, and he sat, facing Pippa and her grandmother. "Just some port," Maxwell told the waiter, "I've already dined. Well, ladies, how are you?"

"Ready for merriment," her grandmother chirped.

Pippa restrained herself from rolling her eyes.

"Not weary after your journey?" he asked.

"You're obviously not," Lady Carstairs said. "Why should we be?"

"But I am," he said after a brief glance at Pippa. "I've only dressed this way because I'm staying with an old friend, and he has guests tonight. I plan to make my way back to his house and my bed as soon as I'm done here. Unlike you stalwart ladies, I need some sleep. I only came to ask after your health and also to ask if you'd care to come to some soirees with me in the coming week."

Pippa let out a relieved sigh. Her grandmother looked disgruntled. Maxwell smiled, took some cards from his waistcoat pocket, and shuffled through them.

"Let me see," he said. "Not the Janeways, no indeed. They're English persons trying to slide into French society. *Bon chance* to them. Nor the musicale at Mademoiselle Pinchon's either. She's a dead bore and her company always tedious. Ah. But yes. Wait. Here it is. I thought you might want to visit at Madame Recamier's salon this Thursday afternoon. Yes, she still holds them. They are something to talk about, if nothing else. And Madame Duchamps is hosting a little soiree this Friday night. They're said to be amusing. And last but surely not least, Monsieur and Madame Fauchard are giving a ball this Saturday. They were supporters of Napoleon and now glory in the role of friends to the First Consul. It is even possible he may grace the company and show his face.

"Well?" he asked, looking up. "That's the best of the lot so far. Which do you prefer? Any? None? Or all?"

"All!" Lady Carstairs cried. "What fun. Now we shall see Paris. Anything on the agenda for tomorrow night?" she asked greedily.

"I'm afraid not," Maxwell said. "Though I should be happy to take you to dinner at a very well recommended restaurant."

"Then it will have to do," she said ungraciously, "that is, if my friends don't get my notes and invite me somewhere first."

Pippa squirmed in embarrassment but saw Maxwell incline his head as he hid a smile.

"But of course, you want to tour the city tomorrow to see how it has changed," he said. "I can be here after breakfast."

"I plan to sleep late. It is the custom," Lady Carstairs said. "But Phillipa rises with the chickens. Doubtless, she'd like a drive 'round Paris."

"I don't wish to trouble you," Pippa told Maxwell.

Now his smile was wide and warm. "Impossible," he said.

"We hired you to find Noel," Pippa whispered. "You don't have to play escort. We should not impose so much."

"And if I don't think of it as an imposition?"

"The fellow is a gent down to his toes," Lady Carstairs declared. She covered her mouth as she yawned. "Demme if you're not right, Montrose. I am tired. Must have been all that sea air on the crossing."

Pippa was too shocked at her grandmother's cursing to say a word.

Maxwell nodded sagely. "It takes its toll. Shall I escort you upstairs?"

"Not a bad idea," Lady Carstairs said on another yawn. "You may stay, Phillipa. Finish your sorbet, it cost enough. I'll see you in the morning."

The lady rose from her seat, signaled to her maid, and, with Maxwell at her side, made her way to the stair.

Pippa sat and watched them leave. She still had her maid watching from a corner of the room. The dining room was full. But she felt very alone.

When Maxwell came back to the table he glanced

at her and frowned. "What is it?" he asked as he took his seat. "Has anyone upset you?"

"Surely, even though you don't know her you can see that my grandmother is changing under our very eyes."

"She's becoming more free with her speech," he said. "But she's not acting strangely. We'll take her to places where she'll be considered merely eccentric. The French believe all the English are that. And then, with your permission, we'll take her home. Unless you want to go on? I would accommodate you with that, but I greatly fear that this peace of ours is fragile. I wouldn't want us to be caught here, trapped in a web of politics.

"Now," he said with more force, "as for Noel Nicholson?" His expression grew serious. He spoke low. "I have heard some things. Nothing tangible but enough, and from so many sources, that I begin to believe them. Your Mr. Nicholson is said to have been seen heading eastward, toward the Alps, and Italy." He held up a hand. "It seems to have been on purpose. No one is traveling with him. No one seems to be pursuing him or guiding him. He eludes capture, and conversation. I'm sorry," he added, looking at her closely, "but whatever his difficulties, it appears that he doesn't want to come home again—if England is his home."

Pippa nodded. She felt very weary. "If you think he isn't in danger . . ."

"I'm certain he's not, except, of course, from you and your family."

"And not even that. Then so be it," she said on a sigh. "I'd love to know what happened to make him flee, of course. But I don't think it had to do with me."

"Neither do I," he said, watching her.

She drew a deep breath. "So what I will do is go home, explain to grandfather, have a notice put in the papers ending the engagement, and go on with my life."

She didn't add that she didn't have great expectations for that life. A jilted lady wasn't considered a great catch. If her grandmother were deemed worse than eccentric she feared her fate would be sealed. She'd probably live on with her grandparents until she herself became an eccentric.

His voice was soft, as though he was reading her mind. "Forget dull sorrow," he said. "We'll enjoy Paris while we can. I won't stop making inquiries. I may yet find out what happened to that wretch, stupid, and blind ex-fiancé of yours."

She managed a smile.

"Now eat up your sorbet— Uhm, I mean syrup.

Your grandmother said it was expensive."

That made her laugh, and he kept her laughing until their waiter had cleared the table.

Maxwell looked up from her at last. The dining room had cleared out. "Come," he said to Pippa. "Your eyes are growing heavy and I'm enough of a conceited ass to think it isn't due to my conversation. No, no, don't apologize. That makes it worse. It's been a long day for you. I'll see you upstairs and then again in the morning. It bids to be fair. If you like, I'll show you Paris in the springtime."

"I'd like that," she said simply, rising and taking his arm.

They went up the stair and then down a winding corridor. Her maid followed at a dutiful pace and then disappeared into Pippa's room as they reached her door. Pippa and Montrose were left standing together in the dim light of a single flickering wall lantern. She realized she still held his arm, took her hand back, and wondered what to say now.

It wasn't dark enough to disguise the fact that he was staring at her. Darkness had no way of hiding the lovely scent of lavender and sandalwood that he wore. And Pippa swore she could feel the warmth of the man radiating toward her even though they weren't touching.

He leaned toward her and then stopped himself. "A kiss to see me through the night?" he asked softly.

She couldn't answer. She simply leaned in toward him.

This kiss was both more satisfactory and more frightening for Pippa than the others she'd shared with him, because it was like sharing their desire and their needs. She opened her lips against his and breathed in the taste of dark warm red wine and spices on his breath, and then the strange and welcome intrusion of his tongue against hers.

He gathered her closer, and she felt her breasts tingling even though they touched nothing but his jacket, waistcoat, and shirt. That was, they did until his hand cupped a breast and she felt the delicious prickling rise of her flesh all the way down to her toes. He seemed to know, and she heard him chuckle as he deepened their kiss. And then the next one, and the next.

It took a while until she let herself realize that the top of her gown was down to her waist, and her breasts uncovered except by his warm hands. She was not so inexperienced that she didn't know it was his arousal pressing into her as she clung to him as though he could hold her from the current of longing threatening to sweep her away.

It took will power, but she breathed deep and stepped back. He immediately dropped his hands. She drew up her gown and then went straight back into his arms, resting her head against his shoulder.

"I don't know what to say," she whispered in confusion. She was embarrassed and aroused, sorry and yet thrilled.

"It seemed," he said, his voice a little rougher than usual, "that you were saying yes. I was too glad of it, I suppose. But we can't, my dear. Not here, and not now."

She was too honest to pretend she didn't know what he meant. But surely he could feel her cheek growing hot against his neck.

"But soon, Pippa?" he asked softly, pressing light kisses on the rim of her ear. "We can make it soon if we can find a place and the time."

She was too honest to lie to him or to herself.

"No," she said. "Yes. I don't know. Perhaps. It may be."

Chapter 14

"I don't know a thing about you," Pippa said suddenly, staring at Maxwell sitting beside her as they drove down the avenue in a jaunty open carriage. "Not really. I know all about Versailles now, thanks to you. And the Cathedral de Notre Dame as well, and even about Charlemagne, so you've obviously been well educated. But where? And where do you live when you're not chasing criminals? What of your family? Your tastes? Who are you, Lord Montrose? I don't know!"

He laughed. "I asked you to make love to me, not marry me! No! Don't jump!" he cried, catching hold of her arm as she tried to stand and get to the end of the long seat. "Not from a moving carriage. I'm sorry. What I said was careless, rude, and unfair. Of course, you're too well bred to make love to a strange man. Although many well-bred women love to do that, I promise you."

"I'm leaving," she said through clenched teeth. "As soon as this carriage stops, wherever it stops." Her face had grown red as the new blown roses in the park they'd just driven past.

"And I'm not going to make love to you," she said in a fierce under voice. "I only considered it because I was carried away by your kisses last night."

She glanced at the stone-faced driver in the seat in front of them. "Are you sure he doesn't speak English?"

"Yes. He's Parisian. He thinks everyone speaks French, and dreams of the day when everyone will. Look, I'm sorry I offended you. But come to think on, my dear, it seems to me that you don't bother to get to know your would-be lovers or would-be husbands very well, do you? You didn't know much about Noel. And now you say you don't know me. It's not necessary, of course, to know one's husband these days. Or one's lovers. But you're intelligent. Why should this be?"

She sat still. Her look of consternation faded as one of dawning wonder replaced it. She looked very fine this morning, he thought. Her petal pink walking dress, striped with spring green, made her skin radiate light. A tiny tilted straw bonnet let the sunlight gleam on her fair hair. She was lovely in a very commonly English sort of way, or so he'd thought when they'd met. There were whole villages filled with glowing fair young English maidens who looked like her. But not quite, he'd realized, because her looks were animated by her wit, her charm, and her boundless curiosity. Her eyes were blue, but never bland. They were the blue of an ever-changing sky. Even that didn't account for her appeal for him. Her face and form were lovely; it was her intelligence and personality that made her beautiful, and unforgettable.

She was courageous too. Most young women of social standing would have withdrawn from Society if their wedding date had been set, their fiancé gone off into oblivion and everyone knew. But she was publicly hunting her lost fiancé, and if she could be believed, was doing as much for his sake as her own. Whatever her reasons, she knew that she was flying in the face of Society.

Bright, brave, and beautiful. The more he knew her, the more impressed he was. She called to him, mind and body. In fact, that beautiful body was calling to him more each hour. But he was wary. She was still a mystery, perhaps even greater the more he got to know her. Why would such a gifted woman still be so determined to find a man who had rejected her? In fact, why was he still on the wretch's trail? Or was it that Noel was too involved with her for her to give up the search?

"You know?" she asked, looking at him with surprise, and interrupting his thoughts. "You're right! I never got to really know Noel, did I? Or you, for that matter, or any man since I reached adulthood. But when I was a girl my best friend was Richard, the gardener's boy. We were of an age, and we played in the fields and daydreamed in the haymows, compared warts, and skipped stones on the pond together. All that changed when I got older and was forbidden to play with him anymore.

"Then, I don't get to meet many men of any sort, actually," she said as though to herself. "They came to visit Grandfather and were only polite to me. At home I got invited to parties and dances, and I knew everyone there. All the men of the proper age for me were deemed to have improper breeding by my grandfather. Anyway, now they are already married, or else they're insufferable. There are seldom new faces, which is why Noel so entranced me, I suppose. Even so, since the debacle with Noel, I'm not asked anywhere. Am I engaged: a jilt or a cast-off? No one knows where I fit any more than I do.

"I suppose," she said slowly, so deep in her

thoughts that although she was looking at him she was obviously not focusing on him. "Meeting new men has been difficult for me. I reckon it's because I came to think of males as a different species, harder to communicate with because they were more important than women."

She turned a shining face to Maxwell. "I'm shy with men!" she blurted. "Imagine that! Or at least I'm so respectful that it banishes any thought of equality, so I don't dare ask anything except for stupid questions about the weather and such. I don't know how to be friends with a male, not since I was a child. I never realized it!"

"And this pleases you?" he asked.

"Oh no! But it explains me. And that's something. I'm so glad I didn't call after you when you left last night," she said impulsively, reaching out and touching his hand.

He blinked. "You wanted to?"

She ducked her head and quickly withdrew her hand "I confess, I think I did. I don't know if I really would have, though. But what folly! I almost married a man I didn't know, and to compound matters I wanted to . . . be close to another male I also didn't know." She frowned. "We're so bounded by rules, how does an adult female get to know a male in this world of ours?"

"Most men talk about themselves, endlessly," he said, sitting back.

"You don't," she countered. "Neither did Noel."

He thought a moment. "I suspect he had something to hide," he finally said. "As for me, I wanted to entertain you and didn't think I was the most fascinating topic. And remember, all this isn't about me anyway. I was merely a hireling. Still, I shouldn't worry were I you. Marriages in the ton aren't usually based on knowledge of one's mate. Certainly, love affairs seldom are. Marriages are arranged, or the participants have known each other since childhood. Love affairs begin and end with mutual physical attraction. Whatever it's called, that's not love."

"You're right," she said seriously.

"There's only one thing I wonder about," he said slowly, unused to confessing his inner thoughts to a woman, especially one he mistrusted. "Why did you decide to chase the wretch from here to kingdom come?"

"I thought he might be in danger," she said. "His disappearance wasn't like him. But now I see I didn't really know what he was like. I'll have to be more circumspect in future. And at the same time, I have to learn to be more straightforward with gentlemen." She frowned again. "And no matter what I discover about Noel, whether he was kidnapped or waylaid on the road, or off to visit his aged mother, or to sell secrets to the tsar, one thing is certain. It's over. I'll officially end my betrothal to him. Immediately."

"Thus ending our relationship immediately?" he asked innocently enough.

She sat up. "No, of course not. I don't want to be abandoned in Paris. Anyway, I can't dismiss you even if I want to. I must write to grandfather, tell him my decision about Noel and why I made it, and have him put the notice of ending the engagement in the papers. Then, I suppose, he can let you go. But you will see us home, won't you?"

"Absolutely," he said.

"Thank you," she said, and fell still, obviously thinking about the future.

Maxwell laid his head on the back of his seat, and tilted his high beaver hat over his forehead as though he wanted to avoid getting sunlight in his eyes. But he hoped to encourage her to speak more, and more frankly. All the revelations she'd spoken of had doubtless been brought on by what he'd said. She'd been insulted and tried to defend herself, but as she spoke she heard herself revealing some long-buried truths that surprised her.

He thought everything she'd said about herself

was true. He hoped she'd go on and learn even more about herself. She could, the mood was upon her. But from long dealings interviewing other tight-lipped persons, like suspected spies and traitors, he realized she'd speak more only if she stayed in this curiously confiding mood and kept on talking. Once she had time to think and digest her thoughts, she might deny them again; and she wouldn't speak more if he kept watching her.

So he sat back, his body stretched out, hat brim shadowing his eyes, a perfect picture of an unconcerned gentleman at ease in the morning sunlight.

"So," she mused after a moment, as he'd hoped, "actually, there's no more reason for me to be here, is there? I don't have to find Noel. In fact, I don't want to find any husband until I know how to deal with men." She was silent for a moment and then blurted, "But I do so want to stay here a little while longer. Please, don't tell Grandmother about my decision? I want—I need to see a bit of the world before I return to England."

"I think your grandmother would have me murdered if I suggested going home now," he commented without opening his eyes.

"Do you think she's able to make any decision now?" she asked in smaller, worried tones.

"I think the lady is as competent as any other English person who is here," he said. "She's changed, you say. I wouldn't know. She seems sane enough, if a little uninhibited, a bit unrestrained. She is. I think she's only reacting to being free and visiting old friends and places where she spent her youth. It makes her less likely to guard her tongue. But I don't believe she's disordered by any means."

He was so attuned to her mood he fancied he could hear Pippa's heartfelt sigh even over the sound of the traffic and their horse's hoof beats. She said nothing more. He realized her confidences had ended and decided that it wasn't good for her to dwell on them.

He tilted his hat back. "Now let's talk about more interesting things," he suggested, sitting up. "I'll stop being a tour guide and will tell you all about me instead of French history. We're almost at the end of our scheduled ride anyway. But your hotel is near a park. When we head back, what do you say we stop awhile and ramble before I take you back to Grandmamma?"

She smiled.

"And then perhaps," he said, sitting up, smiling, and looking into her eyes, "we can think of where and when to meet again without any fuss or notice so I can show you even more about myself?"

She stared.

He nodded. "Yes. Exactly what you're thinking. Darkness doesn't bring on lust. It only uncovers it. Why should we deny it?"

"Why?" she asked in horror. "Because I don't want an affair. I may have been drawn to you, I admit. I am, in fact, as if you didn't know. But no wonder! You're handsome, charming, and very experienced with females. And here I am as good as alone in a strange land, worried to bits about my Grandmother, disappointed in my traitorous fiancé, and feeling utterly abandoned. And you offer me warmth and comfort. I'll admit that. But the last thing I need now is to involve my heart again."

He sighed. "If you recall, I never asked for that part of your anatomy."

"Oh!" she puffed.

"It would have been a great comfort for us both," he went on quickly. "But if you don't wish to make love with me, so be it. Please understand that I will likely be ready and willing to accommodate you if at any time you change your mind."

" 'Will likely'?" she asked, her brows rising. "You have the effrontery to tell me that you mightn't want me, after all?"

"Never," he said, hand on heart. "Only if I'm already promised to another lady of an evening, how could I promise you my instant readiness?"

"You are the worst rogue and roué I have ever met," she huffed.

"How many have you met?" he asked.

She seemed to deflate. "Apart from Noel? Not any, at least that I knew of," she said. "Oh, this is all nonsense. Let me go back to the hotel. I'll write to Grandfather, and explain everything to Grandmother, and we'll go home as soon as may be. I'm not fashioned for this sort of life. I can't swim in your waters."

"Would you want to?" he asked.

She smiled a real smile for the first time in a while. "Sometimes, I think so. But understand I'm alone quite a lot and given to all sorts of fancies. Disregard it, please. And let's forget this conversation as well. I have no doubt you'd make a wonderful lover. But I need a friend now."

He couldn't think of a clever answer. So he only looked at her and nodded.

"Go home? Now?" Lady Carstairs asked incredulously, her voice rising so high that the few others in the hotel's front salon glanced at them in curiosity. "Go home? Are you joking, child?"

"Well, not immediately, but say, by next week?" Pippa said, clutching her hands together. They'd found her grandmother in the front salon, waiting for them when they returned to the hotel. Pippa had decided it would be easier to confront the lady with her decision while Maxwell was still with her, so they'd sat down together.

"But it's Maytime, Grandmamma," Pippa went on. "Think of how pretty everything will be at home. Think about how long we've been gone. Grandfather surely misses us, in his way. So now that I'm not chasing after Noel anymore, there's little point in our staying on here."

"Who said we'd stay on here?" her grandmother asked in astonishment. "Italy is just beyond the Alps, Pippa. Roma! Venezia! Milan, and beyond to Austria, Brussels—I can't think of all the places we could go. Who says gentlemen are the only ones to have a chance at a Grand Tour? It isn't fair and never was. Go home? Are you run mad, child? Tell her, Lord Montrose."

"It is not my decision," he said carefully. "But I must remind you, my lady, that my services were engaged only for when you were searching for the errant Mr. Nicholson. I have no other business with you and could not follow you on your farther journeys."

Lady Carstairs opened her lips but before she could speak, he raised a slender hand. "And surely," he said, "you would not go alone. Certainly, you are far too wise to trust any chance-met characters who would offer you escort through foreign parts."

"'Chance met'?" she retorted. "Hardly. I have friends here, my lord. Respectable, worthy gentlepersons who can give me the direction of suitable escorts."

"But Grandmamma," Pippa said worriedly, "we haven't met any of them yet. Remember?"

"Of course," her grandmother snapped. "I'm not in my dotage. But we've scarcely got here and haven't gone out on the Town. Even so, look—" she said in triumph, pulling a handful of cards from her lap. "I was just going over these invitations that were delivered this morning. We are invited everywhere. Every night. Some are from old friends, and some from persons I don't even recall. But I am not nothing, my love," she added proudly. "I am remembered!"

"Congratulations, my lady," Maxwell said dryly. "But as I am still, in a way, in your employ, may I look over your invitations? Doubtless I'll have no trepidations about your old friends, but when you say you've been invited places by people you don't recall, it becomes my duty to ensure none of them are unsuitable."

"Of course," Lady Carstairs said graciously, handing him the cards. "One doesn't like to put a foot wrong. But why anyone would want to harm us, I cannot say."

"You have wealth, and your husband has a certain renown," Maxwell said softly as he flipped through the invitations. He nodded at some, smiled at others, and then his face became expressionless. He gave a low whistle.

"My lady," he said, handing the card back to Lady Carstairs, "do you know these people?"

She pulled a lorgnette out of her pocket, raised it, and squinted at the card. "Can't say as I do. Are they *comme il fault*?"

"Extremely," he said thoughtfully. "Have you any idea who might have recommended you to these hosts?"

"None," Lady Carstairs said, visibly preening. "But I imagine they have heard of me. Our name is not nothing, you know."

"Why do you ask?" Pippa asked Maxwell.

"This is a grand ball," he answered. "In all probability the First Consul himself will make an appearance."

Lady Carstairs drew in her breath, as did her granddaughter.

"His lady, Josephine," Maxwell went on, "is connected to this Comte Deauville and his lady. Everyone, as you say, will be there. Perhaps you can solve the mystery of your invitation when you get there. Congratulations. You'll see Paris in a new light: amongst the stars of the new regime."

Pippa's eyes widened. "Really?"

"Really," he said, smiling.

"Then we must get new gowns," Lady Carstairs said. "No expense must be spared. I shall send to my friends immediately to get the name of a decent modiste! Let me think who to consult with."

Pippa grinned. "Imagine, hobnobbing with Napoleon himself? Truly?" she asked Maxwell again.

"Truly," he said. "Though you'd best not try any hobnobbing."

Pippa grinned, but her smile soon faded. She leaned toward him. "But I really do wonder why they would invite us."

"It's likely as your grandmother said," he said. "Your grandfather has a certain renown and the French are eager to show the world their new world. Nothing for you to fear."

She bit her lip. "My lord," she asked softly, glancing at her grandmother to be sure she wasn't listening, "will you be there?"

"Assuredly," he said. "I have entree everywhere."

She smiled. "Then I have nothing to fear." She lowered her voice. "Except for you, of course."

"Of course," he answered on a chuckle.

Chapter 15

"Now this is Paris, we've been to teas and receptions, but nothing like this," Lady Carstairs said with great satisfaction.

She, Pippa, and Maxwell stood at the top of a grand stair, looking down into the ballroom of an elegant, ancient town house. They stood in back of other guests, waiting to be announced.

The ballroom was vast, with high vaulted ceilings decorated with soaring and floating cherubs smiling down at the assembly through golden clouds. Satin draperies covered tall windows. In the center of the room, an enormous glowing candle-filled multi-tiered chandelier dripped faceted prisms of glass. Two identical but smaller chandeliers hung to each side at the farther ends of the room. Mirrors were everywhere, magnifying the brightness, size, and magnificence of the room. The walls were covered with expensive floral-patterned stretched papers and, to complement them, blooming floral arrangements that looked like planted gardens occupying every niche. Exotic perfumes, not only from the flowers, drifted in the air.

The babble of conversation that drifted to their ears was obviously foreign. Pippa was well educated and spoke French, of course. But she was too far away to make out a single word.

The guests, in blossom bright garb, their hair, necks, chests, cravats, and fingers crusted with faceted jewels, made the room a whirling, sparkling kaleidoscope of color.

"I thought that after their Revolution there would be no more places or parties like this," Pippa whispered in wonderment to Maxwell.

"This isn't like any assembly before the Glorious Revolution," he said softly into her ear. "The hosts and guests are citizens now, not aristocrats."

She gave him a curious look.

"Not everything was destroyed during the time of Terrors," he added, his warm breath making her hair lift and her spine tingle. "Except, of course, for the aristos. Now they're dead and gone and their gilded palaces have passed to the common man, so all's well."

"But not every common man," Pippa protested. "I've seen as many beggars in the streets here as there are in London, even more, and you yourself refuse to take me to so many historic districts because you say they're squalid and dangerous."

"Hush," he whispered low in her ear, the sibilance making her senses riot. "That's traitorous talk. The Revolution is still fresh, less than a decade past. Tonight: no thinking. Just smile and enjoy yourself. This is no place for politics. Especially not from an Englishwoman."

She changed the subject at once. "The fashions must be the latest. I've never seen such a display. Even the men are more like peacocks than any gentlemen I've ever seen in England. At home, simplicity is the rule: you fellows wear black and white to formal occasions, but it's your unmentionables that are black and linen that's white, with color only in your waistcoats. But here! So many men are wearing white satin breeches and long coats of every color, and look at all the ribbons, medals, and jewels they're sporting! They're almost as spectacularly dressed as their ladies, but no one could be that."

He smiled. "I see you've adopted the latest fashion as well."

She tried not to blush, though she felt her cheeks grow warm. It was true her gown was cut so low that she was afraid to bow. And every time she looked down, she saw two naked white swellings bulging over the top of her gown's neckline.

But the modiste, one of the greatest in Paris, had told her, "Not to fret yourself, mademoiselle. Let your neckline be. If you look down and see a bit of pink showing above the material, you may adjust your gown. Otherwise, the more flesh you show, the better. It is the fashion this year."

It was, Pippa now saw. But that didn't mean she felt more comfortable. "It's what I was told to wear," she said in defense.

His smile grew broader. "I wasn't complaining. And, of course, I should have remembered, you always do what you're told."

She bit her lower lip, seeing he was dressed in sober formal black and white, with a high starched neckcloth and white linen without so much as a smidgeon of lace at the sleeve.

"But you, my lord," she said a shade too sweetly, "obviously don't give a rap about fashion. You're not wearing any colors, ruffles, or jewels, and although I now see that white satin breeches are both elegant and flattering, you still cling to the old ways."

"Me?" he asked, raising a dark brow. "But everyone knows I'm just an Englishman who shouldn't be trusted. I'd shock them and maybe endanger myself if I suddenly became fashionable here in

Paris. And by the by, you didn't hear me complain about your gown, did you? I never would. Not when I can see you have such . . . ahm," he said on a cough, looking down at her with a wickedly tilted grin, "delightfully good points."

She glanced down at herself to see what he was looking at and felt it before she saw it. It was cool and breezy at the top of the stair and her gown was made of thin satin. As the double meaning of his words sank in Pippa wanted to slap him, but he'd turned his head to speak to her grandmother.

She fumed. Her gown was lovely. Light violet, with green at the neckline and hem, it was simple except for a soft pink scarf tied beneath her breasts in the Empire style, and the outline of beautiful violets traced on the front of her gown. Real flowers to match were braided into her fair hair to form a coronet. With a simple string of pearls about her neck, she'd felt like the spirit of spring.

Now she felt like a wanton. And yet she didn't entirely regret it. She was wearing a French gown designed in Paris and she was in Paris. She'd never wear the gown again, in spite of how costly it had been. Tonight would be something to remember.

Her grandmother's neckline was low too, perhaps lower. But there was so much more to her and her costume that her overflowing bosom was scarcely noticeable. Her little round form was draped in a silver net gown. She had a web of diamonds at her neck and some at her wrists and on her plump fingers. An ornate silver coronet sat atop the dandelion shape of her newly poufed bright yellow hair.

Their names were announced before Pippa could think of anything sufficiently blighting to say to Maxwell. Instead, she held her head higher, took one of his arms as her grandmother took the other, and in as stately a fashion as she could, descended the stair, hoping no one was behind her because of what she realized they'd see if they looked down at her and her fashionable neckline.

When they touched down on the ballroom floor, they were immediately surrounded by guests.

Pippa hadn't realized they'd be so popular.

But no one spoke to them. The crowd milled around them, not noticing them any more than they'd notice servants. Lady Carstairs went red, and Pippa looked puzzled.

"There isn't enough room for more people and more people keep streaming in," Maxwell explained. "It isn't because you're not popular. I know you have friends here," he told Lady Carstairs, "but how to find them? As I'm tallest, I'll crane my neck to see if there's anyone I know."

But after a few minutes, there was nothing for it but that Maxwell had to act like a human shield, and let them follow his broad back into the center of the crowd. It was obviously the right thing to do because none of the guests seemed to mind or even notice being pushed aside.

"Stand your ground," Maxwell told Lady Carstairs and Pippa in a voice loud enough to carry over the general babble. "And hold on to me. We'll stay in the middle of things until someone hails us."

Pippa doubted they'd see any of her grandmother's friends. The ones they'd visited so far were too decrepit to socialize much, and, she'd swear, none of them were socially connected in France. They were all English, and she believed they stayed in Paris due to inertia or misfortune at home.

But suddenly, they were greeted. The fair young gentleman Maxwell had spoken to on the packet before they'd left for France hailed them. The crowd made way for him. Pippa doubted they had any choice.

"What ho!" he cried as he came toward them. "Lord Montrose, as I live and can scarcely breathe! What are you doing in this crush?"

"Cyril!" Maxwell said in return as the two men bowed to each other. "What are you doing here? I thought you were staying in England."

"So did I," Cyril said, his lips twisting in a rueful mile. "But plans change, eh? Our mutual friend, Talwin, had other plans for me."

"You remember the delightful Lady Carstairs and her lovely granddaughter, Phillipa? They were on the packet with me. We were invited. How did you get in?"

"Ha!" Cyril said. "It was arranged. Good evening ladies. And so it will be, or at least, it will be interesting. The rumor is that the First Consul and his lady will be dropping by later. Hence: the crush, and the guards at all the entrances and exits. It's supposed to be a ball, but the only dancing that can be done would be on the other guests' heads."

Pippa hadn't noticed the guards before. But now that she looked around she thought she could see glimpses of uniformed men at the fringes of the crowd. This was the most peculiar ball she'd ever attended. She'd hoped to meet some famous French persons so she could tell her grandfather about them later, but she couldn't even see past her escort. For that matter, she'd worn a hideously expensive and lovely gown, she knew she couldn't be seen either. The crowd was too thick and getting thicker. Conversation had been babble before. Now there was such a roar her head was beginning to ache.

She didn't know what the guests were supposed

to do. If there was scarcely any room to move, were they expected to just stand there and chatter all night?

An orchestra had been sawing away somewhere in the background. Pippa only realized it because suddenly it fell still. So, strangely enough, did the crowd. Two trumpeters stood up and blared an ornate fanfare. The crowd began to part.

As though they'd rehearsed it, the crowd separated, half of the guests forming a line to one side of the room, the other half going to face them from the other side. Maxwell and his friend escorted Lady Carstairs and Pippa to the right side. They stood facing the center of the room and waited as all the other guests were doing.

The fanfare flourished once more and then went still; strings took up the music. The crowd stirred, but silently. All eyes were on the grand stair.

At first, brightly dressed soldiers and naval personnel descended in their full regalia and carrying their arms.

The crowd applauded and cheered as they came down the stair in waves, as though the ballroom was being invaded.

Then some elegantly dressed ladies and gentlemen came down the stair. They weren't announced, but the crowd surely knew them. There was more applause as they ringed the crowd and stationed themselves along the walls.

And then, after a silence in which Pippa would swear no one breathed, two figures descended. An elegantly dressed female in a rose-colored gown, carrying a long-stemmed red rose, wearing a golden tiara on her curly brown hair. She wasn't beautiful, or particularly elegant, having a short figure and sallow skin. But her dark eyes were luminous and she bore herself with the air of a woman of some importance.

She held her head high, and walked slowly down the stair on the arm of a much-decorated swarthy gentleman wearing black breeches and a heavily decorated red-and-gold jacket, his chest covered with medals. His dark hair was brushed forward à la Brutus; his eyes were dark and serious, his nose was long, and his brow low. He wasn't handsome so much as rivetingly interesting, Pippa thought.

She took in a breath as she realized that this, then, had to be Napoleon Bonaparte, First Consul of France. She'd seen the pictures in the magazines; she'd seen the caricatures. As he descended she could see that he was definitely England's famous enemy and now friend, General Bonaparte, and ruler of France, whatever he called himself.

The crowd bowed down like Mandarins greeting their emperor as he reached their level.

And then the First Consul strolled to one end of the long lines. Preceded by his guard, and followed by members of his party, he and his lady then made their stately way down the center of the path the crowd had made for him. Their progress was slow as they nodded at some guests, smiled at others, and stopped every so often to exchange a few words with some along the route.

The guests began to whisper to each other as he passed them, and soon a soft susurration began to be heard as they did.

The First Consul was far from where Pippa stood when she broke from her silence, rose on her tiptoes, raised her head, and whispered to Maxwell. "He's not so short!" she breathed in obvious surprise.

"Shh," Maxwell whispered. "Later. For now, just be charming."

Pippa stood waiting as the Consul's party leisurely made its way down the lines of guests. She watched as Napoleon and his lady stopped to chat with a lady here, or a gentleman there. And when they came abreast of her party, Napoleon stopped.

Pippa could feel Maxwell suck in a breath as

his body tensed. His friend Cyril straightened and stood taller. Lady Carstairs visibly swelled with pride and shot a triumphant look at Pippa. Pippa was impressed, if puzzled. Her grandmother had spent days chirping about her old friends and never mentioned that one of them was Napoleon Bonaparte himself?

But the first Consul's dark eyes were fastened on Pippa. So were his lady's. Pippa was shocked to see that his eyes were on a higher level than her own. He was taller than she was!

"Charming," he said in French. "You see?" he asked his lady. "English by the look of her, and yet she wears our symbol."

"But of course," his wife said smiling, and tapping her lips with her red rose. "Who would not?"

"Well done," Napoleon told Pippa. "And your name, little one?"

Pippa curtsied low in spite of her neckline. But she remembered it as she did. She wondered if that was the reason he was staring at her and shot up quickly, pink faced. "Phillipa Carstairs . . ." She paused. Was he a "my lord" or "Sir" or . . . ". . . Your Excellency," she finally said.

"Carstairs? Oh yes, I recall. Clever chit," he said in English. "Your grandfather taught you well. Enjoy your stay with us, mademoiselle."

Then, actually inclining his head in a semblance of a bow, he left Pippa and walked down the line again.

Pippa turned speechlessly to Maxwell. He was looking at her strangely, she thought. She felt a little embarrassed, and yet at the same time immensely flattered and impressed. She tried to regain her composure, swallowed hard, and spoke. "Symbol? What symbol?" she asked him.

"You didn't know?" he asked as answer.

"Well, I wouldn't ask if I did," she said, her spirit rising.

"Those flowers on the front of your gown," he said.

She looked down. "Oh. They're pretty, what of it?"

"They're purple. They're violets. They're his symbol. You didn't know?"

"The royal bee is his symbol," she said, thinking fast.

"And the violet. You have them in your hair too. The man likes symbols." He smiled, at last. "He likes white bosoms too. But his Josephine was with him. My turn for a question. I assume he knew who you were because his spies know everyone who comes into his presence is. But why do you think he mentioned your grandfather?"

"I told you," she said. "It must be because my grandfather has scholarly renown. He knows everything."

"And every one," her grandmother said testily. "So why didn't he stop to talk with me?"

"Because," Maxwell explained, "his admiration for you must know no bounds. There's only so much he can hide from his lady."

For the first time in a long time, Pippa got a glance of the grandmother she knew as that lady stared at Lord Montrose with a wry expression on her face. As her grandmother herself used to say, his explanation smelled so high that it could have been put in a basket and sold at Billingsgate.

"Fiddle," Lady Carstairs said. "Phillipa's got a heavenly bosom. And the man may be careful in his wife's presence but he's still a man. Ah well. He'd have done more than stare at me in my day."

"Without a doubt," Maxwell said as Pippa said, "There's no doubt of it!"

Lady Carstairs looked mollified. Pippa and Maxwell's eyes met and they smiled. But Cyril suddenly started coughing and couldn't say a thing.

Chapter 16

"But I didn't want to leave yet," Lady Carstairs complained. "The shun hasn't rosen . . . risen. No one leaves a ball until the shun, sun, rises."

"In London," Maxwell said gently. "But here in Paris things are different. The First Consul has left, meaning the ball is over."

Pippa thought that wasn't true, but she was glad they'd finally convinced her grandmother to leave the ball and get into a coach. Her grandmother was slowing down, at least she was no longer braying, but only slurring her words. Now they were riding back to their hotel, she and Maxwell flanking her to be sure she didn't try to stand while the coach was moving, or slide off the seat if the coach stopped short. Pippa's maid and her grandmother's sat on the seat opposite them, both looking amazed at seeing a grand lady like Lady Carstairs so drunken.

"And just think," Maxwell told Lady Carstairs, "you'll have had a good rest and will be energetic and bright tomorrow so that you can visit your old friends and tell them about your experiences tonight."

Lady Carstairs bobbed up, sitting like a little girl agog with anticipation. "Too true!" she crowed. "Be sure I'll tell 'em how the Firs' Consul himself stopped to chat with me."

Pippa saw her maid turn her head to stare at her. Pippa shook her head and said nothing. Her grandmother had remade the incident. But what did it matter? It made her happy.

"They've lived here for years and years, and years, don'cha know, and never so much as clapped an eye on 'im," Lady Carstairs gloated. "But he paused, he actually stopped to compliment me. One don' have to be one of his supporters," she told Maxwell with oversized care, "but I believe even so, it was a great honor. And he did it with his Josephine at his side. A great honor," she repeated with contentment. She sat back and closed her eyes.

Pippa spoke quietly. "I think she'll nod off," she whispered to Maxwell.

"I hope so," he said. "Even a wine cask has a bottom. I didn't know she could hold so much."

"Neither did she," Pippa said with a giggle.

They rode on to the hotel in a comfortable silence broken only by the soft buzz of Lady Carstairs's snores.

Once they arrived, they escorted a staggering Lady Carstairs up the stair. It took all three of them: Maxwell steering her and supporting her weight, Pippa murmuring to her about how nice a little nap would be, and the maids following, prepared to catch the lady if she stumbled. They stopped at last in front of Lady Carstairs's room. There, Maxwell handed her over to her maid.

"I think it will take two of you to get her to bed," he told the maidservants.

"And then you're free," Pippa told her maid, Anne. "We did leave the ball too early; it's not very late. And I'm not half ready for sleep myself. I'm going downstairs for a while. Don't wait up for me."

"May I keep you company?" Maxwell asked as they left Lady Carstairs to the care of the two maidservants.

"Certainly," she said. "Let's go to the blue salon."

"You're not worried about the scandal of being alone with me?" he asked.

"I won't be," she said. "That's a salon for the guests and it's always occupied. Anyhow," she said softly, "after Grandmamma bawling 'God Save The Queen' and then dancing with such abandon, I don't worry about scandal anymore. And too," she said, taking his arm as they walked back down the hall to the stair, "this is France, after all."

"And what's said and done here is echoed in London in the time it takes for another packet to sail to England," he cautioned her.

"You? Worried about gossip?" she asked, pausing in the middle of the stair.

"About your reputation," he said.

She shrugged. "I have none anymore."

"Because that idiot jilted you? No, that only makes you more interesting. But sitting alone with me in a hotel? That's not done. Let's see if anyone's in there."

They descended the stair and walked to the blue salon. "You were right," he said, looking in. "There are living souls here," he said, "but just barely."

Pippa stifled her laughter. There was a pair of ancient men playing chess, and three elderly women sitting close together by a flickering fire in the hearth. The hotel had many elderly guests, and evidently the others were already sleeping. But it was a cool, beautiful spring evening in Paris and more guests than Pippa obviously didn't want to sleep all through it.

She and Maxwell sat on a long, ornate sofa to the side of the room.

"At last," he said as he seated himself, "we are almost alone."

She laughed. "I had such a good time in spite of my worries. Thank you."

"For what?" he asked, surprised.

"For being our escort. We had the invitation but no lady goes to a grand ball without a male escort. That wasn't what had been asked of you."

"It was my pleasure, absolutely," he said.

"And I met the Grand Consul of France," she said. "Really met him! I was so shocked that he noticed me."

"Not I," said Maxwell with a smile. "He's many things, but not blind."

"And he's not that small," she said with wonder. "Or at least not as small as I imagined."

"Our journalists and caricaturists like to belittle him, literally," Maxwell said. "It's another weapon against him. The man is said to be in love with himself in word and deed. Portraying him as a dwarf must irritate him."

"But he's not our enemy anymore."

"He's not our enemy at the moment," Maxwell corrected her. "But I'm surprised too. You don't mind being left out of your grandmother's story?"

She shrugged. "What difference does it make, except that it makes her happy? I haven't got a clutch of friends to brag to, the way she does. At least I'll always know that the First Consul of France himself complimented me. Whatever his politics, that was immensely flattering, something to be remembered, and that's enough for me."

"And soon, if rumor is to be believed," Maxwell said slowly, "she may brag that she was singled out by the Emperor of France."

Pippa frowned. "Is that a jest?"

"No, sorry, no," he said. "I wish it were. Peace is lovely. But we fear it will be brief. A First Consul could be a democratic sort of fellow, willing to share with others. But an emperor is never happy with only one country to rule."

"But he was for 'liberty, equality, and fraternity,'" she said. "He promised it. Grandfather thought that was noble."

"A noble speech," Maxwell said, "does not make a noble ruler. But never mind the little—ah, not so little—colonel now. You enjoyed the rest of the ball?"

"Yes," she said, stretching her arms above her head. "I love to dance and was sorry I couldn't, and yet now I enjoy the fact that it's over and I'm free."

"I shall have to take you for another night of dancing," he said.

She gave Maxwell a small sad smile. "That's not necessary. I have no complaints. I suppose that's why I'm feeling strange tonight, because I'm not worrying about anything. The ball is over and I didn't disgrace myself. I begin to see that my grandmother has nothing wrong with her reason. I think she was just kept home and alone too long, away from the Society that makes her so happy. And most of all," she added, "I'm happy because I can give up the search for Noel now. That's done. So I have only to convince Grandmamma to go home, and my problems and my adventure is over."

Maxwell said nothing.

She gazed at him. He still looked ready to take a princess to a ball. His black jacket, knee-length breeches, and black stockings were well fitted and wrinkle free. He scarcely looked as though he'd been in a crowded, overheated ballroom tonight. A person would never guess how often he'd danced, and how well he did it. His high neckcloth was perhaps a bit wilted, but if anything, she thought, it made him look even more masculine.

How handsome he is, she mused. And how

very well he knows it. Look your fill, my girl, she told herself, you'll not meet the likes of him again soon.

"Your adventure is far from over," he mused, cutting into Pippa's thoughts. "Your grandmother won't be easy to persuade. And I can't blame her for it. She's not only accepted dozens of invitations to all sorts of parties for the next few weeks, or so she told me, but I guarantee there'll be dozens more delivered tomorrow, for her and for you. They all saw Bonaparte salute you. Prepare for fame, Phillipa."

" 'Pippa,' " she said absently, and then looked at him wide-eyed. "Fame? Lud! I don't want that!"

"It's what you'll have until you're home," he said. "And even there, if you wish to make a splash in the ton, you have only to pass a season in London now. Everyone will want to meet you. You might even find a gentleman you can care for."

She might have winced but the expression was gone in a moment. She waved a hand. "Oh lovely, just the life for me: a husband who is a figure of fashion and wants a 'famous' bride. No, thank you. I want to go home to the countryside and live with my grandparents. They have no one but me. I won't drag my grandmother through all the fuss and frivolity again either. She may be enjoying herself, but I don't know how good it is for her. I do know this sort of life isn't good for me."

"You prefer a little country cottage with no one to talk to but geese?" he asked.

She laughed. "The Old Place isn't a cottage, or little. And I think all the geese are in London. I like listening to running brooks in the daylight, not the cursing of coachmen and horsemen when the traffic gets tangled. At night, I like to hear an owl, or leaves on a tree blowing in the breeze, and not the howls of roistering young bucks out on the town. And I like horses in the meadows, not clogging the streets, and dogs running at my heels, not cringing at them, as the poor starvelings do here as in London. What about you? A London ball or a harvest dance?"

He thought a moment. "Both," he said. "Each in their season." He straightened and looked around the room. "Ah, the chess masters have gone to bed and the three fates who were sitting by the fireplace have toddled off too. We are alone. And here we are, both free as birds. I'm not sleepy either. It's still Paris too. And so, what shall we do?"

"What do Parisians do?" she asked.

His smile was wide and wicked.

She blinked at what she saw in his eyes. He couldn't mean that. There was only so much one could do in a respectable hotel's salon, even in Paris.

She tried to think of a light answer to turn the conversation. Although she'd loved to be in his arms, his answer was too ambiguous. She wasn't sure she was ready.

"But first," he said, sensing her withdrawal, "let's do as the Parisians do in other ways. I'll get you some wine, and we'll share it by the fireside. You approve?"

She nodded, relieved and yet apprehensive. When he returned with a bottle and two glasses, she was already sitting in a settee by the hearth.

He settled down beside her, poured a glass of rich, red wine, and handed it to her. He poured another for himself, placed the bottle on the floor beside him, and raised his glass to her.

"Confusion to our enemies," he said.

She laughed. "And luck to our friends."

They drank and then looked at each other. She noted he kept gazing at her neckline, and wished she'd taken a shawl with her, though his glances made her warmer, not chilly.

And he watched her face reflecting her emotions, saw her hesitation, and wondered just what it was that she wanted from him.

"So," she said, settling back. "I know I've asked

before, but I must again. How can you know so much about France, and not be a spy?"

"I can't," he said simply, "but I'm not a very active one at the moment."

She tensed. "For England?" she asked.

He laughed. "No, for Iceland. Of course, for England."

"It's a dangerous occupation," she said. She took another sip of wine, and peered at him over the top of her glass. "Doesn't your family worry?" she asked. Her lips opened in surprise at what she'd said. "There it is again!" she cried. "I don't know enough about your family. I'm not even positive you're not a married man, except that a married man wouldn't have . . ." She left the rest unsaid, and felt her face growing warm.

"A married man might," he said lightly. "But I'm not married. And," he added too casually, "I'm not aiming to be, at least, not for some time to come."

She flinched. Her eyes turned steely blue as she looked at him. "I am not angling for your hand," she said through her teeth. "I thought you understood that."

She set her glass down on the floor and stood up, ready to stamp out of the room.

He rose as quickly, and seized her wrist to hold her back. "I didn't mean that."

"Did you not?" she asked, raising one eyebrow.

He foundered and then blurted, "Then why the devil are you alone and here with me now? And what about the way you fit into my arms before? You're an unmarried lady, I'm an unmarried gentleman, the situation is ripe for a proposal. Any man might expect an enraged relative to come crashing in on our tryst, demanding I do the right thing."

"My relative is not enraged," Pippa said fiercely. "You know very well that she's sleeping. And I didn't think this was a tryst," she lied with less vigor.

He didn't smile. "I don't want to mislead you," he said seriously. "I want you, Pippa. Very much. But I can't claim I'm in love. And," he added, as she looked away, "neither can you. Or can you?"

She knew she'd rather eat raw snake than admit to what she was beginning to feel for him. She couldn't blame him for thinking that since she'd given up on Noel she was seeking a new fiancé, any fiancé.

She tried to be flippant, to be worldly, to reassure him. "I can't claim that either," she said. "I'm here now because I wanted to share the evening. Don't you like to discuss your exploits with a friend? And I find myself fitting into your arms far too often because . . . because you are very alluring."

Now he smiled.

She lifted her chin. "But I'm not after you, my lord. Not for a husband. I'm single, but no ingénue. I know I'm almost old enough to be a chaperone. My grandmother proposed a Season in London for me when we return, but the patronesses at Almack's would laugh if I were presented wearing a pure white gown, as ingénues have to do."

He took in a breath. His eyes grew darker, and he narrowed them as he gazed steadily at her. She turned to leave but he held her wrist, and suddenly pulled her into his arms and answered her with a kiss.

It was what she'd wanted all night long. She refused to admit it, but only clung to him, opened her lips and gladly answered his kiss with all her heart. There was an urgency in their embrace, as though the both had yearned much too long for it. Then he took a breath and looked down at her with a tight smile. He started to speak but instead bent his head, gathered her closer, and kissed her again. She knew by the evidence of his need pressing against her that it wouldn't be enough for him—or for her.

"Oh, this gown," he finally murmured into her ear after trailing kisses along her neck. "And its ridiculous neckline. Ah," he breathed as he eased the fragile material down and cupped one of her breasts in his hand. "Tempting me all night."

He kissed her breast and then covered it, the cresting peak rising in the palm of his hand. He put his lips on the other breast, as with her eyes shut to lock out the world, she clung to him. His other hand slowly, softly stroked up her leg to her thigh. She felt the new growth of his night beard rub against her tender skin as he saluted each breast with his lips again, and reveled in the feeling of it because it proved he was real and human and desired her.

He was the one who suddenly pulled back. He quickly drew her neckline back up again.

"Damnation!" he said, running a hand through his hair. "We can't go on like this, stealing kisses and fumbled embraces like a pair of truant adolescents. Come with me now, Pippa. We can't keep pushing toward the edge without falling in. But not here. I want you naked against my own skin. I want privacy in which to explore you. Come to bed with me, my dear Pippa. Let me love you properly."

She was still dazed by the sudden interruption of the most wonderfully sensual pleasure she'd ever felt. She couldn't think of what to reply.

"I can't go to your room," he said in frustration. "But it's nighttime, and all of Paris is on the move and will be until morning. Come to my rooms with me. It's not far and is a decent place," he added quickly when he saw her eyes widen. "There's an experienced concierge whose discretion is absolute. No one will know, except for we two, and I promise neither of us will ever forget."

She stared at him, one hand on her heart.

"I can have you back here before dawn. Blast!" he said. "This is awkward. But how am I to make love to you as we both deserve when at any moment one of the old parties that were just here may totter back looking for their spectacles?"

"To your room with you? Now?" she asked in a faltering voice, playing for time because she honestly didn't know what her answer would be, although she knew very well what it should be.

Chapter 17

"I will admit that it might seem awkward to you," Maxwell said, as Pippa sat wide-eyed after his proposition. "An assignation isn't as exhilarating as an impetuous moment. I realize that you may be loath to just fly off with me now to rush to my bed. It's gauche, to say the least. But at least we can take a stroll in the soft spring night, can't we?"

Pippa hesitated. That sounded lovely. But as she gazed at his face she realized that in the mood she was in, walking close to him in the darkness on this soft spring evening might mean she wouldn't be home until dawn.

"I see," she said slowly. "Could it be that an eventual stroll to your rooms is what you're thinking?"

He smiled. "Clever Pippa. What would be the harm in that?"

She shook her head. "You really ought to write a book for rakes: How to turn an awkward moment into an impromptu moment of passion."

His expression changed. He stood, suddenly rigid, and looked down at her. "Do you think I'm a rake, Pippa?"

She thought about it. "Are you?"

"I've never thought so," he said, his gaze direct, his eyes dark and serious. "I've had affairs of the heart and some were, I admit, of the moment, but I've never preyed on the innocent or ignorant or lied about my expectations. I think that frees me from the taint of 'rake' don't you?"

"I suppose it does," she said. "We don't get many rakes in the countryside, to tell the truth, so I spoke without thinking. I apologize. I didn't know you'd think it an insult."

"Then for your future reference," he said, "a rake is a fellow who lies and cheats in order to take what he wants from women, body and soul, without caring about them. And while any man may behave badly now and then, a rake does it repeatedly, and revels in his prowess. Although my suggestion of a stroll did have ulterior motives, I've never misled you, Pippa, have I? And every advance I've made has been acceptable to you, hasn't it? You're a grown woman, I trust in your ability to make your own decisions. I just wanted to make it easier for you."

"A very rakish thing to say," she said.

He laughed, and sat down again.

But she was thinking, and when she spoke, her tone was serious. "So I see that you didn't believe me," she said. "You think I made love to Noel?"

He shrugged. "Perhaps not Noel, but dearling, be reasonable. You kiss too well to be a stranger at it. And you yourself said you're not an ingénue. I wouldn't want you if you were. You're a fiercely independent lady in spite of your claim to be in the thrall of your grandparents. I know few females who would hare off around the world in pursuit of a vanished suitor, for whatever reason. And you obviously enjoy my company as much as I do yours. So where's the harm?"

She sighed. He was right. But she wasn't ready. To make love to him would be to finally change her way of life. He'd said he wasn't interested in marriage. He'd never said he loved her. But he enthralled her. She'd be going home within the month and doubted she'd meet any eligible gentlemen, enthralling or not, again.

She'd been thrilled with Noel's courtship, although it had lacked passion, because it had been so new to her. Few of the gentlemen who came to visit her grandfather were young or unwed, and if they were their passion for research far outweighed their interest in any mere female. The older ones might show lechery by a pinch or a wink. But none of it had ever been serious. No one, not even Noel, had ever engaged her mind and her senses as Maxwell had.

She knew now that her grandmother would certainly need her company for many years to come, so she'd probably not have a chance at true freedom until she herself was old. And although she wasn't an ingénue, she wasn't really old, not yet. Some nights she ached with longing. It was time to find out exactly what she was longing for. She wanted to experience lovemaking . . . No, she told herself, she yearned to actually make love with this man, only him, even if only once, or with great good luck, twice. And as for the repercussions if it were found out? She had no reputation to lose, after all. It was about time she did something to deserve it.

She was about to say yes and go to her room to fetch a shawl. He must have seen it in her eyes, and he smiled. She returned his smile, but then saw his gaze shift to the doorway. She turned her head.

Her maid stood there, looking terrified.

"What is it, Annie?" Pippa asked at once.

"It's her ladyship," Annie said, curtseying,

glancing from her mistress to Maxwell. "She woke up and cast up her accounts, and now she's moaning and groaning something awful. Her maid says as to how it's only that she drunk too much. But maybe you should get a physician for her?"

"At once," Maxwell said, striding toward the door. "If the concierge doesn't have one close by, I'll find another." He looked back at Pippa. "I'm sure we can help her," he said. "And don't fret. I'll return soon."

"Too much to drink, too much excitement, my lady," the physician told Lady Carstairs in his native French an hour later. "I've powders to make your head feel better and a dose to help your poor entrails. But you must stay in bed for a few days. And when you rise you must be careful of what you eat and drink. You may feel young as a spring lamb. Paris does that to everyone," he added with a touch of pride. "But, my lady, you are not; although you are certainly handsome you are no longer a girl. You must take care of yourself as befits a woman of your years."

Lady Carstairs spoke French, of course. Any educated English lady did. But she pretended she didn't. She looked away and turned her nose up.

Maxwell escorted the physician to the door, as the fellow left, shaking his head at her folly.

"I don't want to stay in bed," she said to Pippa as soon as they'd gone. But it was a weak protest. She was wan and puffy-eyed, her usually gloriously fluffy hair turned to dampened stringy coils. Pippa realized, with a pang, how sparse her grandmother's hair really was under her usual cloud of curls. But the lady didn't seem to care. She was obviously not well.

"We'll see," said Pippa. "He said you should be better soon. So it's up to you now, Grandmamma. Rest, take your medicine, and drink soup instead of sherry, and you'll be right as rain in no time."

"But I'll miss the Comte Bouchard's soiree tomorrow night," the lady wailed. "And you know I wanted to go to my old friends Lord and Lady Ashworth's musicale the next night."

"They'll understand and everyone will think it's very clever of you to dole out your presence," Pippa said, patting her hand. "You're enormously popular now. Your brief absence from the scene will only make you more in demand."

The lady looked up at that. She nodded. "Clever, Pippa. You've your grandfather's wits. All right. But leave now. I think I will sleep. Those powders are better than three bottles of the finest red."

Maxwell was standing in the hallway as Pippa left her grandmother's room.

"It's as well I didn't go for that stroll," Pippa told him in a soft voice. "I'd never forgive myself if I were gone when she needed me."

"I think she'll always need you in future," he said soberly. "But not always in the same way. Perhaps when she's healthy and happy and occupied at some party with her friends, you'll have a chance at your own life."

He drew her into the shadows by the stair and took her in his arms. "Time isn't of the essence for her, or you and I," he whispered as he dropped a light kiss on her forehead. "Paris is full of lovely evenings."

But after Pippa said goodnight to him she couldn't stop thinking about how many lovely available females there were for him on such evenings.

Her grandmother couldn't stop thinking of how many parties she'd been invited to attend. They both had the time to dwell on it because it rained for the next two days and nights. They were showers that drew a soft gray veil over the springtime streets, pretty to see, but not to stroll in. And certainly not fit for a recently recovered invalid to travel through.

It was difficult to know who was unhappier, fretful, and disappointed at being housebound, the lady or her granddaughter.

There were no visitors except for Maxwell, Lord Montrose. Lady Carstairs was new to the city, and new to her old friends as well. And the older they were the less they wished to encounter a contagion, or so she claimed. She was said to be ill, so she was left alone. But Maxwell arrived each day and brought flowers and news of the world to them. Then, with a shrug and a smile, he said good-bye to Pippa and her grandmother, leaving them to another day of aimlessly watching the sky.

And then the sun came out again.

The concierge brought more cards and letters to both Lady Carstairs and her granddaughter. Although she was well now, Lady Carstairs enjoyed lying abed in the morning. The shutters were open, sunlight streamed in, and finally, a floral scent wafted through the room on soft warm breezes. Pippa, in her dressing gown, sat on a chair at Lady Carstairs's bedside. Her grandmother read some of the invitations aloud. She cackled happily over them, and made a special fuss over one inviting her to a party this very afternoon, given by one of her oldest friends.

Pippa read her invitations with little interest

until she saw one card. Her hand shook when she picked it up and read it.

Miss Carstairs,

The sun is out, the air is mild, and Paris smells like a flower shop. Please do me the honor of joining me on a picnic in the park today. I will come for you at one this afternoon, and hope you will come away with me.

Maxwell

Pippa wanted to laugh aloud. She'd go with him if it was still raining and she had to take a rowboat.

"Well, may you laugh, this is excellent," her grandmother said, sitting up. "We've been invited to a impromptu garden party at the castle of my old friend Sir Malden and his wife. It's a real castle, I hear. They got it for a song years ago when the owners had to flee France, or had their heads removed. It doesn't matter. I hear it's a grand place. They say they heard I was feeling better, and they add that they hope I will attend because if I do, I will be the guest of honor. It's not because of friendship, I'll wager. No doubt they'll all want to hear about my adventure with Napoleon himself."

But Pippa didn't want to hear it again, and not just because it was a lie. "Grandmamma," she said, "that's lovely for you. But Lord Montrose has invited me to a picnic in the park with him this afternoon. I should love to go and get some fresh air."

"Is that all you want to get?" the lady snapped as she rang for her maid to help her out of her high bed.

"It will all be perfectly proper," Pippa said, trying to keep the pleading out of her voice. "My Annie will be with me. Come, Grandmamma, since when have you been such a high stickler for propriety? And even if you were, surely a lady and a gentleman at a picnic in the sunshine won't be noted much by any one, especially here in Paris. Nor should it be."

Her grandmother looked doubtful. Pippa didn't know if the lady believed her own fiction now or not. But it was worth trying to test it. She thought a moment and added, "As for your garden party, you don't need me. Rather the reverse, I should think. If you go by yourself you're the only one who can tell them about that glorious night. If I were there and you were otherwise occupied, some eager guests might ask me about the ball and the incident with Napoleon instead."

If her grandmother really realized she'd been twisting the truth to make herself the heroine of the tale, it might do the trick. Pippa fell still and held her breath.

Her grandmother's cheeks turned pink. "Oh, very well," she grumbled, avoiding Pippa's eyes. "You are the one who will be missing the fun. But go, if you must. I will see you at dinner—unless I am begged to stay, or invited elsewhere. I intend to conquer Paris." She laughed.

Pippa couldn't stop smiling as she left the room. Then she raced to her own and hurried to wash and dress. She felt freer than she had in days, and not just because it wasn't raining. She would spend the afternoon with Maxwell. And she didn't have to worry about her rash promise to bed with him, not yet. It was a bright spring day. She'd let the evening take care of itself when it came.

She knew exactly what to wear. She put on a gown to match the day: It had a modest neckline and long sleeves, and was yellow with pink roses at the high waist and hem. Her slippers were each adorned with an embroidered rose. A patterned Madras shawl in rose colors added bright accents when she flung it over her shoulders. A new light straw chapeau would protect her nose from the sunlight. Even so, she wished she were home so she could wear her hair simply tied back at the nape of her neck, so that if it got too warm, she could shake it free.

But this was Paris, and so she let Annie coil it and curl it, and then pin it high on her head so that she looked more like a sophisticated lady than a milkmaid.

She was ready. So was her grandmother. They waited in the hotel's salon and eyed each other.

"You'll do," her grandmother said with a note of satisfaction.

"And you'll do more; you'll devastate them," Pippa said in truth. Her grandmother looked very well, if a trifle too spectacular for daylight. She wore a low-cut scarlet gown with a dazzling necklace of rubies and diamonds, and her earlobes, fingers, and wrists were heavy with sparkling red-and-gold jewelry. She herself actually seemed to glow.

When her coach was announced, Lady Carstairs rose from her chair and went to the door. "Enjoy yourself," she told Pippa. "I know I surely shall."

But when she had left, Pippa began to wonder about her appointment as she waited for Maxwell to come collect her.

She'd never gone out with a gentleman alone, in London or in Paris. She paced the hotel's front salon. She supposed he'd supply their luncheon, since it was his invitation. But what if he simply drove her to his hotel?

She realized how foolish a thought that was. Annie sat prim and expectant, waiting for the excursion. He said he wasn't a rake but even a rake wouldn't try to shab off a lady's maid who was acting as chaperone. Pippa looked around the blue salon, remembering what she and Maxwell had done in there only a few night's past. She didn't know what she'd do this evening, and suddenly she didn't care. They would have a day together, at last.

A young man appeared in the doorway to the salon. He bowed to them. He was fair and blue-eyed and smiling, and even though he was dressed in servant's livery, he looked dashing. "Lord Montrose is without," he announced in stately tones. Then with a charming grin he added, "And he says as how to tell you he don't want to walk the horses so if you'd move it quick, he'd be appreciating it."

Pippa and her maid bounced up and followed the young man out the door.

And there at the curb, in the sunlight, was Maxwell. He sat on the driver's bench of a handsome two-seat carriage, reins held easily in his hands. A team of roan horses waited for his signal to move. Maxwell wore tight buff unmentionables, high black boots, a brown jacket, his linen was white, and a beaver hat was set jauntily on his dark head. He saw Pippa and his smile was sudden and bright. He extended a gloved hand to her to help her up to his high seat.

Pippa forgot her doubts and fears. She went to the carriage and immediately took his hand. After all, it was the only thing she wanted. She clambered up and settled next to him.

The young fellow in livery helped a dazed and delighted, pink-cheeked Annie climb up to sit next to him on the backseat.

"All set?" Maxwell asked.

Pippa nodded.

"Cozy as clams," the young servant in back answered.

Maxwell shook the reins.

"Ready for adventure?" he asked Pippa.

She nodded, and answered. "Never more so," she said.

"Then adventure you shall have," he said, and laughed as the carriage rolled off down the street.

"And luncheon," she said. "Don't forget that, please."

They were both laughing as they drove away.

Chapter 18

"This," Pippa said in wonder as Maxwell helped her down from the high driver's seat, "is amazing."

Once on the ground, she shook out her skirt and looked around. There was new, fresh greenery as far as she could see. Stately trees flanked long neatly cropped lawns bordered by banks of shrubbery in bloom. Meandering pebbled walkways wandered off through the trees.

"This is still Paris?" Pippa asked.

"For a certainty," Maxwell replied.

Pippa stared. This lovely green manicured landscape was within the city of Paris? And yet there was no one else in sight, anywhere.

The other parks they'd driven through or passed: the Bois de Boulogne and the gardens at the Tuileries, had been so filled with people enjoying the mild spring day it had been difficult to see the grass. She'd seen whole families, servants and children, elderly people, working men and women strolling along or sitting on benches or coverlets they had tossed on the grass. There were noble-looking horsemen and fine carriages on the roads through the parks. And everywhere there were pairs of lovers—many pairs of lovers. They made Pippa stare. Lovers in England held hands in public, sometimes. They did far more here.

There were picnics on the grass and picnics with tables and chairs. And since it had been a long time since her meager breakfast of a croissant and dark coffee, Pippa couldn't help her stomach grumbling when she saw the long golden loaves of bread and pots of butter, wheels of cheese, and strings of cured meats being laid out for various luncheons.

But "Too crowded," Maxwell had said at one park. "Congested as a market day," he had commented at another. "There's scarcely room to sit," he'd complained as he drove on. "But never fear, I have a better destination in mind."

They had ridden through the crowded streets of Paris, and then they took a turn to a smaller road with rows of pleasant houses at its sides. They turned again, and rode down a narrow road a long way until they had to stop because of a pair of high iron gates that blocked their way. There was no one about, but there was a quaint cottage by itself at the side of the road.

Pippa was about to make a wry comment until she saw how patiently Maxwell was waiting. She heard nothing but birdsong and saw nothing stirring, until an old woman in an apron stepped out of the cottage, came to the carriage, and bowed to Maxwell. He handed the reins to the curly-haired boy in livery and jumped lightly down from the driver's seat. He spoke to the woman in low tones Pippa couldn't quite make out, but she saw him reach into his jacket and hand the woman something. She bowed again.

Then he came back to the driver's seat, and took up the reins. He waited for the woman to produce a key from her apron pocket and unlock the gates. Then Maxwell waved to her and drove on.

Pippa looked her question at him.

"It's a deserted estate," he said. "There's a walloping big castle miles from here. Empty, except for a few rooms where the caretakers live. The owners left with the revolution, as my own mama did. Being dedicated to keeping a head on their shoulders, none chose to come back and live here.

But the absent owner keeps the place up. I've been here before and, you'll grant, that's a perfect place for our picnic."

"Why didn't the government confiscate it?" Pippa asked.

His smile was tight. "Because the old owner played both sides of the game. He had some political power. And the new owner pays taxes."

"Are you sure we're welcome here?" she asked.

"Never more certain of anything," he said with a laugh.

They drove for a bit, then Maxwell stopped the carriage. "Do you fancy this spot?" he asked Pippa.

"What is not to fancy?" she asked softly. "This is lovely."

They'd come to the edge of a long green lawn surrounded by trees and edged on one side by a burbling stream that banked a bluebell-carpeted forest.

"So I thought," he said, leapt down from his seat, and went around to help Pippa down.

By the time she alit, his servant had hauled two wicker baskets from the backseat. Her own maid carried the blanket taken from there. Before Pippa could wonder where to put it, they'd spread it near the stream and under the trees.

"There's bread, cheese, and wine," Maxwell said. "That's if you want to be a purist. But we've also got sliced meats and pâtes, aspics, and little cakes, or so I was told."

"Perfect," Pippa said, watching as the servants spread the feast on the blanket. But then she hesitated. "Where do we sit?"

"On the ground like true picnickers," Maxwell said. "Unless, of course, you want to do it in high British style, and then we'll have to drag some boulders over to sit on, because I didn't bring chairs."

"No, this is fine," she said, looking at the blanket with trepidation and wondering how she could sit down without exposing and embarrassing herself. "But I haven't done this since I was a girl."

He smiled, and held out his hand. She took it, and carefully lowered herself to the ground. Once here, she arranged her skirts and grinned up at him. "Done!" she said.

He smiled and lowered himself to sit beside her. "Now," he said, "we shall dine. Samson," he told his servant, "I think we can manage on our own from here. Do you want to go for a stroll in the wood to find your own picnic spot? There's a feast packed for you too."

Pippa looked up to see his servant exchange a

longing glance with hers. "You can go as well, if you wish," she told the girl.

Annie blushed, curtseyed, and then took the young man's proffered arm. "I'll be within calling distance if you need me," she assured Pippa. "Won't I?" she asked Samson.

"Aye," he said, patting her hand. He picked up the other basket and strolled off with her down a path though the wood.

"Will she be?" Pippa whispered to Maxwell.

"Of course," he said. "Samson gave his word."

When Annie and Samson were out of sight, Pippa felt a moment of panic. She was utterly alone with Maxwell now. But it was broad daylight. She relaxed.

They drank rich red local wine, and the music they dined to was the sound of the singing waters as they tumbled along the rocks in the stream bed, accompanied by the bright songs of the birds in the trees.

"I can't eat another thing," Pippa said at last. "That was delicious."

"Because it was flavored by fresh air," Maxwell said. "Now," he said, "in many countries the right thing to do is to nap for an hour or so. But you don't have to if you don't want to. You can just shut your eyes and rest awhile, if you wish." He smiled at her, lay back on the blanket, folded his arms on his chest, and closed his eyes.

She looked down at him. His expression was serene. It was warm here in the spring sunshine. The air was fragrant. She was full of good food and red wine. So she eased herself down and lay beside him, balanced on one elbow, her head held up on her hand. She looked down at him. His skin was clear; his expression serene; his eyelashes were so long. She sighed and finally lay down and closed her own eyes.

But she didn't doze. She listened to the birdsong and the tumbling water of the stream, and wondered what she was doing here, with him. Or rather, what he was doing here with her, because she didn't trust this odd moment of peace for a moment.

And then she heard him move, and felt the light touch of his breath on her hair. Her eyes opened to see his looking down into hers.

"Don't feel like sleeping?" he asked softly. "We can do other things."

"We're in broad daylight," she whispered.

"With no one around," he assured her. "No one comes here. Martin won't be back for another hour. I told him to take his time. We have more privacy than we would at an inn or hotel. Only the birds will know, and they certainly don't care." He dropped a light kiss on her mouth. "And so?"

And so, she thought suddenly, why not? If they didn't make love now when would she have the chance again? Certainly he had every right to expect her to, because surely, in the back of her mind, she'd known what he was up to since they'd arrived at this deserted estate. She could have stopped this long before this moment. But she hadn't because she wanted him and had promised herself this.

"And so," she whispered as she closed her eyes, "yes."

They kissed for a long time. She drank in his kisses, squirmed under his hands and was glad she'd shut her eyes when she felt him begin to pull up her gown. She helped him by raising herself; she encouraged him by holding his shoulders tightly, she spurred him on by sighing and shaking as he kissed each hidden part of her body as he slowly uncovered it.

His hands skimmed her legs, her abdomen, and her hips, setting silken fire wherever he touched. His mouth saluted her breasts, her stomach. He lingered over parts of her body she herself had been taught never to touch. She had never felt anything so wonderful, except perhaps, for the feeling of his sun-warmed broad back, which her hands slid over, the solidity of his chest, his taut abdomen, and then the shocking, thrillingly wondrous long warm velvet part of a man that she'd never touched before. She could not see any of it except through her fingertips, because she kept her eyes so tightly closed.

"But look," he said at last, laughter in his voice, "and see. You're beautiful."

She opened her eyes to see only that she was stark naked in the open sunlight. She slammed her eyes shut again. Brazen was one thing, but this was quite another. She was as excited as embarrassed. "But you're completely dressed," she said breathlessly. "I feel like a wanton."

"Good," he said as he dragged off his neckcloth and cast it off. Then he pulled his shirt over his head.

"You are beautiful too," she whispered, seeing his lithe, lean, unblemished torso, his chest lightly dusted with dark hair.

"Thank you," he said a little breathlessly as well, and reached down between them to fully unfasten his breeches and push the flaps apart. "And now," he said, raising himself on his elbows and looking down at her, "are you ready?"

"Oh yes," she said, flinging one arm over her eyes and lying back.

There was a moment of silence.

"Are you sure?" he asked, his voice unsteady.

She opened her eyes to stare into his. "Yes, what's wrong?"

He drew back with a frown. "You're ready to make love to me?"

Her brow furrowed. "Yes, I said yes. What do you want me to do?"

He shut his eyes. She saw the tendons in his arms straining. "Damnation, Pippa, are you serious?"

"Yes," she said in confusion. "What is it you want of me?"

"You don't know," he said, but not as a question.

She stared at him. "Of course, I do," she said. "You want to make love to me."

"And you say you're ready?"

"Of course," she said, now a bit unnerved.

He threw back his head. "The woman doesn't know," he told the air. He flung himself away from her, turned his back, and sat up. "You've never done this before," he said flatly.

"No," she said.

"And so why then did you say you couldn't wear white to Almack's, and that you weren't an ingénue?"

She saw her gown on the blanket beside her, snatched it, and clutched it to her breast. "B-because I'm four and twenty and I'd look foolish in a young girl's white gown, of course. And because at four and twenty, I'm certainly no ingénue. What's the matter?"

"You're a virgin," he said with loathing.

She nodded, though he couldn't see it. "But I want to make love to you," she insisted, though the desire to do that was fading by the minute.

"I don't despoil virgins," he said through tightly clenched teeth.

"I wouldn't be despoiled," she argued. "I want to do it."

"I told you," he said, pulling his shirt on over his head, "that I'm not a rake. I don't take advantage of women. You don't know what you want."

"Why do you say that?" she asked in a somewhat muffled voice as she struggled into her gown again.

"Because a woman who is ready to make love doesn't lie back like a corpse, tight and tidy. You didn't even part your legs."

"Oh," she said, ashamed of not knowing that she had to do that, before she realized it was a strange thing to be ashamed of. "But you could have asked me. I would have."

He did up his breeches, but didn't move away.

"I went too fast," he said bitterly, "faster than

I should have because I thought it was what you wanted. I didn't know you didn't know what to want. And what if I did oblige us, and my usually impeccable timing had failed me?" he asked angrily. "You moved me greatly, you know—or rather you don't know."

"What?" she said.

She saw his back heave as he sighed. "What if I couldn't stop in time, and you found yourself encumbered? Blast it, Pippa, an experienced female would know what to do before she made love, as well as what to do if a lover left her with bread in the oven."

"Oh!" she said. "That. But that never happens the first time."

"Good God," he said.

They sat in silence.

"I can't get up now," he said in a strained voice. "Not without embarrassing you. But listen, Pippa. I had no intention of seducing an innocent. I wish I did. But I don't want entanglements, and charming and delicious as you are, you would certainly be that."

She didn't know what to say. She didn't know where to go. The breeze seemed cooler now, and she shivered.

"Here," he said, "sit back to back with me, as

though we were a pair of bookends. That way, I can talk without the distraction of your face and form. I think we need to talk, because not only did I not want to seduce you, I didn't want to hurt your feelings. I just wanted us to share some moments of pleasure on a fine spring day. But we can't. It's not your fault, either."

After a moment's hesitation, she moved and positioned herself so that she sat back against his long lean back, and waited.

"My father," he said into the air, "has his faults, to be sure, but, in all, is a good man, but unfortunately not lucky with women. My mother was, I understand, a lovely little thing, an escapee from the Terror. She had dark hair and beautiful dark eyes, a charming trace of a French accent, and a clever mind. He adored her, and she, him. But she didn't live long after I was born. She died when I was an infant, and my poor distracted father took to drink.

"He wasn't a nice man when he did it, but was wise enough to know that wouldn't help him. He needed a mother for me but, mostly, a companion for himself. He was lucky enough to meet a lovely Scots woman before he became a complete sot. She was beautiful and in no way like my mother, being a tall and hearty sportswoman. She was a merry soul, with red hair and a flashing smile. I do remember her. She bore my father another son, and then when he was still in small clothes she was thrown over the head of her horse while riding, and died on the field.

"This time, Father was desolate. So he reasoned that it was bad luck to marry for love and believed he was king of bad luck. But he couldn't face living without a woman. So he married the Honorable Harriet Broome. She had neither charm nor beauty nor wit. But he was right. Father's luck did change. She bore him another child. The problem is that the child is a terror, and Father can't bear to be in the same room as his wife, nor can anyone else. She's a nag with the soul of a fish. And she flourishes like the green bay tree.

"And so," he said, "you can see why I choose to live independently. I never wanted to deceive you, Pippa," he said, turning his head toward her. "I thought you were an experienced woman. I just wanted us to share some light and aimless pleasure before we parted, and thought you felt the same way."

"Well, who said I didn't?" she asked, somewhat childishly, even to her own ears.

He laughed. "Oh, Miss Phillipa, you didn't know what you wanted, and I apologize for that. But you are a lady, and I am a gentleman, and we may both regret it, but there it is. What we must do now is to wait for Martin and your maid, pack up, and take you home. And then send you and your grandmother all the way home."

"What you must do," a deep voice said, "is to see if there's anything left in that basket for me."

Maxwell sprang up, fists clenched. A tall, lean, auburn-haired gentleman stood smiling at him. "I'm glad you're disarmed," the gentleman said. "Literally. I mean, with your pistol out of reach. I wouldn't want to be perforated for my jest."

"By all that's unholy," Maxwell cried, "Duncan! What are you doing here?"

The man limped toward him, and the two embraced, clapping each other on the back.

"I've been following you," the man he'd called Duncan said as he stepped back. "Trying to keep you out of trouble. I wasn't very successful, was I? Good afternoon, Miss Carstairs," he added.

She'd never seen the man before, but he knew her, and lord knew what more. How long had he been watching? Pippa ducked her head, feeling her face flaming.

"Oh. Miss Phillipa Carstairs," Maxwell said, "may I present my brother, Duncan, Lord Sutton." He turned to his brother again. "I saw you, but never recognized you," Maxwell marveled. "That limp deceived me. It's real, is it? What happened?"

"The war," Duncan said with a shrug. "Do you have any bread or cheese left? I'm starved."

"First, why the devil are you here?" Maxwell asked, his hands on his hips.

"I am my brother's keeper," Duncan answered piously and then grinned. "Father's orders, Lord Talwin and the war office's permission. The cheese, please? And Miss Carstairs," he added, as he sat down next to the picnic basket, "don't worry. I saw nothing, there was nothing to see."

Pippa couldn't color up any more than she already had. She nodded. He was lying, but she was grateful for it. And now all she wanted was to just go home, all the way home.

Chapter 19

"Bad form," Duncan said.

He seated himself in a chair before the hearth in his brother's rooms and grunted as he used both hands to raise his leg and rest it on a padded bench before him.

"Is that leg hurting?" Maxwell asked. "Why don't you use a walking stick?"

"You're avoiding my comment," Duncan said, "but as a matter of fact, a glass of something warming might help it a lot. What I was saying before you so rudely interrupted was that it's bad form to seduce a female and then leave her before the job is done. You and I both know it's no pleasure to be abandoned, unfulfilled. The Carstairs woman seemed too well bred for that sort of thing anyway. You shock me, brother."

"Because I tried to seduce her, or because I didn't do it?" Maxwell asked as he went to a nearby table, picked up a bottle, and poured a glass of cognac.

"Both," Duncan said, taking the glass from his brother. He drank, and shuddered. "Not Scot's made. But it will have to do."

"I tried to seduce her because I thought she was up to snuff," Maxwell said, sitting down opposite his brother, head down, hands clenched and hanging between his knees.

"And adorable," Duncan added.

"Yes," his brother admitted. "Very much so. And willing. But she didn't know exactly what she was willing to do, and of course when I realized that, I would not and could not accommodate her."

"Ah. You like her?"

"Yes. But before you begin playing matchmaker, remember that I'm not planning on marriage, and she deserves nothing less. And I'm promised to find her damned runaway fiancé for her. I don't think she'll know what she wants until we find him or what happened to him. Why don't you use a walking stick?"

"Sensible idea," Duncan nodded. "A spy trailing after someone while using a cane. He certainly wouldn't be noticed. Very clever."

"You shouldn't be a spy. You've done your bit."

"And my further bit is to protect you. I must add that our father was greatly relieved when I told him that I would. He dotes on you, you know."

"And you," Maxwell said. "The thing is that he doesn't dote on either of us when we're around."

"A secret doter, in fact," Duncan said.

The two men threw back their heads and laughed. Only then was their family resemblance clear to see.

Maxwell arose and took his brother's empty glass. "More?"

"Aye," Duncan said.

Maxwell went to the table again, and picked up the bottle of cognac. He gestured to his brother's leg. "Shot or sword?" he asked as he filled the glass again.

"Horse. It fell on me. I'm lucky to be walking, even hobbling as I do. There's hope it will strengthen in time. So, as for the lovely Phillipa? You intend to just let her go?"

Maxwell sat again, this time with his head against the back of the chair. "S'truth, brother, I don't know."

They sat in silence until they heard someone at the door.

"You don't actually expect me to get that, do you?" Duncan asked.

"No," Maxwell said, rising. "I hesitate because I have a feeling that the way things are going there won't be good news on the other side of that door."

He opened the door. His curly-haired servant stood there, smiling. "Note for you, my lor'," he said, touching his forehead. "I thought you'd want it right off." He winked. "It's from you know who."

"Ah, my faithful correspondent, you know who," Maxwell said, taking the note. "Thank you, Samson."

He closed the door, unfolded the note, and read it. His expression grew grim.

"It's from Talwin," he said in a tight voice before his brother could ask him. "All our plans are shattered. The peace of Amiens is broken. We're at war again."

Duncan whistled, low. "Not expected, but not a surprise either, I suppose. And your commission to find the lady's lost fiancé and discover if he was only fickle as to his promises to her, or in deeper, spying for someone else while using her grandfather for information he could pass on? Talwin told me everything, you know."

"All I know is that all of it is over. He wants me, and you, and the Carstairs women home again."

"Good luck to us," Duncan said. "What with the young Carstairs furious at you, and the older one, I hear, not too steady in her mind."

"Nevertheless, we have our orders. By luck, or force if need be, we are all going home," Maxwell said, with more confidence than he felt.

"I really do think we should go home," Pippa said.

"And I really do think we ought not," her grandmother replied. "Never have I had such a lovely trip," she went on as she inspected her maid's work on her hair in the mirror. "Everyone is so pleased to see me. And I am thrilled to see them."

"But, Grandfather—" Pippa began to say.

"Your grandfather," Lady Carstairs said, "probably has not noticed I'm gone yet."

Pippa fell still. This might well be true. Not in the sense that her grandfather's wits were so far gone that he didn't know his wife wasn't at home. But now she realized it was true that he paid little attention to her when she was.

"I know," Pippa said desperately. "But grandmother, I want to go home. I know now that I won't find Noel, and I don't want him even if I do. That's the reason we came here, and now that reason is gone. I miss the peace and quietude of the countryside. I don't thrive on social gatherings as you do, and in fact, you didn't used to either. Haven't you had enough of it?"

"There is never enough gaiety in this world," her grandmother said, nodding at her reflection in approval and sending the purple plumes set in her bright hair swaying. She wore an elegant spangled purple gown with yellow flowers set at the neck and sleeves.

Pippa sighed and took in a breath. "Then I'll wait for you to come around to my way of thinking. But, Grandmamma, don't you see? We don't have an excuse to be here anymore."

"We need no excuse," her grandmother said. "We are Carstairs, and free to do as we wish."

"So then I'm free to not go to the party tonight," Pippa said sadly. "And I don't want to. I'm exhausted."

Lady Carstairs turned to look at her granddaughter for the first time since Pippa had come into her room. Then she noted that Pippa wasn't dressed for an evening out. Her hair was simply tied back at her nape, and she wore a plain blue day gown. Her mood obviously matched it.

"Are you sickening?" her grandmother asked.

Pippa wanted to say yes, but refused to lie. She didn't want to tell the truth either, which was that she was deeply humiliated, disappointed, embarrassed, and feeling more worthless and cast off than ever. Noel had run away rather than marry her. She hadn't felt half as much for him as she did for Maxwell, but Maxwell had refused to lie with her even without any promises given on either side. She was done with men, and wanted only to go home and hide her head and grieve.

"I'm sick of frivolity," she said.

"Then I'm sorry for you," her grandmother said, turning back to her looking glass.

Pippa rose and went to the door. When she opened it she startled—the page from the hotel was standing there. He bowed. "Visitors, mesdames," he said, presenting a card to her. "They wait. Do I tell them you come?"

Pippa took the card and read it. Her hand shook.

"Well, hand it here, Phillipa," her grandmother ordered. She took the card and her face became wreathed in smiles. "Tell the gentlemen we shall be down tout suite," she told the page. "Well, my love?" she asked Pippa. "Surely you feel good enough to see Lord Montrose and his brother?"

"Surely," Pippa said dully, because for all she didn't want to, she supposed she was a true Carstairs too. She refused to run away.

They didn't look like brothers, Pippa thought again when she saw them waiting in the downstairs hallway. They both wore immaculate evening clothes, neither gaudy nor opulent, but rather, neat, clean, and well fitted, in the style of English gentlemen. Duncan was very tall, with dark auburn hair, and his striking eyes were crystal clear, blue ice, not a deep warm brown like his brother's. But Pippa could see a certain resemblance in their well-shaped mouths and occasional fleeting expressions.

"Ladies," Maxwell said after he'd introduced his brother to Lady Carstairs, "can we go into the salon? There's important news I must share."

Pippa was apprehensive. Her grandmother only gave him a stately nod and took Maxwell's arm. She went with him into the blue salon, Pippa following, accompanied by Duncan. She didn't dare look at or speak to Maxwell's brother, because she was sure he'd seen more of her botched misadventure with Maxwell in the grass than he'd admitted.

Oddly, for this hour of the evening, the salon was otherwise unoccupied. Maxwell exchanged a knowing look with his brother as the ladies were seated.

When Maxwell was sure they were the only ones in the room, he spoke. "The peace is ended," he said abruptly.

For a moment Pippa thought he was saying that he was angry at her. It took another moment for the real import of his news to occur to her. "France broke the treaty?" she asked in horror.

"No, England. But it hardly matters. Neither side wants peace. I think it was just a brief respite for both sides, a time to gather troops and make plans. Perhaps the news of Napoleon's real intentions reached us and alarmed us. He's not through with his ambitions; we knew that. So we're nominally at war again. I believe it's time for you ladies to return to England."

Pippa sighed with relief.

Her grandmother swelled with indignation. "Carstairs do not run from danger," she announced.

"Is there rioting in the streets?" Pippa asked anxiously. "Are English persons being arrested?"

"No, in fact, it's strangely quiet," Duncan said.

"We think neither side is ready for out and out warfare just yet," Maxwell said. "But it won't be long."

"Or ever, possibly," Lady Carstairs said with a sniff. "And so we shall see. I have an appointment for the evening and I shall keep it. It is a party in the best part of Paris. If there is any difficulty, then I will think about retreat. But even then, I won't return to England until I know what my friends are doing."

"Packing, if they have wits," Duncan murmured.

Maxwell bowed. "Then so be it. We don't advise it but are sworn to protect you. We'll come with you, my lady, and judge the situation ourselves. But please remember to tell your English friends that France is no longer a comfortable place for us."

Lady Carstairs smirked. "What, with thousands of us already here? I doubt we'll come to harm. There are no jails big enough to hold all of us."

"I'm not so convinced," Maxwell said. "Rather the opposite. There are worse things than jail, and ransom is very profitable. But the end of peace was just announced. We'll be with you tonight and at the first sign of danger we'll leave. I want you to test the waters and see the truth for yourself, my lady." He glanced at Pippa, his expression bland. "Now we have only to wait for Miss Phillipa to dress and we'll go," he said.

"She's not coming," Lady Carstairs said bluntly. "Refuses, in fact. Not sick, she says. She's homesick, I think. She'll be well enough staying here. Unless," she added with a smirk, "you think a battalion of French soldiers will burst in and abduct her."

"I doubt that," Maxwell said.

"I want to stay here," Pippa put in quickly.

"Then, we'll go without you," Maxwell said

with a frown. "But, my lady," he asked her grandmother, "may I have a word alone with her before we leave?"

"Of course," Lady Carstairs said. "I must send for my wrap before we go anyway. We shall wait in the hall. It's a mild evening, but it is spring, and one never knows how quickly the weather will change."

"I wish she really understood that," Maxwell said to Phillipa when Lady Carstairs and his brother had left them.

She stood facing him, refusing to look down at the floor, though she longed to. They made a handsome couple, he, tall and straight, only his dark head bowed to her; she, shapely and slender, looking up into his face.

"I'm sorry," he said softly. "The whole episode wasn't worthy of you or me. If I were another sort of man, I'd offer for you straightaway. If you want me to, I will, no matter my mode of living."

"Oh," she gasped. "No, please. I wouldn't say yes. Let's forget it."

"I can't," he said simply. He took her cold hands in his warm ones, and looked down at them. "I wish I were like other men. That I didn't have so many reservations, that I could be free to do as I want, without pondering the matter over and over.

You didn't deserve the treatment you received from your unworthy Noel, nor did you deserve my blundering, licentious actions.

"Again," he said, "I apologize. None of it is due to any fault in you. Please know that if things were different—if I were different, I'd ask for your hand and never let it go."

He slowly opened his hands and let hers free. Then he looked down into her face again. "You'd be within your rights to despise me whatever I say. I can only hope someday you'll forgive me, even though I don't deserve it. We will continue to search for Noel Nicholson, one way or another. But I'll stay with you until you're returned safe to England. And I promise, I'll do all I can to speed that day."

She nodded, not contented at all by what he'd had to say.

Chapter 20

Pippa sat in a chair in the blue salon and waited as the night hours passed. She blamed herself for not going with her grandmother on what could be a night of danger. She reassured herself that her grandmother's two clever escorts would be able to protect her. And she listened for noises from the street.

But everything was still. The guests at the hotel were long abed. She was alone in the room and had been for hours. A footman had brought her a cup of tea a few hours past, for which she was grateful. But her grandmother hadn't returned.

Pippa couldn't forget that she was suddenly an enemy alien in a land with which her country was at war. It was true that thousands of her country-men were in the same position, but it was an un-comfortable one. Pippa had teethed on stories of what happened to the aristocrats in France when the Revolution came. Then later she'd shivered in horror at the stories she'd read about their fates. She could easily envision dark dank dungeons, tumbrels rolling through the narrow streets of Paris again as enraged crowds of Frenchmen screamed for her to be brought to the guillotine.

And there was her grandmother, out for a night on the town in a town that was now at war with her, and her grandmother not able to understand. Pippa sat and listened. It was a quiet night. No rioters, no tumbrels or carriages either, nothing but silence in which to blame herself for anything that might go wrong.

Finally she heard noises. Laughter. It was her grandmother's. Pippa jumped to her feet. The front door to the hotel opened and there she was coming into the hall, flanked by her two escorts. Lady Carstairs looked jubilant, pink-cheeked and merry. Her escorts, Pippa noted, were expressionless. They walked into the hotel.

"Why, there she is," Lady Carstairs cried, stopping by the entrance to the salon. "Still in the salon. My own little Ella, sit by the cinders. Oh, Phillipa, my love, what you missed!" her grandmother went on. "It was a grand soiree. Everyone was there. My English friends all gathered together and we talked about what we ought to do next. And would you believe," she asked with pride, "many of them thought I would know, since I was a personal friend of the First Consul."

Pippa's eyes flew to Maxwell.

He shook his head and looked grim.

Pippa had accepted her grandmother's lie about their meeting with Napoleon. "But Grandmamma," she said, using that incident as a wedge, "I was there. Having him acknowledge you in the receiving line was very gratifying, but not exactly a vow of friendship. I doubt you could demand his attention if you were in difficulty now."

Her grandmother's smile was beatific. "Ah, but you don't know everything, my Phillipa. You couldn't hear what he said to me, or what he promised to say when we were alone together."

Pippa's shoulders slumped. She'd put her grandmother's recent antics down to confusion, or self-aggrandizement. This, however, was madness. She looked at Maxwell again, her desperation clear to see.

"I think we ought to sleep on this," Maxwell said.

"A good idea," Lady Carstairs said with satisfaction. "We're all meeting again in a week's time to decide what to do. Some are already leaving for home or going farther abroad. I heard there's not a space to be found at any price on the next packets to England. But I think we should stay and wait. This may all blow over. For now," she said, stifling a yawn, "I must have my beauty sleep. Good night, Phillipa, gentlemen."

Maxwell shot a look to his brother.

"If I may assist you up the stair?" Duncan asked Lady Carstairs.

"With that poor leg?" she said. "I think not, thank you."

"Then I will, if you please," Maxwell said, offering her his arm. "Duncan, will you stay and wait for me? I'm sure Miss Carstairs will want to hear more about tonight's doings."

"I would," Phillipa said quickly.

She watched her grandmother make her way up the stair with Maxwell and then went back into the blue salon with his brother. She sank into a chair and heaved a great sigh.

"How the devil am I going to get her home?" she asked him.

He settled himself in a chair opposite her. "Devil a bit, if I know," he said. "Kidnapping, I think."

"It may come to that," she mused. She sat up straight. "Is there any truth at all in her thoughts about the safety of the English here? Is this as temporary a war as it was a peace?"

He shook his head. "No. This time the war will be ferocious. Napoleon won't stop until he owns the world. Or we, until we've defeated him."

She looked down at her lap. "Is there any possibility that by any chance she does have any personal connection to him?"

He understood at once. "No," he said. "None. So the war has also convinced you to give up your search for your lost fiancé?"

Her laugh was bitter. "Didn't your brother tell you? I did that a while ago. I wish I'd never had such a mad fancy. If Noel came to harm, I'm sorry for him. If he simply wanted to be rid of me, then I'm not. Whatever it was, it was for the best. He may have had no manners for leaving me in the lurch, but I had less pride by following him. Rather," she said, cocking her head to one side, thinking about it, "I think I had too much pride, I couldn't believe he would simply jilt me.

"No matter. That's done with now," she went on with a crooked smile. "Because now I haven't a shred of pride left and it serves me right. I was a fool for pursuing him. I wasn't even thinking correctly when I got here. I felt cast off and abandoned and wanted someone to love me. What a farce I made of that!"

She ducked her head, raised it again, looked him in the eyes, and added, "All I want to do now is go home and live quietly. Although with the way the world is going, and my grandmother's state of mind, I have doubts of being able to do it. But the world will go its way, and maybe being home again will steady my grandmother's wits."

"And my brother?" he asked simply.

"What of him?" she asked as answer.

"You're also giving up on him?"

This time her laughter was real. "Oh, my goodness, my lord. There's nothing to give up. I don't blame him for having no plans to change his life. He was, in fact, as you know, a perfect gentleman at a . . . difficult moment. You should be proud of him. Now. How do we get my grandmother to go home?"

"I have a few ideas," Maxwell said as he came into the room. "As of the moment, she refuses and thinks it a foolish idea, and only wants to stay here and enjoy herself. She puts great stock in what her old friends are doing."

"And they are doing what?" Pippa asked.

"Waiting, as she is," Maxwell said. "The clever

ones have already removed themselves from the scene. The foolish have gone on to Italy, Spain, or farther abroad, ignoring the fact that Napoleon's reach is growing longer."

"I'll write to my grandfather immediately," Pippa said, "and finally tell him the whole truth. I concealed a lot for her sake, but now that time is critical, I'll tell all. He'll insist she come home."

"In a month or so," Maxwell said. "But we don't have that much time. The post isn't that swift and I don't know how quickly your grandfather will respond. Doubtless some English persons will stay here that long. But I won't and my brother won't either if I leave." He paced a few steps. "I don't fancy ferrying home an outraged dowager. So I think we'll have to somehow engineer the lady's departure, and although I don't shrink at actually bodily removing her after enough powders have been dropped in her wine, it might not be necessary. We'll wait on it."

He stopped pacing and looked at Pippa. His eyes were dark and serious. "What you have to do is to keep her here, in the hotel, for the next few nights. At least until her next grand party with her friends. Do you think you can do that?"

"I will," Pippa said, rising from her chair and

standing tall. "One way or the other, I will."

He smiled. "I believe you. But as a precaution, I'll have someone watching your hotel."

He took Phillipa's hand in his and said soberly, "There's more I have to say to you, but now is not the time or place."

"I'll just go and see if our coach is ready," Duncan said, awkwardly rising from his chair.

"That won't make it the right time or place," Maxwell said over his shoulder. He pressed Pippa's hand, let it go, and then bowed. "Good night, Miss Phillipa. Don't worry. Whatever else may be, this time you're not alone."

Pippa watched the brothers leave, although it was hard to focus on them because her eyes were suddenly so misted.

"You're going to stay here, with me," Maxwell said bluntly.

"I have engaged rooms," his brother said. "I'm all grown up now, and besides," he added in a deliberately childish voice, "Father sent me to watch you, not the other way around."

"That was folly," Maxwell said. He was pacing the sitting room in his own rooms. "You've been wounded. How bad is it, by the by? Truth now, if you please."

Duncan sat back in his chair. "I deal with it. We don't know if and when it will completely heal, and won't until more time passes. It's been set and stitched together again. I won't pretend it's been easy. But I persevere. Actually, it's good for healing parts to work rather than rest. Speaking of which," he asked, "how is your heart doing?"

Maxwell turned around to stare. "By which you mean?" he asked, his eyes narrowing.

"A fool could see you're smitten," Duncan replied idly. "And only a fool would deny it, so don't bother. And why not? She's lovely. Well-bred, intelligent, sensitive, and . . . honorable."

"How long were you watching us in the meadow?" Maxwell demanded.

"Not that long, and I certainly would have left had things gone further. In fact, I was beginning to go when events suddenly turned. I don't know where you get the control, Maxwell. That's a thing I wish you'd teach me. Although I confess I don't entirely understand it in this case. You want her. She wants you. You're both of age and free, so where's the hindrance? And don't try to tell me that virginity withers a fellow's desires. She may have believed you, which just goes to show what an innocent she is. I am not."

Maxwell sat down and knotted his hands together. His eyes were clear and candid as he looked at his brother. "The hindrance is that she doesn't know what she's doing any more than her daft grandmother does just now. Her worm of a fiancé left her at the altar. I don't think she's been thinking straight since then, else why would she have gone tearing off to find him? She's not that forward in anything else. She seems attracted to me, I'll grant. But how can I know how much of that is just reaction to what happened to her? I care for her, very much. Who wouldn't?

"But I can't dally with her. And I won't enter into a marriage without knowing all that I can before I do. If I'm devastated by fate after that, so be it. But it's not a light undertaking. I learned from Father. He loved too much twice, and too little once. None of it made him happy. In fact, it's what set him to drink. Is he still overindulging again, by the by?"

Duncan shook his head. "He gave that up. Strange, but I think he's actually gotten to like our Theo the Terror, which gives him an interest in the world again. Another benefit to him, I suppose, is that his wife hates that."

Both men chuckled, thinking of their obstreperous sibling and their detested stepmother.

"So," Duncan continued, "no matter what Talwin wants, am I to assume that if you found

Miss Phillipa's confounded fiancé and saw her reaction to him you'd know where her heart really lies? Reasonable. But what if he's dead? You'd just let her wilt on the vine?"

Maxwell scowled. "As with your confounded limb, brother, we'll just have to wait and see."

"At last!" Lady Carstairs said. "I am free! You are finally well enough to go out, and I am conscience free to do as I please. Almost a week of ill health, never have I seen you so susceptible, Phillipa," she said, turning from the looking glass in her chamber to scold her granddaughter. "One night you were succumbing to coughing spells and the next a stomach upset. Then you suffered the headache, and then the toothache. The physicians who came didn't know what to do for you, nor did I. I confess, I'd have gone out of an evening anyway, but you made me feel too guilty to enjoy myself."

"I merely said that if I expired alone, Grandfather would be upset," Pippa said meekly.

Pippa shot her maid a sharp glance and stopped her incipient giggles.

"But here you are, up and about and looking fine as five pence," Lady Carstairs said with approval. "The enforced rest seems to have done you good. And myself as well, I admit."

Lady Carstairs smiled at her reflection. Her gown was red as a rooster's comb, and her bright yellow hair was done up with red plumes and topped with a ruby-encrusted tiara. She looked like rising dawn in a henhouse, Pippa thought. But her grandmother preened in front of the glass.

Pippa stood quietly, wearing a dark blue gown with a modest neckline, with a lighter blue sash tied under her breast. The French modiste had said it would suit her perfectly. It did. Her pale hair was drawn up and back and she wore a cameo on a black ribbon at her neck. Her attire was simplicity itself, and she was pleased with herself.

"And now," Lady Carstairs said, rising and pulling on her long gloves, "we'll go out for the evening as a visitor in Paris is supposed to do. Doubtless Lord Montrose and his charming brother will be delighted to see us. They sent bowers of flowers to you, the dear lads. Life must have been dull for them this past week."

Pippa followed her grandmother down the stair. Neither Maxwell nor his brother, awaiting them in the front hall of the hotel, looked particularly deprived she thought as she first caught sight of them. They looked dapper, elegant, and at ease. She wondered what female Maxwell had found to help him while away the lonely hours, and hated herself for caring so much.

"Ladies," Maxwell said, bowing. "How good to see you again. So my lady, we go to your friends the Chestertons' house this evening. I hear they're generous hosts. Do you think that you'll discover what they and the rest of your compatriots are planning to do now that we are at war with our other hosts?"

"I shall," Lady Carstairs said with certainty. "And I would have found out sooner had my dear Phillipa not been so ill all week. But I could scarcely leave her to her own devices, could I? A doctor a day, we had here, I think, and none able to cure her. It is the water, I told her again and again. She should emulate me and drink only wine and tea. But that is the past. As for tonight, she's fine again and I am set on having a good time this evening. I know you all will as well."

"Are you sure you're well enough to go out on the town tonight?" Maxwell asked Phillipa solicitously as Lady Carstairs's maid brought her a shawl.

"Absolutely," Pippa said. "Positively." She thought of the endless games of cards she and Annie had played to pass the hours, and unable to say more now, added, "Although I must admit that at times I felt it might be fatal. When I wasn't being vilely ill, I was bored almost to death."

"A worse fate than dying of some mysterious French malady," he said with a smile, and added in a whisper, "Well done!" before he turned to take Lady Carstairs's arm.

"You are a gem," Duncan told Pippa with admiration as they left the hotel.

"I promised," she said simply. "And I keep my promises."

Chapter 21

The Chestertons lived in a huge old town house near others of the same type in an area that had somehow escaped the fires of the Revolution. By the number of carriages arriving in the drive, Pippa thought the enormous house would be crowded to the doors and steeled herself for another night of her grandmother's idea of frolic: food and drink, dancing and gossip, the entire house filled with the deafening noise of music, conversations, and shrill laughter.

But when they entered, the place was strangely still. There was the murmur of conversation and, in the background, a trio of string musicians from somewhere behind the ferns playing soft reflective melodies. The dance floor of the ballroom was filled with guests, most of a certain age. But none were dancing. Rather, they stood in small groups talking in lowered voices. At least, the English guests did. Pippa realized there must have been French citizens at other parties but she'd never particularly noticed them before. Now it was obvious. They were the ones who strolled the room, smiling broadly and talking in normal tones. They were the only ones who seemed in the mood for festivity.

The other Frenchmen were impossible to ignore. There were a number of French army officers in brilliant military regalia. Yet in spite of their finery, they didn't seem festive either.

Maxwell and his brother exchanged looks.

"It's more like a wake than a party," Maxwell said in a hushed voice.

"Then I shall have to awaken them," Lady Carstairs said confidently. "Come, my lords, let me introduce you to our hosts. I warn you, they may put on airs, but they are the Chestertons from Middleborough, and have little to give them entrée into London Society but their money, as is evident here as well."

The Chestertons were in the midst of a knot of guests to the right of the room. They looked up when Lady Carstairs and her party approached.

"Monroe," she said, greeting her host, "so still? Has there been a recent death?"

The tall thin elderly man she addressed winced.

"No, my lady, but these are serious times."

"All the more reason for frolic," she answered.

No one smiled.

Maxwell deftly introduced himself, his brother, and Pippa. "More the time for careful planning, I should say," he said. "Are all the English leaving?"

"Really? A pity. I would dislike losing your company," a new voice intruded. The speaker was a short, swarthy gentleman dressed in high fashion so new it almost seemed foolish. He had a French accent, dark eyes, and a penetrating stare. His words might have been meant to be pleasant, but they didn't come out sounding that way.

"Monsieur Denton, welcome," his host said, bowing. "I hope you enjoy yourself this evening."

"As do I," Denton said. "Merci," he added with a light laugh before he strolled away.

"A parvenu, to use their own words," one of the guests said low and with disgust. "He was made by Bonaparte and now plays the high lord. Beware of him. He doesn't care who he climbs over."

Pippa watched the French gentleman as he roamed through the knots of other guests, ignoring them. Instead, he was looking at furnishings as though they were up for auction.

"Yes," her host said with a sigh. "So it is now. All

the jumped-up citizens are looking to rise to new heights, and they don't care who they throw off the top in order to reach them. Homes are being taken over without restitution or so much as a by your leave. It doesn't matter to us anymore. We're going to leave, and soon. This night is to be our farewell to France for a while or forever. Most of the homes on this street are being abandoned because the owners are aware they are about to lose them anyway. Better to lose your roof than your head. You can see for yourself that our home is already obviously being measured for new draperies."

"Grim talk!" Lady Carstairs said sharply. "Brought on by fear. That is a great weapon by itself. The French are subtle. It may be the rude fellow we just met has no evil intentions, only few manners. I shall go have a chat with him and find out what his intentions really are. I too, after all, have an acquaintance with the First Consul, you know."

The other guests gaped at her.

Pippa paled. "Grandmother, no!" she exclaimed in shock.

She felt a light pressure on her arm.

"Grandmother, yes, I think," Maxwell said into her ear. "It may be the only way to convince her that times are changing and she no longer belongs here. Don't worry. Even if he hates us, the rude gentleman won't hurt anything but her feelings here and now. I'm certain he doesn't want to make an incident, at least, not yet."

"But we are at war," she protested.

"And the first shot hasn't yet been fired," he said. "Let's go see what ammunition the fellow has."

Lady Carstairs detached herself from Maxwell's arm, and marched after Monsieur Denton. Maxwell and Pippa followed a few paces behind her.

"Monsieur, if you please," Lady Carstairs cried out as she bustled closer to him. He stopped and turned around.

"Madame," he said, making a curt bow. "What is it you wish of me?"

"My Lady," she corrected him.

His smile was not amused. "But no. You are not in England now. Here in the new France, we no longer use titles, madame."

Lady Carstairs looked taken aback. But she rallied. "Monsieur," she said, "since you are so outspoken, you are the very person I must speak to. My friends and our hosts believe you mean them no good. They are preparing to leave France. As someone who is friends with the First Consul, I feel I have the right to ask your intentions toward them and the thousands of English persons now on your soil."

Monsieur Denton's lips curled. He drew himself up and looked at her with contempt. "I was at the reception where you saw Bonaparte, madame, and I also saw that he spoke only to your so-pretty companion, not to you. And at that, only a word of praise for how she looked in her gown in his colors. We know what you have been saying too, and excused you much because your wits are obviously overturned by age. But we are no longer amused. The First Consul doesn't know or care for you. As for your friends, they are wise to leave here with all speed. You would be as well. I like this house. It will be mine. I like your ruby red tiara too, madame," he added maliciously, eyeing it, "and if you stay, it will be mine as well, whether I pluck it off your head while it is still on your shoulders, or not."

"There's not a chance of that, Denton," Maxwell said, stepping forward, glowering at the man.

Denton looked up at him. He nodded. "True, monsieur. Not now. But soon, eh? And you know it. If you have a care for the women you are with, send them home. If you have a care for yourself, leave as well. We know who you are and what you do. But be aware, France is for the French once again. There is no point in further conversation. Good evening, and *bon chance*. You will need it."

"Hush. Oh, hush," Pippa said as her grandmother lay shaking in her arms.

They were in the carriage on the way back to their hotel, Lady Carstairs weeping all the way.

"What a fool I was," that lady said through her tears. "I don't know what got into me. You won't let that dreadful man get near me, will you? He hasn't even seen my diamond tiara. Oh, I want to go home!"

"And so we will," Pippa said in soothing tones. "How soon, do you think?" she asked Maxwell, where he sat in the carriage opposite her.

"As to that, my brother and I will seek all possibilities," Maxwell said. "He's already off trying to find us passage. But you, Phillipa, are you ready to give up your hunt?"

"I've been ready for weeks now," she said stiffly. "I told you that. Nothing has changed my mind. Hush, Grandmother, didn't you hear Lord Montrose? We'll be leaving as soon as we can. There's nothing to fear anymore."

But there was, Pippa thought as she sat cradling her grandmother. Because she knew that as soon as they returned to England, she'd say good-bye to Maxwell, and likely never see him again. That frightened her perhaps even more than her grandmother feared strange Frenchmen wrenching her jewels and her head away from her.

Maxwell was a man the likes of whom she'd never seen before and knew she'd never see again. He acted a fop when he had to, and as a spy all the time. He was handsome and clever and made her laugh or tingle whenever he wanted to. But withal he was a truthful man, with morals. He desired her but didn't love her. He wouldn't marry her, neither would he seduce her, and she mourned that more than she'd mourned Noel's desertion. Or did she?

She no longer knew. She and her grandmother had changed on this trip and she no longer knew herself. But she vowed not to be a fool. She'd say good-bye to Maxwell and smile as she did it, and then would have the rest of her quiet life to remember, and think about where she'd gone wrong, or right.

The carriage stopped, and Maxwell helped Lady Carstairs out and into the hotel. It seemed she didn't care whose arms she wilted into.

"She's had a shock and fright, but no more than that," Maxwell told her maid. "Does she have any sleeping powders?"

"Yes, my lord," the maid said. "We don't travel without them. I'll give her some and make her comfortable, don't you worry. There, there, my lady," the maid said as she helped steer Lady Carstairs up the stair, "don't shiver and shake so. We'll have you in bed and comfortable in no time."

"I wish I could say the same to you," Maxwell told Pippa as they went down the stair after leaving her grandmother in her maid's tender care.

Pippa held her head high. "That you do not," she said. "I'd have to lie with a dozen men before you thought me ready for you." There was nothing more to lose; she was weary and frightened too, so all she could speak was her utmost resentment.

He stopped on the stair. "Touché," he said after a moment. "A direct hit. But surely not a dozen men?"

Absurdly, she felt herself smiling. "Why not?" she said airily. "I dashed my reputation by coming here even more than Noel did when he deserted me."

They reached the bottom of the stair and he stopped and looked down at her, his expression serious.

"It's not your reputation but your heart that I fear for," he told her softly. "You don't know how you feel about me, Pippa. You met me at the wrong time for the wrong reasons, when your heart was wounded. I refused to hurt you more. Is that so cruel of me? For all we know you may go home and meet a stranger you care for, or find an old friend that you didn't realize you cared for. You're in no condition to fall in love now, and for that matter, never for such a fellow as I am. I was a determined bachelor and may still be. But I'm as turned about in my head these days as anyone. We'll take you home and then we'll see."

She nodded and looked away, unable to meet his gaze.

"But Pippa?" he said in a strained voice. "This much I can tell you. I want you so damned much my bones ache. We have to wait no matter how I feel. Things have happened too fast all around. We'll leave this place and let time do its work, shall we?"

She stood and stared at him. The hotel was quiet, nothing stirred except for her pulse as she gazed at him. He was so close and yet so distant. A mad idea came to her, but this was a mad night and she was at the end of her reason.

"No," she said. "Who knows what cruelties time may bring? Tonight should be our night, if you want me. There's no one about. I'm so very alone.

I don't care about tomorrow. Can you be with me, tonight, now, please?"

A sad smile appeared on his lips. "Oh, Pippa," he said on a long exhalation. "I want to." He ran a hand through his dark hair. "But I can't for too many reasons," he said. "You may choose to ignore it, but I always think about the future. Again, what if my usually perfect timing fails? You still don't completely understand? That confirms my resolve. Forgive me in advance, Pippa, but the truth is as they say: a gentleman leaves before he comes. I grant they don't say it in places where you go, and I should be shot for saying it to you. I don't want to be scientific. And if you want to be treated as a carefree, care-for-nothing female who is up to scratch, it's a thing you must fully understand."

Her eyebrows descended; she looked less shocked than puzzled.

He chuckled, reached out and tucked a strand of her hair back behind her ear, and then stepped away as though he had touched flames. "As I thought. What it meant was that if we made love, I would have to leave you before my moment, so that you wouldn't have to bear the weight of my mistake," he explained. "Neither of us needs or wants a forced marriage. And a lady can't raise a child by herself, nor would I want you to."

Her eyes went wide.

"Ah, I see, you do understand," he said. "The thing is that superb a lover as I am, it's possible I might not be able to stop myself; I'm very moved by you. And even if I did, what if we were discovered? What if . . . there are so many reasons why pleasure must wait on reason tonight that I can't say them all.

"Go to sleep, Pippa," he said softly. "This isn't your last chance at love, whatever you think now. Your emotions are overwrought, as are mine. I'll see you in the morning, and with any luck, we'll soon leave this country together and then . . . and then, who knows? Good night," he said and hesitated. Then he dragged her into his arms and kissed her.

She clung to him, needing his warmth, his strength, and his need of her.

But then he disengaged and quickly stepped away. "Good God, Pippa. I keep making the same mistakes, don't I? I'd blame it on Paris and springtime, but we both know it's how I feel about you. I'm leaving. We've neither of us anything to regret except for missed chances, and they're easier to bear than chances taken and misused. I have work to do tonight. I have to find us safe passage home.

The sooner we leave, the sooner we'll be safe, and hopefully in our right minds again. Good night."

She whispered good night and watched him leave. She shook her head, wondering with despair how many times she'd belittle herself by offering what wasn't wanted.

"Never again," she whispered to herself, "I vow it." Then she slowly turned and went back up the stair.

"It's not the packet but it's not an old tub either, and there's room for all of us," Maxwell said as they stood on the dock and watched Lady Carstairs being helped aboard a spanking white, freshly painted yacht. "It took a few days to arrange it, and I know you were anxious, but even so I consider us lucky."

They stood on the dock, his coat of many capes being blown by the freshening wind. Pippa had tied her bonnet on, but the breeze flung her skirts around with abandon. Duncan stood apart from them, facing the wind, smiling as it tossed his auburn hair about.

"It's a neat sloop, and won't take more time than the packet would," Maxwell said. "In fact, we'll get home faster. And it's a sturdy craft. But we go to Dover, not Folkestone. A carriage will be waiting for us when we land; we'll make haste to your home. I'll make my bows to your grandfather, and then see what life holds in store." He smiled down at her.

Her heartbeat quickened but she refused to show it. He'd already refused her direct offers twice, she'd promised herself there would be no more embarrassing moments between them. But still he was hinting at something, she was sure of it. And even if he weren't, they would have hours to talk on the way home. The recent past might have been terrifying, but the future seemed cold and lonely. She took comfort in the fact that they'd be together for the journey across the channel and all the way home.

After that? He was right. She knew she needed time to know herself again and see if she really wanted him, or only a man who was strong and able in order to restore her sense of worth.

"Your grandmother already seems calmer," he said, watching the servants leading the lady to the deck. "Leave your troubles behind you, as she's doing."

He took her gloved hand and they walked to the ramp leading to the yacht.

"Ho! My lord Montrose!" a voice called.

They both turned to see a young, harried rider

galloping down the strand. He slipped down from his horse as soon as he reined it in, and ran to Maxwell. "Just in time, a message for you, my lord," the lad panted, holding out a roll of oiled cloth.

Maxwell took it, opened it and unfurled a letter. He scanned it quickly. His smile turned to a frown, and then to a smile again.

He looked up. "Duncan!" he said excitedly as his brother strolled over to see what the fuss was about. "New information. I can't go home yet. I need you to see the ladies home safely."

"You need me to help you," Duncan said sternly.

"Not in this case," Maxwell said. "Bostwick and Sir Charles will be meeting me. They've discovered a clear trail. Do you know any better fellows for the job? No, I didn't think so. I hope to get the matter done with quickly. You see Pippa and her grandmother safely home, brother, and I'll see you soon."

He turned to Pippa. "I dislike leaving you to this churl, but he's good at what he does. I have business to attend to. I'll see you when I can."

"But isn't France dangerous for you now?" she asked in confusion.

He grinned. "For m'lor' Montrose, perhaps, mademoiselle. Not for who will be traveling through

France. Farewell," he said and with a jaunty wave, strode back to the shore with the messenger.

"He didn't seem very sorry," Pippa said to the breeze.

"He is, and he isn't," Duncan said. "When he's on a scent, the world fades away from him. Come," he said, taking her arm. "I promised to protect you. Don't want you blown into the sea before I even get a chance."

She went with him, but turned her head to see Maxwell striding away, wondering if he'd ever return, or if he did, if he'd ever return to her.

Chapter 22

"Your grandfather would like to see you in his study, Miss Phillipa," the butler said as Pippa entered the house.

She nodded, took off her sunbonnet, and bought some time by using the looking glass in the hallway to smooth her hair. It was midday. They'd had visitors since she'd come home in May but none of them had concerned her. Now it was July, and though her hopes had dwindled, they weren't dead. There were two carriages in the drive that she'd never seen before.

She walked slowly, in trepidation, and tapped on her grandfather's study door.

"Enter," her grandfather said.

She pushed open the door to see that the room seemed filled with men. There were three standing to one side, and two to another, but her eyes instantly arrowed to only one. Maxwell didn't look very much like the man she'd last seen on the dock in France months ago. He wasn't dressed like an immaculate gent, but casually, like a country squire or a sportsman. His face had lost its gentleman's pallor and had been sun touched to golden hues. His hair was longer; he wore a scarf around his neck instead of an immaculate neckcloth. But it was Maxwell, however he dressed and whatever he looked like, and she couldn't look away from him.

She thought his face lit with sudden joy when he saw her, but now he stared at her with no expression. She took a step forward toward him, her eyes never leaving his.

"Phillipa," her grandfather said. "These gentlemen have found your fiancé."

She blinked. Her spirits plummeted. She was still a fool. He wasn't here for her; only to show her he had done his job. That was why he hadn't greeted her, why he didn't smile at her. Instead, he dragged his eyes away from hers and looked to his right. She followed his gaze.

"Phillipa," a hesitant voice said. "It is I. Noel."

And so, she realized, it was. He hadn't changed. He looked wearier and subdued, but it was Noel Nicholson. He didn't look half as well as she remembered, though. He was stockier than she'd thought he was. His eyes were dark brown, but there was no lively sparkle in them, and she realized there never had been. His hair was slicked back, and black, not brown; his face was amiable, but not thrilling. In all he was just a young gentleman with nothing to dislike in him but nothing particularly memorable about him either. She stood in shock. Whatever he was, he was here now.

"I've returned," he said.

"Under duress," one of the other gentlemen growled. "We tracked him across England and off across the Continent, but here he is."

"I was going to come here," Noel told Pippa, his eyes pleading, never leaving hers. "As soon as I'd cleared up matters of business, as I said in my last note to you. It took longer than I'd thought, Phillipa, and I was too harried to write to you again. But I was never going to abandon you."

The man next to him opened his mouth to speak again, but Maxwell held up a hand, and he fell silent.

Pippa stared, but said nothing.

"Phillipa," Noel pleaded, "say you forgive me. Say something, please."

She held her silence for another moment. "Why did you go? Why did you come back?" she finally asked.

His eyes darted from side to side. "If only I were

alone with you," Noel said desperately. "You'll hear many stories. But you know me. What I need to know first, for the sake of my soul, is if you still love me and wish to be with me, Phillipa. Will you still marry me?"

The men in the room looked incredulous, some made sounds of protest. But Maxwell help up his hand again and stared intently at Pippa, awaiting her answer.

She didn't look back at him. Instead she kept staring at Noel. At last, she shook herself as though she was coming out of a deep sleep. She grounded herself by setting her feet apart and placed her hands on her hips like a battling washerwoman.

"I never loved you, Noel," she said angrily. "No more than I now believe you loved me. I came to see that. I'm glad you left when you did and gladder still that you stayed away because if you hadn't we'd have been wed, and what a fiasco that would have been for me. I was lonely, you were clean and educated and civil, and I thought my liking for you was love. Now I know it wasn't.

"I wouldn't marry you if you'd spent the past year in a pirate's cave hunting for treasure and came to me with your pockets full of jewels. I wouldn't marry you if . . ." she paused. "I wouldn't marry you for anything. And to think I was fool enough to believe you were dead or in distress," she marveled, "and so went tearing after you to find out what happened, ruining what was left of my reputation in the process. You behaved like a cad, Noel. But I was a plain fool. Now, go away."

"I shouldn't ever have let you go," her grandfather said sadly.

"What?" she asked. "And have me stay home, pacing and worrying and dwindling in my soul? Never. I went looking and though I didn't find Noel, I do think I found myself. Don't have regrets, Grandfather, for I don't." Her eyes narrowed as she looked at Noel again. "But why has he got such an escort? Is he under arrest? Is he a spy?"

"Perhaps," Maxwell said smoothly. "That's possible too. But more to the point, he's a bigamist."

Pippa blinked. Noel shrank.

"He was going to marry you, Miss Phillipa," Maxwell said formally. "But first he had to be sure his other wife was unaware. She lives in a village outside of London, and is known as Mrs. Nelson, as he is Mr. Nelson when he's there."

Phillipa goggled at Noel, who seemed to be shrinking in size before her eyes.

"And then," Maxwell said, "he had to make certain things were stable with his wife Elise, in France, and his wife Francesca in Spain, and the former widow Mrs. Sabatini, now Mrs. Noel Norwood, in Italy. He has four wives, though it's hard to credit that."

"But it was you I loved, Phillipa!" Noel cried.

"And all of them wealthy," Maxwell continued blandly. "He also loves money and we suspect he was also a courier when it was asked of him, but not for us."

"One thing's certain," one of the other gentlemen said, "Mr. Nicholson won't trouble you again, Miss Phillipa. If we don't deal with him promptly, his wives certainly will. Some of them, along with their papas and brothers, are already en route, on their way to meet with him here."

Noel's eyes widened.

"Please escort the gentleman back to the carriage, and then to London," Maxwell told the two men holding up the now-collapsed Noel. "That is, if neither Lord Carstairs or his granddaughter have anything more to say to him."

"Not I," Lord Carstairs said with a dismissive wave of his hand.

"I do," Phillipa said.

The men in the room waited breathlessly.

"Good riddance!" she shouted at Noel, and then stormed from the room.

Maxwell found her walking in the gardens an hour later. Her head was bowed; she was obviously deep in thought. She didn't look up when she heard him coming, although the pebbles on the path under their feet announced him long before he caught up with her.

"Who would have thought it?" she asked in wonder after he'd paced by her side awhile. "A bigamist! He's not that handsome, or rich. He's not a seducer. How does he do it?"

"You gave him your hand," Maxwell said. "How did he get you to do that?"

She shook her head. "I don't know. Except that he seemed to know my loneliness as well as all the right things to say. I feel like a fool."

"Don't," he said simply. "Just consider yourself lucky. How is your grandmother?" he asked as they walked farther into the gardens.

"Better," Pippa said. "Not exactly herself again, actually, that may or may not come to pass. Grandfather blames himself for neglecting her in favor of his studies for so long, as well he should. Now they pass every evening together. He reads to her or talks to her and it appears to help them both.

But you must have known that, you were with my grandfather awhile before you came out here, weren't you?"

"I was," he said simply. "I didn't know what else to say to you then. I still don't. You seem to be angry with me. But I couldn't write lest it was traced back to me. I'm much in demand by the French now, you see, and was traveling across the Continent and then trying to hurry home again. It's getting more difficult to do as Napoleon tightens his grip. Are you angry with me?" he asked, gazing at her downturned head.

She stopped beside a fountain where a marble nymph was coyly bathing. Pippa finally looked up at him. Her eyes were clear, her expression calm. "No," she said. "I'm certainly not angry with you. It's just that I don't trust my judgment anymore. Don't let it bother you. You have better things to do."

"And you?"

She shrugged. "I live my life. And it's not that dreary, after all. I help my grandparents. I read and dabble with paints; I ride and garden. And I have peace. The neighbors don't have much to do with me, but that's all my own doing. I cut a scandalous figure, didn't I? A jilted, vengeful female traipsing across England and France in the company of a strange man, saying she was searching for the fiancé who had thrown her over? I wouldn't have had any respect for me if I'd been here, hearing about my scandalous exploits. And now it turns out he was a bigamist and maybe a spy? Ha! I doubt even the sheep will talk to me in future. But it will pass. I certainly don't want to go to London again. I'm not entirely alone. I can visit with grandfather's scholarly friends."

She grinned at last, and looked up at him. "He makes sure that they're married and over fifty before they can meet with me. This is my home. I like it here, my lord, so for heaven's sake, don't pity me."

"You didn't miss me?" he asked, his dark eyes searching her face.

She lowered her gaze. "And if I did? You told me your plans for the future, and they don't involve me." She looked him full in the face again. "I'm no longer the daring young woman I was in France. I thank you for not taking advantage of me then."

"You don't want me anymore?"

She stamped her foot. "Now what's the point of asking that?" she demanded.

"Only that I asked your grandfather if I could marry you and he said I could if you agreed. But he said that first he'd send the notice of your broken engagement to the newspapers so you wouldn't be considered a kind of bigamist too. Then," he said, "if you agreed, we could post our banns and get it over with. I think he's hurrying because he worries that I may turn out to be some sort of scoundrel too. But I'm not, so will you?"

She studied him. He was even more devastating to her senses now, but she was far more cautious than she'd ever been. "And as for your plans?" she asked. "Your distrust of marriage? Your hatred of virgins?"

He laughed and touched her chin with one finger. "I don't hate them. I'm just wary of them. I was, that is to say. I don't care if you were a nun or a tart, the truth is I missed you, Pippa," he said sincerely, taking her by her slender shoulders and looking down into her face. "Almost from the moment I left you on the shore. I liked you, Pippa. And I wanted you. But when you were gone, I realized it was far more than that. I needed you. I do love you. I never said that to any woman. Be damned to my father's bad luck! I'm not my father. I'll chance anything in order to be with you for the rest of my life. I'll be faithful and honest and a dead bore, if you want. Will you have me?"

She didn't answer right away, though her eyes filled with tears.

"You grandfather will," he added hopefully.

She laughed and threw herself into his arms, holding her face up to his.

"Oh no," he said as his hands went to cup her face so she could look at nothing but him. "You have to say it."

"I will," she said, "I do. I do love you. You showed me what love is. Oh please, kiss me."

"Of course," he whispered against her lips.

They kissed and both sighed with relief and pleasure. But he quickly drew away as though her lips were really fire instead of just feeling like it against his own.

"Now let's not shock your grandfather, or my brother," he said breathlessly. "They're both watching from the window. I don't want his invitation withdrawn. He's offered me and Duncan houseroom here until the wedding. Does that please you? Or do you think distance lends enchantment?"

"Oh, wonderful," she said, "I am already enchanted."

He tucked her arm in his and they began strolling back to the house. "Of course, we'll have my family here before the wedding. I wish everyone could come to my father's house, but it appears that the thought of any travel distresses your grandmother now. That may pass. I thought we'd post the banns and marry here, if you like. Or at my father's home if you prefer. Which do you want?"

"You," she said, smiling. "You."

The house was quiet, the night deep and soft. September had come, but it still bore August on its scented breath. Maxwell couldn't sleep. His window was open so that moonlight bleached the room and the draperies puffed out with every breeze. That wasn't what was keeping him up. He liked the cool night air. But he slept less and less as the days and nights went on.

It was almost painful for him to be so near to Pippa, to see her every day and night, to remember more intimate moments and how her body had felt pressed against his; to laugh with her and walk with her, play cards and read with her, and when he could, kiss her. He wanted her more and with so much urgency it embarrassed him and denied him sleep. At least, he thought, turning in his wide bed again, it was only a month until they wed. If, he thought glumly, he lived that long.

He was thinking that no one died of desire anymore than they did of a broken heart, when he heard a slight sound in the velvet night. He sat up. His chamber door was opening. Duncan, he thought, unable to sleep and here to talk with him.

Only Duncan usually slept like a rock cast in the sea. He hoped nothing was the matter.

He sat up straighter when he saw who slipped through the door and closed it softly behind her. She wore filmy nightclothes and seemed to float toward him. But fairy apparitions didn't have such high jutting breasts that swayed as they moved. He stared, unable to speak.

"Move over," she said in a hushed voice as she came to his bedside. She giggled as she hopped from foot to foot. "Move, I said, it's chilly in here, selfish one."

He reached over and pulled her up into bed with him. She was all suppleness and softness in his arms. He buried his face in her neck. He was actually trembling, trying to keep himself under control.

"What are you doing here?" he asked in a hoarse voice.

"Well—" she began to say as she threw the coverlet back and crawled under it. She stopped. "Oh," she said, "you're not wearing anything!"

"It was warm in here," he managed to say.

"Good," she said. She swallowed hard and steadied herself, so that he wouldn't guess how worried she was, or how much courage it had taken to get her here. "The thing is, Maxwell," she said, "that we're to be married in a matter of weeks, and I remembered something."

"What?" he asked, staying as absolutely still as his unruly body allowed while she curled closer.

"I realized there was an impediment," she said as she hid her heated face by kissing his neck.

He grew hot and cold. "What the devil are you doing?" he demanded.

"Hush," she said. "The walls are thick but I'm not deaf. Don't ruin the mood. What I realized," she said as she placed a kiss on his cheek, and then one lightly against his lips, "is that you wanted to marry an experienced woman. So I'm here for the experience before we marry. Can you help me?"

It seemed an eternity to her before he answered. And then he laughed and drew her to himself, settling her on his hard chest. "Oh yes," he said. He wanted to say many more witty things, but couldn't. She kissed him and he was lost to her.

She stopped being afraid once she was in his arms. She was warm and pliant, and moved with him like a true apparition in some rare, erotic dream. She followed his lead and he led her as far as he could and still keep his control. When he was certain her naked body was as slick and heated as his was, he rolled her back to the feather tick, and paused on his elbows above her.

He'd touched her and kissed her and set her to tingling and aching, and made her shudder with new releases, but wonderful as it was, it wasn't enough for her. She knew there was more. Overwhelmed by her own desire, she no longer knew what to do except to have him even closer.

She relaxed, opened herself to him body and soul and looked into his eyes. "Please," she said.

He sighed and moved to her, and after one moment of difficulty, was within her. She arched her back and clung to him. He tried to be slow, he tried to be gentle, but it was over quickly. The storm of his desire ended their moment too soon for his liking.

"I'm sorry," he said when he was able, as he lay breathing hard at her side. "Did it hurt?"

"A bit," she said, raising herself on one elbow. "Is that what you're sorry about?"

"That, and the fact that I was too hasty. I didn't give you time to share everything I felt." He pulled her close again. "You made me lose control, just as I feared."

"There's nothing to fear anymore," she said seriously.

"No, and there never again will be, you wonderful, brave, and brazen creature," he said, his hand warm on her back.

"At last," she said, and rested her head against his heart. But then she raised her head. "You make it all sound so final. There's not going to be more of this for us?" she asked with a quizzical smile, gently brushing his hair back from his forehead.

"Oh, for a certainty there will be," he said. "Give me a moment."

"And you? Were you pleased with me?" she asked.

"Too much, as I said," he answered ruefully.

"How can I learn to please you less?" she asked, smiling.

"That is not our aim," he said, his lips curling in a smile too.

"Ah!" she said softly. "But what can you possibly want then?"

He laughed.

She sighed. "Obviously," she said, brushing a kiss across his lips, "I'll need a great deal more experience then, won't I?"

Chapter 23

It was a perfect morning for a wedding, and so said all.

The families took their seats at either side of the old Norman chapel. All were radiantly dressed, as might be expected. Both families were wealthy, after all. And both sides had military gentlemen in attendance, as well as some persons with names of note in London and across the known world. There were others with names of note that weren't so well known and neither were they supposed to be, except at the highest levels of the government.

A renowned scholar's granddaughter was marrying into an ancient dukedom.

Everyone present felt privileged, though they showed it in different fashions.

The scholar's family sat to the left of the aisle with long-lost relatives and students of all ages from many places. The thin and bent old gentleman who was recognized as the bride's grandfather was clearly pleased. His wife, an improbably yellow-haired squab of a lady, was quiet. But she smiled a great deal.

The duke's family sat to the right. The tall, icy-eyed duke was unbent just enough to be seen as both proud and satisfied. The groom's brother Duncan was beaming. His stepmother, a pinch-faced female who looked like an illustration of bad temper in a medical text, turned her thin lips up in an attempt at a smile. The duke's youngest child looked as though she'd been dragged through a hedge backward, as some whispered. She'd originally been carefully dressed in white with a wreath of flowers in her hair. Now she looked as though she'd been savaged by the shrubbery outside the church. But young Lady Theodosia seemed pleased and proud as well.

The bride and groom at the altar noticed none of this. They had eyes only for each other.

"At last," the groom whispered to his lady.

The bride grinned. She had no words for her happiness.

When at last man and wife, they embraced.

And for the first time in the history of the ancient chapel, the wedding guests spontaneously applauded.